BATTLES OF DESTINY

WINGS OF THE WIND

AL LACY

With the exception of recognized historical figures, the characters in this novel are fictional. Any resemblance to actual persons, living or dead, is purely coincidental.

WINGS OF THE WIND

published by Multnomah Books
a part of the Questar publishing family

Edited by Rodney L. Morris and Deena Davis
Cover design by D[2] Designworks
Cover illustration by Vittorio Dangelico

International Standard Book Number: 1-57673-032-8

Printed in the United States of America.

For information:
Questar Publishers, Inc.
Post Office Box 1720
Sisters, Oregon 97759

LIBRARY OF CONGRESS CATALOGING-IN-PUBLICATION DATA

Lacy, Al.
Wings of the wind/by Lew Lacy. p.cm. -- (Battles of destiny; 7)
ISBN 1-57673-032-8 (alk. paper) 1. Antietam, Battle of, Md., 1862--Fiction.
2. United States--History--Civil War, 1861-1865--Fiction. I. Title. II. Series:
Lacy, Al. Battles of destiny; bk. 7.
PS3562.A256W5 1997 96-46777
813'.54--dc21 CIP

97 98 99 00 01 02 03 — 10 9 8 7 6 5 4 3 2 1

To my sweet little niece,
Pami P-Nut,
who hangs on the breathless edge of anticipation
for another one of Uncle Al's novels to come off the press.
(I think)
I love you, P-Nut!

PROLOGUE

On September 3, 1862, four days after the Confederate Army's stunning victory at the Second Battle of Bull Run, General Robert E. Lee sat down and pondered the situation. In the aftermath of routing the Federals for the second time within thirteen months, on the same battlefield, two courses lay before him: Go forward or go back.

The decision was not easy. His men were weary and tattered.

Lee considered what it would mean to go back. He would withdraw south below the Rappahannock River. There he could rest his exhausted army, which as one of Lee's generals phrased it, "had been marching, fighting, and starving" since the Seven Days' Battles around Richmond, Virginia, in late June.

To stay in northern Virginia and rest his troops was out of the question. Thousands of foraging soldiers had already stripped the fields there, and the Confederate supply lines were overextended. Lee lacked the wagons to carry sufficient food for his army and fodder for his horses over the one-hundred-mile route from Richmond. If he withdrew, he would have to drop below the Rappahannock to find crops to feed his men.

To make this move, however, would allow the Union Army of the Potomac to reorganize and perhaps launch another drive against the Confederate capital at Richmond.

Lee reasoned that if instead of withdrawing he forged ahead and invaded Maryland, he could achieve his immediate military objectives. Such an invasion would not be with the purpose of occupying Union territory, but rather to harass the enemy on his own soil. Lee could feed his army and horses on Maryland's rich autumn harvest while luring the bulk of the Federal forces away from Washington, preventing another enemy march on Richmond before winter set in.

Lee knew the Union cause was at its nadir. A strike and a victory on Union soil could very well turn the tide for the South and win independence for the Confederacy. Ever since the Baltimore riots early in the War, there had been signs of pro-Confederate sympathy in Maryland. Many Marylanders were serving in the Rebel army. Their presence on Maryland soil could rally the citizens of that state on the side of the South.

Lee reasoned that another advantage might be gained by his invasion of Maryland. There was growing opposition to the Civil War throughout the North. An invasion of Confederate troops across the Potomac no doubt would strengthen anti-war Democrats in the upcoming November elections and so galvanize discontent that President Abraham Lincoln would be forced to settle for peace.

Furthermore, reports from abroad indicated that European powers were watching Lee's progress intently. Great Britain and France had greeted the recent Confederate victories with favor. A successful foray into Union territory might induce the British, as well as the French, to accord the Confederacy diplomatic recognition and even intervene in the War on its behalf.

In spite of all these potential advantages, Lee had to weigh one great drawback: the frightful condition of his army. In addition to the men's physical and mental weariness, they were short on supplies and feeble in the means of transportation, because so many horses had been killed in the last three months of battles. And the men needed clothes and shoes.

Still, Lee reasoned that the morale of his men had never been higher. The recent rout at Bull Run had their spirits high, and the spirits of the enemy troops were at an all-time low.

Lee made his decision.

He wrote a long letter to President Jefferson Davis. It began: "The present seems to be the most propitious time since the commencement of the War for the Confederate Army to enter Maryland."

With those words, Lee announced his intention to carry the conflict onto enemy soil for the first time in the Eastern theater. Little did he know that his campaign on Union soil would culminate in the fiercest single day of combat in American history.

The letter was sent to Jefferson Davis by midday, September 3. Lee was so certain Davis would sanction the invasion that he prepared his army that afternoon and moved them north on Thursday morning, September 4. It took them the better part of three days to move fifty thousand men onto Union soil, along with what wagons and animals they had. As the ragtag army's last troops were wading across the Potomac on September 6, President Davis's sanction of the invasion was in writing and in Lee's hands.

To meet the Confederate threat, President Lincoln commanded General George B. McClellan to move his Army of the Potomac westward.

Eleven days later, on September 17, 1862, the two armies clashed head-on along the banks of Antietam Creek near Sharpsburg in western Maryland. Of all the days on all the battlefields where American soldiers have fought, the most terrible in loss of life and limb was on that bloody Wednesday in the pastoral Maryland countryside.

When the fighting ended at dusk on September 17, 5,818 men lay dead and 17,292 lay wounded in the meadows and fields and along the banks of Antietam Creek. The creek flowed crimson with blood while the wounded moaned and cried out for water.

Night came, bringing a mournful chorus of suffering from the lantern-lit tents, barns, sheds, and houses where weary surgeons, aided by equally exhausted nurses, removed bullets, stitched up bayonet wounds, and sawed off mangled limbs. The same mournful chorus came from the deeply shadowed hollows, woods, fields, meadows, and roads where the wounded and dying men of both armies lay beyond the reach of help.

Near midnight, Confederate Major General Thomas J. "Stonewall" Jackson sent his young aide, Henry Kyd Douglas, on an errand across the fields in the pale, misty moonlight. Later, Douglas wrote:

> The dead and dying lay as thick over the land as harvest sheaves. The pitiable cries for water and appeals for help were much more horrible to listen to than the deadliest sounds of battle. Silent were the dead, but here and there were raised stiffened arms; heads made a last effort to lift themselves from the ground; prayers were mingled with oaths, the oaths of delirium; men were wriggling over the earth; and the midnight hid all the distinction between the blue and the gray.
>
> My horse trembled under me in terror, looking down at the ground, sniffing at the scent of blood, stepping falteringly as a horse will, avoiding human flesh; afraid to stand still, hesitating to go on, his animal instinct shuddering at this cruel human mystery.

The Civil War's bloodiest battle left the residents of the Maryland countryside in and around Sharpsburg stunned and sleepless for days. It was a full week before all the dead had been buried and the wounded had been carried away. The stench of decaying flesh hung in the air for a long time, even after the bodies had been interred. It took the powerful sense of death's awful presence even longer to fade.

Within the next few weeks and months, several thousand more men died of their wounds, or of disease brought on by the wounds.

As I write, several history books lay at my fingertips. In these written records is abundant evidence that the battle along Antietam Creek was the most bitter and savage of the American Civil War.

However, the mercy and compassion of men and women of the medical profession on both sides shone through. The story of one of those gallant physicians began in the small town of McCann's Run, Virginia, in May 1840.

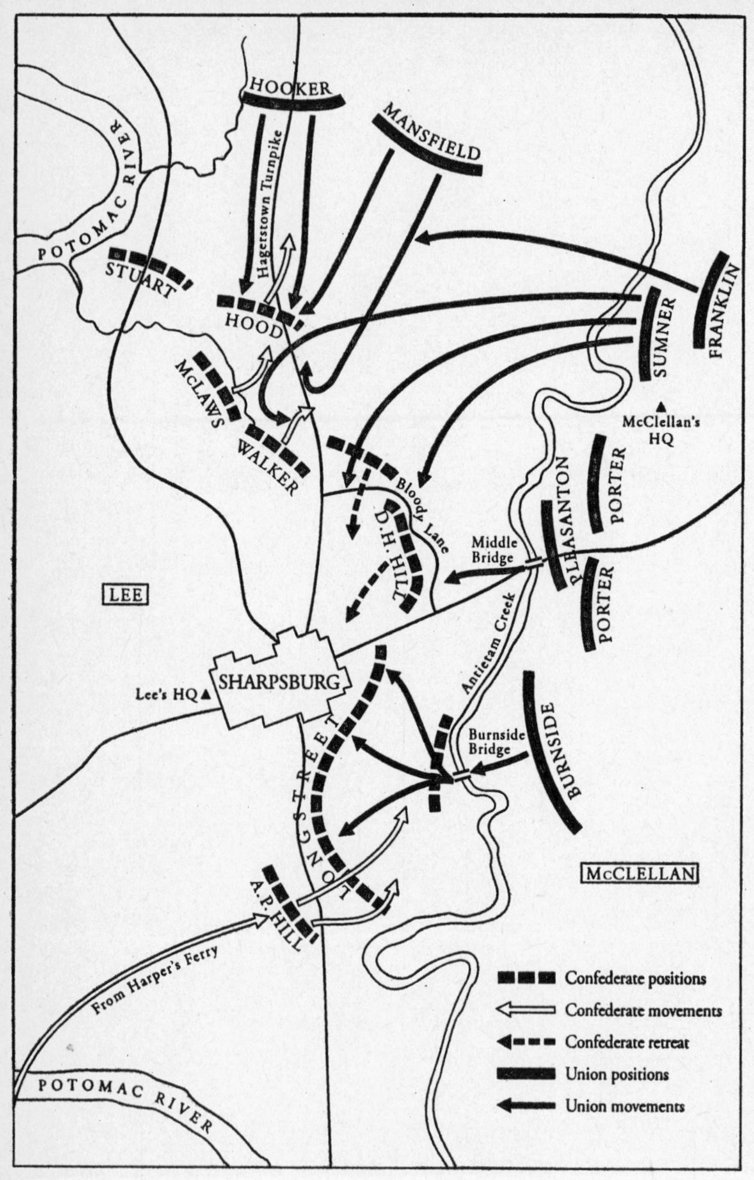

BATTLE OF ANTIETAM
SEPTEMBER 17, 1862

WINGS OF THE WIND

CHAPTER ONE

Five-year-old Hunter Newman Jr. stood at the door of his mother's bedroom, fear clouding his eyes. His arms and legs felt heavy and his pulse raced as he watched Thora Kemp and Bessie Caterson labor over his mother.

Florence Newman had come down with a severe case of typhoid fever. It had been two days since Dr. Riley had examined her.

Hunter bit down hard on his lower lip when his mother rolled her head and shook as if she were penetrated to the core by incredible cold. Was he going to have another living nightmare, as when his father had died almost a year ago in a hunting accident?

Although Hunter had been only four years old at the time, he had taken his father's death hard. For the first three months after his father was killed, Hunter had awakened his mother and baby sister two and three times a night, screaming. Though the nightmares had almost stopped by the time his father had been gone six months, Hunter still remembered, and he trembled at the thought of them.

Now Hunter stood at his mother's bedroom door and looked on in horror as her rapid breathing grew raspy and shallow. She was so pale. Emblazoned in Hunter's mind was the picture of his father's body in the coffin. Hunter feared his mother would die and leave him, too.

Thora and Bessie tirelessly bathed Florence in cool water, trying to reduce her fever. Dr. Riley, the only physician in a thirty-mile radius, had left medicine when he'd been there last and told Bessie and Thora what to do to help keep the fever down and relieve her suffering as much as possible. If she got worse they were to send for him.

While the women continued to wring out cloths in the cool water, Bessie whispered, "Hunter's at the door. The little guy looks scared out of his wits."

Without glancing at him, Thora said, "Why don't you take him outside and talk to him? I'll look after Florence."

Bessie wiped perspiration from the sick woman's brow for the hundredth time that day and handed the cloth to Thora.

Florence laid glassy eyes on Bessie and asked with thick tongue, "Is Hunter all right?"

"He's just worried about you, honey. I'm going to talk to him."

Florence swallowed hard, trying to focus on Bessie's round face. "Tell him...tell him I'm going to be fine."

Bessie nodded and turned away. She walked quietly to the small sandy-haired boy and said, "Hunter, let's go out and see how Jane Louise and little Lizzie are doing."

Hunter shook his head. "No, ma'am, please. Mama's gonna die. I don't want to leave her."

Bessie bent down to Hunter's height, looked him in the eye, and said, "Your mama's awfully sick right now, but Miss Thora and I are working on her. Jesus will help us to make her well. Come on, let's go see about little sister."

Hunter stiffened, gazing toward his mother. Thora spoke to him gently, "Hunter, it will make your mama feel better if you go outside and see about Lizzie."

Florence rolled her head on the hot, damp pillow and choked

out the words, "Son...Miss Thora's right. And let Miss Bessie talk to you."

Hunter nodded and let Bessie take his hand. "Come on, honey," she said. "You can come back and see Mama later."

Hunter glanced once more over his shoulder as Bessie led him away from the door and through the house to the porch. It was early May in western Virginia, and in spite of the heavy gray sky, the air was warm.

Jane Louise, Thora Kemp's fifteen-year-old daughter, was sitting on the porch swing, holding little Lizzie Newman. Lizzie was two years old and, in contrast to Hunter, had dark eyes and hair. She was chewing on the hand of her rag doll when she saw her brother. "Hunna!" she said, and smiled.

Hunter dearly loved his little sister. He managed a crooked grin. "Hi, Lizzie."

Jane Louise gave Bessie a look and said, "How's she doing?"

"Not very good right now. Your mom's staying with her so I could bring Hunter out here for a while."

Hunter let go of Bessie's hand to stand close to his little sister. "Mama's real sick, Lizzie, but Miss Bessie says she'll be okay."

Lizzie nodded as if she understood, then held up her rag doll. "Hunna wan' play wif Daisie?"

"No, Lizzie. You play with her."

"Hunter," Bessie said, dragging two straight-backed chairs close to the swing, "come and sit down so we can talk."

The boy climbed up in the chair, looking at Bessie with eyes longing for assurance, and waited for her to speak.

Bessie leaned close and took both of his hands in hers. "Hunter, in the Bible Jesus said, 'I will never leave thee nor forsake thee.' Do you know what that means?"

Hunter adjusted his position slightly. "Mm-hmm. Mama read that to me out of the Bible not very long ago. It means that Jesus is always with us, even though we can't see Him, and He will never ever go away."

"That's right, honey." Bessie smiled, squeezing his hands. "Jesus won't ever leave your mother, either. He's right here to take care of her."

Some of the fear went out of Hunter's eyes. He knew that Bessie Caterson and her husband, Bill, had a close relationship with his parents—as members of the same church and as good friends. Bill Caterson and Hunter Sr. had spent a lot of time together. Bill had been on the hunting jaunt along with two other men, Zack Peterson and Dave Mullins, when Hunter Sr. was accidentally shot and killed by Zack Peterson. Shortly thereafter, the Petersons had left McCann's Run and moved to Richmond.

The Catersons, along with widow Thora Kemp, had stayed especially close to Florence and the children after the accident. Bessie knew that Hunter Jr. had been asking Florence a lot of questions about Jesus and the cross and sin but didn't yet understand it all. Bessie prayed quickly for guidance as she chose her words carefully. "Hunter, Jesus loves your mother, and He loves you and little Lizzie. And because He does, He will always watch over all three of you."

Hunter looked at the porch floor, his mind working out what she had said. At the same time, Lizzie wanted off Jane Louise's lap to play. Lizzie carried her rag doll to the edge of the steps and looked back at her brother. "Hunna pway wif me."

"He will pretty soon, sweetie," Bessie said. "We're talking right now."

Lizzie nodded and looked down the dusty road to the east. Her attention was drawn to a horse and buggy in the distance.

At last Hunter said, "Miss Bessie..."

"Yes, honey?"

"If Jesus is going to take care of Mama, why couldn't He take care of Papa when Mr. Peterson's gun went off and killed him?"

Bessie's heart ached for the boy. "Well, honey, it wasn't that Jesus couldn't take care of your papa. He could have kept that gun from firing."

Hunter searched her eyes as he asked, "Why didn't He want to keep Papa from being killed?"

Bessie silently asked God for wisdom, but before she could put the words together, Jane Louise spoke up. "Hunter, Jesus wanted your papa up in heaven with Him. He had a special place of service for him there. So your papa is with Jesus now, serving Him in heaven."

Hunter pondered Jane Louise's words for a long moment, then said with quivering lips, "Maybe Jesus wants to take my mama to heaven, too…and she's gonna die like Papa did."

Bessie and Jane Louise exchanged a glance as if to decide who would answer. It was Lizzie who got them off the hook. "Tom!" she squealed, pointing at the rider turning off the road toward the house.

The two-year-old laid down her doll and clapped her hands as Tom dismounted from his horse and picked her up, lifting her above his head. "You're just getting cuter every day, Lizzie!" he said.

Hunter, who considered sixteen-year-old Tom Jackson his best friend, slid off the chair and bounded down the steps. Tom held Lizzie in one arm and hoisted Hunter up in the other. For the first time that day, Hunter smiled and relaxed. "Can I help you chop wood, Tom?" he asked.

"You sure can!" Tom drawled. "It always goes faster when you're there to pick up the wood and stack it."

Tall, black-headed Tom Jackson lived with his Uncle Cummins and Aunt Ophelia Jackson at Jackson's Mill, some four miles west on the road toward Clarksburg.

Tom's father, Jonathan, had been a lieutenant at the head of a cavalry company in the War of 1812, and several men on his father's side of the family had fought in the American Revolution. As far back as Tom could remember, he had wanted to be a soldier. He was planning on a military career once he finished high school. He had already contacted his congressman, desiring entrance into West Point Military Academy.

When Tom's father died of typhoid fever at the age of thirty-five, Tom was only three. His mother, Julia, died three years later, and Tom was obliged to live with his Uncle Cummins and Aunt Ophelia. His siblings went to other relatives.

Cummins Jackson was a hard-drinking man, but Ophelia was a member of the Presbyterian Church in McCann's Run and had taken Tom to church with her ever since he had come to live with them. At nine years of age, Tom had asked Jesus Christ to be his Saviour.

For the past year—since Hunter Newman Sr. had been killed—young Tom had come to the Newman house twice a week to do the necessary chores, such as chopping wood, cleaning the chicken house, weeding the garden, repairing worn and broken things. He knew the Newman family well from church, and did the work for Florence without pay.

While holding the Newman children in his arms, Tom looked at Bessie and Jane Louise. "How's Mrs. Newman doing?"

Bessie frowned. "Not very good, Tom, I—"

"Oh, Tom! I'm so glad you're here!" Thora had come out onto the porch. "I heard your voice from the back room. We need your help."

"Yes, ma'am?"

Thora looked at Bessie. "Her fever is getting worse...much worse." Then to Tom, "Will you ride to Smithburg and bring Dr. Riley? He told us to send for him if Florence's condition worsened."

Hunter's face turned white as Tom set him down and placed Lizzie in Jane Louise's arms. Tears welled up in Hunter's eyes and he dashed up the steps of the porch and bolted through the door, heading toward his mother's bedroom.

Tom vaulted into the saddle and galloped away as Thora turned to Jane Louise and said, "Run to the parsonage and bring Pastor Poole! Hurry!"

As Thora and Bessie, who carried Lizzie, approached the bedroom, they could hear Hunter sobbing, "Please don't die, Mama! Please don't die!"

"Hunter, listen to me," Thora said. "Tom is going after Dr. Riley. He will come as quickly as he can."

Florence was shaking with chills, even as perspiration flowed down her brow. She clumsily patted her son's tear-streaked face and said in a slurred voice, "Hunter, don't cry now."

Soon Lizzie leaned forward in Bessie's arms, extending a small hand toward her mother, and broke into tears. "Mama-a! Mama-a!"

"Hunter," Florence choked out, "you're scaring Lizzie. She needs to see you be strong. Remember, you're the man of the house."

Hunter had taken pride in that title since his father's death and had done his best to live up to it. His mother's reminder took hold, and he looked around at Lizzie. She was sniffling, her eyes fixed on him.

He slid to the floor and walked over to her, waiting for Bessie to lower his little sister to the floor. Then he put his arms around her and said, "It's okay, Lizzie. Jesus is here with us, and Dr. Riley's coming."

CHAPTER TWO

Inside the Riley Clinic in Smithburg, nurse Linna Bittner finished bandaging a small boy's hand and gave him a piece of horehound candy.

Dr. Riley's wife, Alfreda, sat in a chair against the wall looking on, commending Timmy for being such a brave boy and not crying. Alfreda often stopped by the clinic during her daily walk.

When Timmy and his mother had reached the door, Linna offered a final word of admonishment. "No more playing with your mother's butcher knife, Timmy."

"Yes, ma'am," he said, looking at his bandage as he followed his mother outside.

Alfreda sighed and said, "Boys will be boys."

"Oh, won't they," Linna said with a chuckle, her Scandinavian accent coming through. "I'm sure we treat ten times as many boys for cuts, bruises, and broken bones as we do girls."

"Well, Chet and I raised three boys and two girls. I think between those three boys, one of them always had a splint or a bandage or iodine showing somewhere." A faraway look came into Alfreda's eyes as she sighed again and said, "Sometimes I wish they were still little and running around the house."

"They do grow up fast," Linna said, as she cleaned the examining table. "Seems like just yesterday that my two girls were little. And now, here they are married and both expecting their first babies."

"Well, honey, I'll say this—the first time you hold one of those precious grandchildren, you'll be glad your daughters grew up and got married. When I start pining for the days when they were little, I remember that if they hadn't grown up, I wouldn't have those wonderful grandchildren. Why, I remember when our first grandchild was born—"

Alfreda's sentence was cut short by the sight of a surrey pulling up in front of the clinic. Linna followed Alfreda's gaze, focusing on the man who jumped down and, instead of helping the woman, hoisted a wheelchair from the back of the surrey.

Linna squinted and frowned slightly. "I don't recognize either one of them. I wish Dr. Riley was here. Who knows what kind of problem I might face with a wheelchair patient."

Alfreda suddenly stood up, smiling. "Oh, I know them," she said, and hurried toward the door.

Linna followed and stood just inside the doorway as Alfreda moved onto the porch. Linna judged the man and woman to be in their late thirties. As the man eased the woman into the wheelchair, Alfreda hurried to them. "Jason! Ellie! How wonderful to see you!" She embraced the man and leaned over to put her arms around the woman.

Linna heard the man say, "Some people on the street told us where you live and where the clinic is...we went to the house first. When we found no one home, we figured you might be here."

"Linna," Alfreda said, "I want you to meet Dr. Jason McGuire and his wife, Ellie. Linna Bittner has been the doctor's nurse ever since he came here to go back into private practice."

Linna stepped forward as Jason began to pick up the wheelchair. "Here," she said, "let me help you."

"It's all right, ma'am. Ellie's not heavy. I'm used to it, but thank you anyway." As he spoke, he lifted the wheelchair and set it on the porch.

Once inside, Jason looked around the clinic expectantly. "Is Dr. Riley here?" he asked.

"No," Alfreda said, "he's at a farm some twenty-five miles south of here, delivering a baby, and there's no way to know when he might be back. Can you stay for the day?"

"No reason we can't," Jason said. "I noticed a hotel as we drove into town. We'll even stay the night if that's what it takes to see Dr. Riley."

"If you stay the night, it won't be in the hotel. You'll stay with us—we have plenty of room."

Ellie spoke up. "We...we wouldn't want to be a bother, Mrs. Riley. We—"

"Hush, now!" the older woman said in mild rebuke. "You could never be a bother." Then, turning to the nurse, Alfreda said, "Linna, I'm sure you know that Doctor taught at Harvard Medical School before he came here five years ago..."

"Yes."

"Well, Jason—I mean Dr. McGuire—was one of his students. One of his most brilliant students, I might add."

McGuire shook his head modestly as Alfreda continued to speak. "Dr. McGuire is a prominent physician and surgeon in Boston." Then, looking at Jason, she asked, "You are still practicing in Boston?"

"Yes, ma'am."

Alfreda nodded. "And to what do we owe this wonderful visit?"

"Well, we're on a little vacation," he said. "Ellie's parents live in Parkersburg, and we came here to see them. They moved from Hudson, New Hampshire, about a year ago. We sure couldn't get this close to the Rileys without stopping by."

"Oh, I'm so glad you did," Alfreda said. "Chet is going to be so happy to see you! Well…why don't we just mosey on over to the house so Ellie can be comfortable?"

A half-hour later, Alfreda Riley and her guests were sitting in the parlor, sipping tea and talking of old times at Harvard. When the talk began to dwindle, Alfreda looked across the tea table and said, "The last time we saw you—what was it, nine years ago?—you were talking about adopting a child. I assume it has never come to pass."

"Ah…no, it hasn't," Jason said.

"Are there still plans to do so?"

"We decided against it," Ellie said. "It was my decision actually. I'm afraid I wouldn't be able to care for a child properly from a wheelchair."

"I offered to hire a nanny," Jason said, "but Ellie wouldn't hear of it."

"I don't want to bring up a child with a nanny as its mother. If I can't be a mother to our child, I'd rather not try it at all."

"I can understand that," Alfreda said.

"So tell her what you *are* doing, honey," Jason said.

A broad smile spread over Ellie's slender face. "Well, to satisfy the motherly instinct the Lord put inside me, I work with sick and injured children at Boston Hospital, where Jason does his surgeries and sends his patients."

"Well, wonderful!" Alfreda said.

Ellie hunched her shoulders and tilted her head. "It's not the same as actually being a mother, but I can handle what I do from the wheelchair. The work is very satisfying."

"I'm so happy for you, Ellie," Alfreda said. "What a wonderful way to spend your time."

*****

Tom Jackson bent low over his horse's neck and pushed her hard. His heart was heavy for Florence Newman and her children. "Lord, that dear lady and those sweet kids have had an awful hard time of it since Hunter was killed. I'm not questioning Your ways. You know that. But I'm asking You to take care of them…and if in Your wisdom You see fit to take Mrs. Newman home to heaven, please take care of those little children. Give them a good Christian home to be raised in."

Twenty minutes later, young Jackson galloped into Smithburg, ignoring the gawking people, and made a beeline for the clinic, skidding the puffing mare to a halt. He slipped from the saddle and bolted through the door.

Linna Bittner, busy with filing, greeted him with, "Tom! What's wrong?"

"It's Florence Newman. Her typhoid fever's getting worse. She needs Dr. Riley immediately!"

"I'm sorry," Linna said, pulling a folder from the drawer. "Doctor is not here. He's delivering a baby twenty-five miles south of here."

Tom's countenance fell. "Ma'am, it's really bad. Mrs. Kemp is worried that Mrs. Newman will die if she doesn't get help. What am I going to do?"

"Tom, I don't know what to tell you. The mother at the farm has had some serious complications carrying her baby. Her life and the baby's may be at stake, too. I'm not sure what to do. If only there was another doctor nearby. But the nearest one is—"

Tom saw Linna's eyes widen.

"Yes?"

"There's a doctor and his wife from Boston visiting Mrs. Riley at this very moment," Linna said.

"He's a regular-type doctor?"

"Yes. Physician and surgeon. If Florence can be helped, he can do it."

"Then I'll go ask him."

"Tell Dr. McGuire that I sent you. Explain about Florence, and I'm sure he will go with you. Tell him to stop here if he needs any medicine."

Pastor Nelson Poole sat beside Florence's bed while Thora and Bessie bathed her face and arms. He had prayed with Florence upon arriving at the house, then sat down and read Scripture to her. Now he was speaking in soft tones, trying to encourage her.

The fear Hunter felt at seeing his mother so deathly pale and hearing her ragged breathing was taking its toll. He pictured the last time he saw his father in the coffin. Now it was his mother he saw lying there, lifeless and chalky white.

Wild panic filled him. He felt his pulse pounding at the back of his eyes, on top of his head, in his throat. A cry was working its way up when the pastor turned and saw the panic on Hunter's face.

"Hunter," Pastor Poole said calmly, "why don't you go outside and see if Tom and Dr. Riley are coming?"

Hunter had been out to check the road six times already, but he obediently turned to go. As he passed through the parlor, he saw that Jane Louise was sitting on the couch with Lizzie asleep in her arms. He shifted to walking on tiptoe, and Jane Louise smiled at him.

Outside Hunter looked westward and saw Mr. Wykopf's Guernsey cow crossing the road. Bertha was always getting out. Hunter wondered why Mr. Wykopf didn't mend his fences. Then he saw a rider galloping his way with a surrey following.

Hunter charged through the front door and yelled, "Tom's coming with Dr. Riley, Jane Louise!" He bolted down the hall into his mother's room and repeated the good news.

Bessie and Thora sighed with relief. Pastor Poole patted

Florence's clammy arm and said, "You hear that, Florence? Doc Riley's here."

The sick woman ran a dry tongue over chapped lips and nodded. Bessie gave her water and said, "You're going to be all right, now, honey. You'll see."

Tom Jackson skidded his lathered and panting mare to a stop and dismounted while the surrey was bouncing up behind him. Hunter stood waiting beside Bessie and Jane Louise.

Bessie fixed her eyes on the man at the reins and said, "Tom, that's not Dr. Riley..."

Tom walked with Dr. McGuire up the steps and said, "Mrs. Caterson, Jane Louise, this is Dr. Jason McGuire. He and his wife just arrived in Smithburg to visit the Rileys. Dr. Riley is delivering a baby way out in the country."

"Ladies," McGuire said, touching his hatbrim. His gaze settled on Lizzie and Hunter. "And these are Mrs. Newman's children?"

"Yes," Tom said, laying a hand on Hunter's head. "The little lady is Lizzie, and this little friend of mine is Hunter."

Dr. McGuire looked at Lizzie with kind eyes and stroked her cheek. "Hello, Lizzie. You're sure a cute little thing. I wish I had a daughter like you."

Lizzie smiled, warming up to the doctor immediately.

McGuire then looked down at Hunter and placed a hand on his shoulder. "Hunter, eh? That's a strong masculine name, and you look like you're all boy. I wish I had a son like you."

Hunter managed a smile. Jason McGuire eased down on one knee and looked Hunter straight in the eye. "I'm going to do everything I can to help your mother. I want you to know that."

"Thank you, sir. My papa died when I was four. I don't want my mama to die."

"I know about your papa, son. Tom told me. I'll do everything I can for your mama."

Hunter reached out with both arms, and McGuire gave him a hug. Then the doctor patted Hunter on the back and said, "Let's go see about your mama. Will you take me to her?"

Bessie and Jane Louise followed as Hunter took the doctor's hand and led him inside. Tom trailed along.

Dr. McGuire set his black bag on the bedstand and Florence looked up with languid eyes. "Mrs. Newman," he said, "I'm Dr. Jason McGuire. I'm from—"

"I heard, Doctor. If you studied under Dr. Riley, I trust you completely."

"Thank you, ma'am. Now let's check your temperature."

Dr. McGuire placed a thermometer in Florence's mouth and checked her pulse. He also quickly checked her eyes and throat and listened to her heart. He read the thermometer and placed it back in his medical bag, his expression remaining impassive.

He glanced from time to time at the children who looked on and then set soft, gentle eyes on Florence and said, "Mrs. Newman, I understand from Tom that you are a Christian."

Florence smiled slightly and nodded.

"I just want you to know that I am too, ma'am. Jesus Christ saved me when I was nineteen years old under the fiery message of a Baptist preacher."

Pastor Poole stepped closer, smiling, and laid a hand on McGuire's shoulder.

Tom excused himself, saying he would go do the chores around the Newman place. "Want to help me, Hunter?" he asked.

Dr. McGuire saw Hunter's hesitation and said, "You go ahead, son. It'll be good for you to spend some time with Tom."

The five-year-old nodded and walked to his mother's side. "Mama, I'm gonna help Tom with the chores. I'll be back pretty soon."

"That's fine, honey," Florence said hoarsely. "You go ahead."

*****

Soon the sun was setting, and Florence's fever rose higher. The doctor made no comment when he read the thermometer.

"Worse?" Thora mouthed silently from the other side of the bed.

The doctor nodded.

The room had been silent for some time, except for the sound of the women dipping cloths in water and wringing them out. Florence swallowed with difficulty and fixed torpid eyes on McGuire. "I'm...I'm not going to make it, am I Doctor?"

McGuire hesitated, then said, "I cannot lie to you, ma'am. You won't make it through the night."

Thora and Bessie exchanged sorrowful glances, then looked at their pastor. Nelson Poole's face was pale.

No one had noticed that Hunter had returned to the open doorway and heard what the doctor said. He blinked rapidly, as if startled by a loud noise, and charging toward the bed, he cried, "No! No, Mama, no-o, please don't die! Mama-a!"

He managed to climb onto the bed before anyone could stop him and threw his arms around his mother, continuing to call her name.

Dr. McGuire feared that typhoid might be contagious, in spite of what the medical experts were saying. He wanted to pull the boy away from danger but refrained.

Jane Louise, still carrying Lizzie, had come back into the bedroom. Even though Lizzie didn't know exactly what was going on, Hunter's sobs upset her and she began to wail.

Florence kissed Hunter's forehead and said calmly, "Honey, you have to be brave. You're making Lizzie cry. C'mon, now. Be Mama's big boy."

The sandy-haired child nodded and released his hold on his mother. She was going to die, but for her sake, and for Lizzie's, he would be brave.

CHAPTER THREE

Dr. McGuire looked at Nelson Poole and nodded toward Florence. The doctor had done all he could; she needed her pastor now.

McGuire laid a firm hand on Hunter's shoulder and looked down into widened, fear-filled eyes. He tried to smile at Hunter but couldn't quite manage it.

"Florence," the pastor said, "you're in the Lord's hands. He will not fail you now. He—"

"I know that, Pastor," she whispered. "I have no fear, even as David in Psalm 23. My Shepherd is with me. You...you will see that the children are taken care of?"

Poole was not sure what he was going to do about the Newman children, but he nodded silently.

Florence saw his nod, and said, "Would you let the children come and sit beside me?"

Jane Louise carried Lizzie to the bed and Dr. McGuire helped Hunter to climb up.

The dying mother raised a shaky hand and stroked Lizzie's cheek. "Mama loves you, sweetheart," she said. "Jesus will take care of you and brother."

Lizzie leaned over and hugged her mother's neck, then straightened back again into Jane Louise's arms. The two-year-old was touched by the emotions in the room, but didn't understand what was happening.

But Hunter knew. He embraced his mother, fighting the urge to cry. He swallowed hard and bit down on his lower lip.

Florence ran her dull gaze from one child to the other, then lifted her eyes toward heaven and said in a half-whisper, "Thank You, Lord, for being so good to me. You saved my soul when I was thirteen. You gave me such a good husband...and these two wonderful children. Please, Lord, take care of Hunter and Lizzie."

Florence looked at the pastor's Bible on the bedstand. "Pastor," she said, "would you read my favorite praise verse? Psalm 104:1. I love the way it exalts the Lord."

Tom Jackson was now in the room. Tears were streaming down his face as Nelson Poole read the words, pushing them past the lump in his throat:

> Bless the LORD, O my soul.
> O LORD my God, thou art very great;
> thou art clothed with honor and majesty.

"Thank you, Pastor," she whispered. "The third verse is also one of my favorites. Would you read it to me?"

Hunter recalled so many times that his mother had referred to that verse in the past year, especially on a windy day. She would look heavenward and say, "Hunter, see those big white clouds up there? Psalm 104 verse 3 says Jesus makes the clouds His chariot. And sometimes He steps out of His chariot and walks on the wings of the wind, looking down at us. The day Papa left us, Jesus came walking on the wings of the wind, reached down, and lifted Papa up into His mighty arms and took him home to heaven."

Hunter felt Dr. McGuire's hand squeeze his shoulder. He liked this man who reminded him of his father—strong yet gentle.

Florence spoke again, her hoarse whisper even weaker. "Hunter...Jesus is coming on the wings of the wind to take me to be with Him and Papa. But someday, Son, He will walk the wings of the wind and bring us together again—all four of us." She swallowed with difficulty and tried to speak again, but her strength was gone.

Hunter looked up at Dr. McGuire, then at the pastor, who had a grip on his mother's hand. Florence's chest rose and fell a few more times, then her head fell to one side and she stopped breathing.

Pastor Poole placed her hand gently on the bed and stepped back to allow Dr. McGuire room. The doctor checked for a pulse but could find none. He pulled the sheet up and covered Florence Newman's chalky-white face.

A strangled moan escaped Hunter's lips and his whole body trembled. He could hardly breathe.

The kindly doctor turned and said, "She's with Jesus now, Hunter." He dropped to one knee to be able to look into Hunter's eyes. "Jesus will make everything all right for you and Lizzie, Hunter. You'll be happy in your new home."

"Who are we gonna live with, sir?"

McGuire looked to the pastor, ran his gaze to the women, then back to the pastor. "Have some arrangements been made for their care?"

"Not yet, Doctor," Poole said. "We were so confident God would spare Florence's life."

Hunter ran from the room, his heart pounding in his ears as he ran. When he was deep into the woods, he threw himself on the ground beneath a giant oak tree and sobbed out the pain in his young heart.

"Aren't there any relatives who could take them in and adopt them?" Dr. McGuire asked.

"None that I know of, Doctor," Poole said, softly. "I'll do everything I can to find someone to adopt them, but everybody around here is poor."

"I'll talk to Bill," Bessie Caterson said. "Maybe we could adopt Lizzie. I...I haven't told any of you this, but Bill and I just learned yesterday that we're moving to Greensboro. Pastor, you knew Bill had applied for a job there. With Florence so sick, I just haven't thought to tell any of you that the letter of acceptance came yesterday. We'll be leaving in a few days. He'll be getting a raise in pay, so he just might go along with adopting Lizzie. But we couldn't afford to take both of them. I love Hunter too, but I think for me, Lizzie would be easier to raise."

"I'd hate to see Hunter and Lizzie separated," Tom said. "They are brother and sister. They should be raised together."

"By far that would be best," Poole said. "The children shouldn't be separated."

"I'm a stranger, here," put in Dr. McGuire, "so I have no say in anything about this. However, I'd like to put in my two cents' worth. I agree with Tom and Pastor Poole. Hunter and Lizzie should be raised together. Of course there may be no choice. They must have a home, even if it means separation. But one thing's for sure, they must be adopted by Christian people."

Jane Louise was sitting on a straight-backed chair, holding a squirming Lizzie, who pointed toward the body that lay covered on the bed and said, "Mama."

"We ought to move to the parlor," Thora said. "And someone ought to check on Hunter."

Quickly the women moved through the house, calling the boy's name, but there was no reply.

Darkness had fallen, and the stars were twinkling in a velvety black sky. Tom ran to the backyard, calling for Hunter, and the pastor and the doctor checked in front and down the road. When everyone had returned to the parlor, they began to talk about scouring the town.

"Before you do that," Jane Louise said, "you'd best look in the forest. Florence has told Hunter over and over not to go there—even in the daytime—but he told me more than once that he feels close to his father out there."

"Have you any idea where, Jane Louise?" the pastor asked. "It's a pretty big forest."

"Well, I've never seen the spot where his father was killed, but that's where he goes." She put a hand to her temple. "I'm trying to remember what he said about it. I think there's a huge oak tree there...and a small stream that runs by it."

"I know the place," Tom said. "I'll light a lantern and go after him."

"We'll light a couple of lanterns," the pastor said. "I'll go with you."

"I...ah...would like to go along, too, if you don't mind," Dr. McGuire said. "I want to be sure the little guy is found before I head back for Smithburg."

Hunter had no more tears to cry and was sitting with his back against the oak tree. Owls hooted, and strange night sounds filtered through the forest, but the boy was too wrapped up in his grief to be afraid of the night around him.

Memories of his father and mother rushed through his mind. He was glad, at least, that his mother had been able to talk to him before she died. His father, on the day he had died, had walked out of the house with his musket in hand, saying he would bring some meat home that evening.

The boy's mind once again ran to Lizzie and what would happen to the two of them. Who would take them in? Pastor Poole loved them, and so did Mrs. Poole, but they already had three children. Maybe five would be too many. The parsonage was pretty small.

Hunter wouldn't mind living with Tom Jackson, since they were best friends. Tom's Aunt Ophelia was a nice lady. She always cried in church. Tom had told him she cried a lot because his Uncle Cummins wasn't a Christian, and she didn't want him to go to hell. Hunter had seen Uncle Cummins a few times. He was always using bad language and he was real crabby. For sure, Uncle Cummins wouldn't let Lizzie and Hunter live in his house.

He thought of the different families in the church. He liked everyone. Well, except for Mrs. Ballard. She always smelled strongly of something like flowers, and whenever she kissed his forehead she left it wet. She talked so loud it hurt his ears, and in church she sang louder than everybody else. Anyway, Mrs. Ballard was real old. His mother had told him she was forty-six. Anyone that old wouldn't want children living in her house.

And, of course, he wouldn't want to live with somebody who didn't really love him and Lizzie.

Love. He suddenly thought of Dr. Jason McGuire. Dr. McGuire hardly knew him, but he sure did show Hunter that he loved him. So much like Papa. A warm feeling came over Hunter when he remembered Dr. McGuire saying, "I wish I had a son like you."

But Dr. McGuire lived in some big city somewhere, and was awfully busy with his work. Besides, maybe Mrs. McGuire wouldn't—

Hunter lifted his head and listened. Someone was calling his name. It sounded like Tom. Hunter got up and looked toward town. He could see twin lights winking through the trees. Then he heard it again: "Hu-u-nter-r!"

It was Tom's voice, all right.

Hunter wondered who else was with Tom. Probably the pastor. Would he be angry? Hunter hadn't meant to upset anybody.

The lights were getting nearer. Hunter cupped his hands to his mouth and shouted, "I'm over here!"

It took only seconds for them to hurry toward him. Hunter

saw Tom carrying a lantern, and Pastor Poole carrying another. It was the third man whose presence pleased Hunter the most. Dr. McGuire hadn't left yet for Smithburg. He had come with Tom and Pastor Poole to find him.

"Hunter, we were worried about you," Tom said.

"You shouldn't have run off like that, Hunter," Poole said. "Especially into these woods at night. There *are* wild animals out here, you know."

"Yes, sir. I...I just wanted to be near Papa. He was killed back there by the big tree. I—"

"It's all right, son," Poole said. "You gave us a pretty good scare though."

The boy dipped his chin. "I'm sorry."

Dr. McGuire moved forward and said, "Come on, son. We'll take you back home now." The doctor picked Hunter up and cradled him in his arms.

There was something about being in Dr. McGuire's arms and hearing his voice that went all the way to Hunter's heart. It was the closest to a father's touch he'd felt since his father died.

As they walked back toward town beneath the towering trees, Poole said, "Hunter, when we get back, we'll arrange a place for you and Lizzie to stay tonight. I'm calling a special meeting of the church tomorrow night to find a family who will adopt you and Lizzie. How does that sound?"

Hunter hesitated and then nodded his head.

When they arrived back at the Newman house, Bill Caterson was sitting at the kitchen table with Bessie and Thora, holding a sleepy-eyed Lizzie. Jane Louise had gone home. Everybody smiled and felt a moment's reprieve from the sad events of the day when they saw Hunter in Dr. McGuire's arms.

Bill said, "Hey, Hunter, you really had us worried."

Hunter did not reply, but when Dr. McGuire started to put him down, his little arms tightened on the doctor's neck. McGuire sat down near the table with Hunter on his lap.

Tom and the pastor doused their lanterns and remained standing as Bessie introduced Dr. McGuire to her husband.

Bill then turned to the pastor and said, "I was just telling Thora that Bessie and I'll take the children for the night."

"Did the ladies tell you I'm calling a special meeting of the church tomorrow night to find a family who'll take Hunter and Lizzie?"

"Yes," Bill said, looking down at the sleepy little girl in his arms. "Pastor, Bessie and I would love to adopt both of these children, but even with my new job in Greensboro, we couldn't afford it. I agree that the ideal thing would be for them to both be adopted into the same home, but if that doesn't work out, we'll take Lizzie. Bessie feels she's best suited for raising a little girl."

Poole nodded. "I understand. I'm trusting that the Lord will work it out according to His will." He rubbed his tired eyes and said, "We'll have Florence's funeral day after tomorrow."

Dr. McGuire gave Hunter a squeeze and lowered him to the floor. "Well, folks, I've got to head for Smithburg. I haven't seen Dr. Riley yet. Sure hope he's home when I get there."

Everybody followed the doctor onto the porch where he turned and bent down to hug Hunter once more, saying, "I'll be praying that you'll be adopted into a real good home, Hunter. Good-bye."

Hunter nodded, wishing Dr. McGuire didn't have to go. McGuire told the others good-bye and turned toward his surrey. Nelson Poole called after him, "Oh, Doctor! Florence didn't have much in the way of money. If you'll give me a figure, I'll take a special offering at the church to see that you're paid."

McGuire paused and raised his hand in a wave. "No charge. The smiles I got from Lizzie and the hugs I got from Hunter are pay enough."

CHAPTER FOUR

The night was dark except for the shimmering stars as Dr. Jason McGuire drove west toward Smithburg. The clip-clop of the horses' hooves echoed across the fields and was swallowed up in the dense stands of trees that lined the road.

McGuire could not shake the heaviness he felt for the Newman children. He would have adopted them in the blink of an eye if he could have. But with Ellie in a wheelchair, it was out of the question.

He considered talking to Ellie again. A nanny would make it possible. But he remembered Ellie's words the last time he had suggested adoption and hiring a nanny. McGuire shook his head. His desire was an island, gradually succumbing to the tides of reality.

When the surrey pulled into Smithburg it was after midnight, and most of the town was asleep. But he saw light glowing in the Rileys' parlor windows.

As McGuire guided the team toward the barn, a side door of the house opened, sending a slanted shaft of light into the darkness. He recognized the silhouette of the elderly physician and heard a familiar voice call out, "Jason! That you?"

"Yes, sir."

Riley walked toward him as he drew the surrey to a halt beside the elder doctor's buggy. McGuire slid from the seat and the two men embraced, pounding each other on the back.

"I just got back about half an hour ago," Riley said.

"Get the baby delivered all right?"

"Mm-hmm. What about Florence?"

"She...ah...she died."

"Oh, I'm so sorry."

"She was critical when I got there. I knew when I took one look at her that she would never pull through. Went peaceful, though, with her faith anchored in her Shepherd. Pastor Poole was with her."

"Praise the Lord. I assume the preacher will see to it that the children are placed in a good home."

"Let's talk about it after I get these horses in the corral. Can I buy some feed from you?"

"It'll cost you somewhere around fifty thousand dollars," Riley said.

"Charge it to the dust and let the rain settle it," McGuire bantered back.

Moments later, the two friends entered the house and broke the news of Florence Newman's death to Alfreda and Ellie.

"Pastor Poole is calling a special meeting of the church tomorrow night," McGuire said. "He's going to see if there's a family who will adopt them."

"Do you know if the prospects are good?" Riley asked. "The folks in that area are pretty poor."

"He knows it might be difficult. You know Bill and Bessie Caterson?"

"Sure do."

"They're moving to Greensboro, North Carolina, and they've offered to adopt Lizzie if no family will take both children."

"Separate them?" Ellie said. "That would be terrible. Mrs. Riley told me about their father being killed a year ago. And now they've just lost their mother. Certainly they shouldn't be separated."

"I agree," Jason said, "but they may have to be separated if one family can't take both of them."

"Be a shame," Riley said.

Ellie's eyes misted and her lips quivered. "Poor little dears. Mrs. Riley said the boy is five and the girl two."

"Yes," Jason said. "And they're both beautiful children. I especially got attached to Hunter. Wonderful little boy. Little Lizzie is pretty as a picture. Captured my heart with her smile."

Ellie was quiet for a moment, then looked at her husband. "I would say let's adopt them, but there's no way I could take care of them...at least the little girl. A two-year-old would be out of the question. I guess the boy might not be a problem for a mother in a wheelchair."

Jason's heart leaped in his breast. He turned to his wife and said, "Really? You think you could handle a five-year-old boy from your wheelchair, Ellie?"

Ellie smiled at him warmly but didn't comment.

He shrugged his shoulders and said, "Surely some family in the church will adopt them both. Of course, if they don't, the Catersons will adopt Lizzie and take her to North Carolina. Then...ah...someone in the church certainly will adopt Hunter."

"Of course," Ellie said.

Silence prevailed.

Jason cleared his throat. "On the other hand, maybe the poor little fellow will be left out in the cold."

Ellie sighed. "Well, if that happens, I guess we'd just have to take Hunter back to Boston with us."

Ellie's words started a riot inside Jason. Was she serious? No, she couldn't be. Dare he ask her? After all, even a five-year-old would demand a lot of attention. It would be too much to put such a load on Ellie. Of course, with a nanny...

"Jason," Alfreda said, "have you had anything to eat? Chet ate supper at the farm where he delivered the baby."

Food was the furthest thing from Jason's mind. "Oh...ah...no, ma'am, but really I'm not hungry."

"You're sure? I could fix some leftovers from the supper Ellie and I had."

"No. Really. I'm fine, thank you."

"Well, then," Alfreda said, sighing. "It's late. We'd best get to bed."

"Sounds good to me," Ellie said.

When Jason neither responded nor moved, Ellie said, "Sweetheart—"

Jason was lost in his own thoughts. He returned to reality with a start when he heard his wife say, "Sweetheart, where have you been? We've been talking about retiring for the night."

"Oh! Sure. I guess we'd better. We sure appreciate you two taking us in like this."

"Happy to do it," the older physician said. "After all, you and Ellie are just like family—like our own kids, you know."

Jason smiled. "Thank you."

Riley cocked his head. "Jason..."

"Yes, sir?"

"Your mind is still in McCann's Run, isn't it?"

Jason rubbed the back of his neck. "I...I just have to know if those little ones find a good Christian home. Tell you what. If you don't mind, Ellie and I will stay a little longer than we had planned. We'll drive over to McCann's Run day after tomorrow and see how the church meeting turned out."

"Of course we don't mind," Alfreda assured him. "Do we, Chet?"

"Not in the least. In fact, I'll just take Jason to the clinic with me tomorrow. Maybe since he's one of those hotshot big city doctors, he can teach this old country doctor something."

"Not in a million years," Jason said. "You've already forgotten more than I'll ever know." Then to Ellie: "Is that all right with you, sweetheart? Staying over and going to McCann's Run on Saturday?"

"Certainly. You're not alone in this, darling. I too want to know if those dear children will be adopted."

On Friday evening the members of McCann's Run Presbyterian Church gathered in their white frame building with the steeple on top. The pastor was in conversation with Thora and Jane Louise Kemp and Bill and Bessie Caterson, who sat on a front pew with the Newman children. Thora's other children were on the pew behind her. Tom Jackson and his Aunt Ophelia were on the front pew across the aisle.

At seven-thirty on the dot, Nelson Poole stepped behind the pulpit, called the meeting to order, and asked one of the men to open in prayer.

Four people slipped in just after the "Amen." Poole waited for them to take a seat, then said, "All of you know why I've called this special meeting." He looked over the congregation and did a quick survey, telling himself there were three families missing. He was about to proceed when a couple filed through the door. The sound of wagons rattling to a halt outside told him more were arriving.

Poole waited patiently for the others to enter. These people were farmers, and he understood the necessity of getting cows milked and stock fed after working in the fields all day. The three missing families were now in their pews.

"All of you know why I've called this special meeting. You've had time to think about the situation and make it a matter of prayer, so I'll get right to the point. Do we have a family willing to adopt Hunter and Lizzie Newman?"

People looked around at each other, waiting for someone to speak up. When no one did, the pastor said, "Mrs. Poole and I would love to do it, but you all know the size of the parsonage, and you all know my salary. We just can't do it."

A man stood up. "Brother Jenkins," Poole said in acknowledgment.

"Pastor, Audrey and I would love to adopt those precious kids, but we already have five. I just don't know how we could afford two more."

Others stood up one at a time, expressing the same reality. They couldn't afford to adopt even one of the Newman children, let alone both of them.

"Well, folks," Poole said, "since there's no one who can adopt Hunter and Lizzie, I have an alternate plan. I would like to see them stay together, so how about if we pass them from family to family a week at a time? That wouldn't impose a financial burden on anyone. With our small house, it will mean a couple of children sleep on the floor, but we can manage that when our turn comes. In fact, Mrs. Poole and I will take them the very first week."

A low rumble of discussion among the people went on for the better part of a minute, then Bill Caterson stood to his feet. "Pastor," he said, "the offer Bessie and I made to you last night still stands. We will adopt Lizzie. I wish we could afford to adopt both of them. We'd sure do it if we could. I don't like the idea of them being shifted from home to home every week. I know this would keep them together, but they need a home and family to call their own. That's what Bessie and I wish to do for Lizzie. We'd like to know that we have your blessing and the blessing of the church on our adopting her."

There was much discussion, but the final consensus of pastor and congregation was that the Catersons should adopt Lizzie and give her the home and security she needed.

Several families volunteered to take Hunter for a week at a time, and Mrs. Poole wrote down their names. The pastor then told the volunteers that his wife would set up the schedule and post it on the church bulletin board so each family would know when it was their turn.

When the meeting was dismissed, Hunter began to cry, saying he didn't want to be separated from his sister.

Bill Caterson knelt down beside Hunter and said, "North Carolina isn't real far away. We'll try to work it out so we can have you down once in a while to spend a few days with Lizzie. Would that make you happy?"

The boy nodded, wiping his tears.

"Then we'll work on that," Bill said, patting the boy's arm.

Tom Jackson sat beside Hunter with his arm around the boy, and the families who had volunteered to take Hunter gathered around him, letting him know they would be glad to have him in their homes.

The next day, Jason and Ellie McGuire arrived in McCann's Run at 9:30 A.M., figuring they would talk to the pastor before the funeral. But as they rounded the corner on the dusty street where the church stood, they saw wagons, buggies, and surreys pulling into the churchyard.

"Looks like they have their funerals early around here," Jason said.

Inside the white frame building, a closed coffin decorated with flowers rested on a stand in front of the pulpit. People quietly filed in while the woman at the pump organ played a hymn. Six men who had volunteered as pall bearers sat on a front pew. Across the aisle on the second pew, Bill and Bessie Caterson, with Lizzie, were sitting with Mrs. Poole. Hunter sat next to Mrs. Poole with Tom Jackson on his other side.

In an attempt to avoid looking at the coffin, Hunter kept turning around to glance toward the rear of the church. He happened to be looking that way when he saw Dr. McGuire enter, pushing a lady in a wheelchair. His heart beat faster. He looked up at Mrs. Poole and whispered, "Dr. McGuire just came in.

Could I please go see him for a minute?"

"All right," she replied, "but don't stay very long. The service will be starting in a few minutes."

Hunter looked up at Tom as he slid off the pew and said, "Dr. McGuire's here!"

"Yes, I saw him," Tom said.

Mrs. Poole leaned toward Tom. "Maybe you'd better go with him so he's sure to come back in time."

"Yes, ma'am. Come on, Hunter."

Compassionate eyes from the people in the pews watched little Hunter Newman as he walked in front of Tom Jackson to the back of the church. There was a space behind the last row of pews, then a final pew was positioned against the back wall. Jason had parked Ellie's wheelchair next to the side wall and was just sitting down beside her when he saw the little boy hurrying toward him with Tom on his heels.

Ellie McGuire watched her husband lift the bright-eyed child into his arms and felt a lump rise in her throat when she saw how Hunter clung to Jason's neck. Then Jason set the boy down and said in a subdued voice, "Hunter, this is my wife, Ellie. Ellie, this is Hunter Newman."

Hunter was taken aback for just a second at the sight of the doctor's wife in a wheelchair, but he covered his surprise quickly. She was very pretty, and he could tell by the look in her eyes that she liked him.

Ellie opened her arms, smiling. "Could I have a hug?"

Hunter complied, squeezing her neck hard. Tom greeted Ellie, then took the boy back to the front pew.

As her husband sat next to her, Ellie leaned over and said in a soft whisper, "I can see why you had such an instant attraction to the boy. He's precious."

*****

Later, at the cemetery, when the graveside service was over, the McGuires waited patiently while the mourners moved past Hunter and Lizzie. Pastor and Mrs. Poole stood close by and also greeted the people. The McGuires were listening as the pastor explained what had happened at the church meeting.

"I hate to see Hunter and Lizzie separated," Jason McGuire said, "but I'm glad Lizzie will have a good home. But this bouncing Hunter from family to family bothers me. He needs a permanent home, too."

"I agree," Poole said, "but we don't have any choice. At least he'll have good care. I can assure you of that."

McGuire rubbed his chin for a few seconds and then said, "Pastor, would you excuse us for a moment? I need to talk to Ellie alone."

Jason leaned close to Ellie and said, "Darlin', I...I really feel the Lord wants us to—"

"Adopt Hunter?" she said.

"Yes. It's been all I could think of for two days."

"I realize that. And I agree with you that the circumstances seem providential for Hunter to have parents and for us to have a son."

"Do you mean it?"

"As long as there's no talk about hiring a nanny. I told you Thursday night that I could handle a five-year-old from my wheelchair. If Hunter becomes our son, I don't want some nanny raising him. I want us to raise him. I'll be everything to him a mother can be, I promise you."

Jason's whole body tingled. "All right. Let's talk to the pastor."

McGuire saw Poole looking their way and motioned to him. As he approached McGuire said, "Pastor, would there be any objection to Ellie and me adopting Hunter?"

The preacher's eyes widened. "Why, of course not. I think it would be wonderful. My only concern is the...the wheelchair. Can you handle a five-year-old boy, ma'am?"

"I can," Ellie said firmly.

"Well, I certainly can be a character witness for you, if you'd like to take care of it on Monday at the same time the Catersons adopt Lizzie."

"The only thing left is to present this to Hunter," Jason said. "I want him to be in total agreement."

"Certainly," Poole said, turning to call to the boy. "Hunter, would you come over here?"

He had been watching the McGuires and Pastor Poole and he came on the run.

His eyes flitted from Ellie to Jason to Nelson Poole as the pastor said, "Hunter, Dr. and Mrs. McGuire would like to talk to you about something very important."

"Yes, sir."

McGuire dropped to one knee and said, "Hunter, as you can see, Mrs. McGuire—Ellie—is in a wheelchair."

"Yes, sir," Hunter said, setting his sky-blue gaze on Ellie.

"And...well, Hunter, she can't have babies and be a mother like other women. Like your mother did. So we don't have any children."

"Yes, sir."

"Thursday, when I came to your house to see if I could help your mother, I saw right away that you are a very special boy. You've been taught well by your parents. You're respectful to your elders, and you're a good brother to your little sister. Well, Hunter, we just told Pastor Poole that we will adopt you, if you want to be our son."

Hunter's smile spread from ear to ear. "Oh, yes, sir! Yes, sir!"

Jason took the boy in his arms and held him, trying to keep from breaking into tears. "Then on Monday, Hunter, Ellie and I will go with Pastor Poole to the county magistrate's office and adopt you."

"Oh, thank you, sir!" Hunter rushed to Ellie to give her a hug and thank her too. Then he said to both of them, "Couldn't you adopt my sister, too?"

Jason explained that the Catersons had already set their hearts on adopting Lizzie, and that Ellie's being confined to the wheelchair would make it impossible for her to take care of a two-year-old. He promised Hunter that they would make arrangements with the Catersons for Hunter and Lizzie to see each other often.

The next day, the McGuires attended the services at McCann's Run Presbyterian Church. The news was out, and people looked on with pleasure as they saw Hunter sitting on the pew next to Dr. McGuire and his wife.

Pastor Nelson Poole preached on adoption, showing from the Bible that Christians are not only born into God's family by receiving Christ into their hearts, but they are also given the status of heirs of God and joint-heirs with Christ through adoption.

On Monday, Nelson Poole accompanied the McGuires and the Catersons to the county magistrate's office, and the children were legally adopted. Bill Caterson assured Dr. McGuire they would keep in touch by mail. McGuire told them he would finance any trips to Boston the Catersons could make, and that from time to time, he and Ellie would come to Greensboro with Hunter.

Early the next morning, Bill and Bessie loaded their wagon and were ready to pull out. The McGuires had driven to McCann's Run with Hunter so he could say good-bye to his little sister. Pastor Poole and Tom Jackson were also there.

While Ellie looked on from the surrey seat, Jason led Hunter by the hand to the Caterson wagon.

Tears were streaming down Hunter's cheeks as he hugged his little sister and said with shaky voice, "Good-bye, Lizzie. I love you."

Hunter's tears caused Lizzie to start crying. "Wuv you," she said, sniffling.

Bill handed Lizzie back to Bessie. "God bless you all!" he said, as he climbed aboard.

"We'll write you as soon as we get settled in Greensboro!" Bessie called.

As the wagon pulled away, Jason picked Hunter up and held him.

"It'll be all right, Son," Jason told him. "We'll make sure you get to see Lizzie real often."

When the Caterson wagon was out of sight, Jason said, a quaver in his voice, "Well, I guess we'd better get going."

Tom moved close to Hunter and laid a hand on his shoulder. "Well, little friend," he said, blinking back tears, "I don't know when we'll see each other again, but I'm going to pray that the Lord will make it happen."

The best friends hugged and told each other good-bye, then the surrey moved west and Tom was lost from Hunter's view.

CHAPTER FIVE

It was Sunday afternoon, May 20, 1855. The sky was threatening rain over Cambridge, Massachusetts, and had forced the graduation exercises of Harvard Medical School indoors.

The great auditorium was slowly filling up as family and friends of the graduates made their way inside hoping to find choice seats. A section directly in front of the platform was roped off for seating the graduates.

Dr. Jason McGuire, his hair now streaked with silver, wheeled Ellie through the front door and down the center aisle. Ellie was as pretty as ever, even with a few lines added to her face and some threads of silver in her hair.

When they came near the section just behind the roped area, a young man with a white armband greeted them.

"Good afternoon, folks. This section is reserved for the immediate family of the graduates. Do you have a ticket?"

"Yes," Jason said with a smile, reaching inside his European-made black suit. He produced two tickets and handed them to the young Harvard student. "Our son is graduating today, young man. Would there be a place where I could stash this wheelchair? I'd like his mother to sit in one of the seats."

"Of course, sir. I'll take it over there by the west wall for you."

Other people were filling in the special section as Jason lifted Ellie from her chair and placed her in one of the opera-type seats.

Soon the auditorium was packed, and at three o'clock the band struck up a lively march and the school officials filed onto the platform, clad in gowns and mortarboards with tassels swinging. When the faculty and staff of the Harvard Medical School and top officials of the university were seated, the band struck up an inspiring processional.

Everyone on the platform rose to their feet, and then the audience stood. The standing audience blocked Ellie's view of the graduates as they moved down the aisle from the back of the auditorium, but she would be able to see her son when he passed her row.

Ellie saw Jason's mouth quiver and watched him brush moisture from his cheeks. Then Hunter came into view, looking like a prince to Ellie. Just the sight of him was enough to start her crying softly from joy and pride.

Hunter had grown into a tall, athletic young man. He stood two inches over six feet and was ruggedly handsome.

When the graduates were all in their places, the president of Harvard University introduced Dr. Gabriel Rains, pastor of Boston's Broadway Baptist Church, asking him to say the opening prayer.

Rains's prayer exalted Jesus Christ and asked His blessings on the graduates who would go out to serve mankind. At his "Amen," the great audience sat down, and the ceremonies began.

After the commencement address, the graduates walked to the side of the platform to receive their diplomas in alphabetical order.

When the name "Hunter Newman McGuire" was called, tears spilled down Ellie's cheeks. Jason put an arm around her as Hunter walked to the center of the platform to receive his degree. Jason leaned close to whisper, "That boy has made me so proud."

*****

When the graduation exercises were over, and the graduates were being swarmed by their families and friends, Hunter McGuire hurried back to where he knew his parents were seated. As he approached them through the crowd, Jason smiled and said, "Hello, Dr. McGuire."

Hunter embraced his father. "Thank you, Dad, for being my inspiration all the way through medical school. I hope I can be half the physician and surgeon that you are."

"You'll be ten times what I am, Son."

Hunter then leaned over and wrapped his arms around the woman who had so wonderfully cared for him. As he held her close, he said into her ear, "I love you. Thank you for being my mom."

"Thank you for being such a wonderful son," Ellie said warmly.

"Hey, Hunter! If you don't quit hugging that beautiful lady, her husband will probably break your neck!"

Jason laughed as Hunter turned around to face John Brinton with his fiancée, Betty Miller. "Well," Hunter said with a chuckle, "if it isn't *Doctor* John Brinton."

"Yes! And don't you forget it, *Doctor* Hunter McGuire!"

The McGuires offered congratulations to John for his graduation and imminent marriage. Betty then turned to Hunter and said sincerely, "I've said this several times before, but I must say it again. Thank you for caring enough about John's eternal destiny to lead him to Jesus. If you hadn't won him to the Lord and brought him to church, we would never have met."

"My pleasure, Betty," Hunter said, then blushed as she raised up on tiptoe and planted a kiss on his cheek.

Ellie smiled at Betty and said, "Well, dear, by this time two weeks from today, you'll be Mrs. Dr. John Brinton."

"That's right," Betty said. "John and I will have been husband

and wife for nearly two hours by this time in two weeks." She turned and said, "And Hunter is going to be best man!"

"I disagree with that," John said. "If Hunter was the best man at the wedding, *he* would be the one with the bride!"

Everyone laughed.

John clapped a hand on Hunter's shoulder and said, "Well, Hunter, maybe you'll catch the bride's bouquet and finally find a woman who'll have you!"

Hunter playfully clipped his dark-haired friend on the chin and said, "Oh, yeah? I've had women swarming all over me since I was ten years old. I have to beat them off with clubs."

John waggled his head. "Well, lah-dee-dah! How come you aren't the one getting married, then, Romeo?"

"Simple. The right little gal hasn't yet walked into my life. When she does, I'll know it, and grab her."

"Well, I hope she shows up before you're sporting a cane and living in a rocking chair!"

No rain had fallen yet, but the dark clouds were still hanging low as the McGuire surrey rolled off the campus with Hunter at the reins. Ellie sat between her two men.

"Son," Jason said, "I want you to know how proud Mom and I are of you. What a joy to watch our boy walk across that platform and receive his degree. And on top of that, to hear you listed as an honor student."

Ellie turned to smile at her son and saw the shadow of sadness that suddenly clouded Hunter's face.

"Hunter...what's wrong?"

"I...I sure wish Lizzie could have been here to see me graduate."

Jason reached around Ellie's back and squeezed Hunter's shoulder. "I wish she could have too, Son."

*****

The Brinton-Miller wedding took place as scheduled on Sunday afternoon, June 3. After the reception in the fellowship hall at Broadway Baptist Church, John and Betty stepped out the door where a decorated buggy waited with a "Just Married" sign on the back.

The crowd looked on gleefully as the young unmarried women collected, each one hoping to catch the bride's bouquet. There was much laughter as Betty tossed the bouquet into the air and it bounded off hands and fingers for a few seconds before a young woman caught it. Then the crowd made two lines for the bride and groom to run between so they could pelt the couple with rice on their way to the buggy. Hunter McGuire had rice in both hands.

Just before John and Betty started their run, one of Betty's friends dashed up to her with a second bouquet and whispered in her ear. When the couple headed for the buggy, ducking their heads against the flying rice, they paused long enough for Betty to toss the bouquet straight at Hunter. He caught it in a reflexive movement and stood with a bemused look on his face as everyone laughed.

He continued to hold the bouquet, turning it in his hands as the buggy bounded down the dusty street, noisily dragging old pots, pans, and buckets.

CHAPTER SIX

Afternoon sunshine cast long shadows across the Virginia countryside as the train chugged toward Lexington on Wednesday, June 6, 1855. Dr. Hunter McGuire was about to begin his internship at the Kurtz-Aaron Medical Clinic.

As the coach rocked soothingly, Hunter let his gaze roam over the rolling landscape. Wildflowers picked up the gold of the lowering sun and the evening breeze tufted the grass. His eyes and ears were attentive to every tangent and curve, to the rhythm of the wheels on the rail joints, to the flow of the train along the smooth tracks.

Suddenly the rear door of the coach opened and closed with a brief rise in volume of the clacking wheels. The conductor's high-pitched voice filled the coach, "Lexington, ten minutes! Lexington, ten minutes!" and then was gone as the man passed through to the next coach.

The train ran on without breaking stride for another five minutes, then the engine's long whistle blast fled by the window in gusty waves, and the town came into view.

Soon the engine was chugging into the depot with the bell ringing. When the brakes squealed and the engine released steam with a loud hiss as it came to a halt, the young doctor stretched his arms and yawned. The other passengers were gathering their belongings as Hunter hoisted his long, muscular frame and stood up in the aisle. He reached for his bag and hat in the overhead bin and moved slowly toward the front of the coach.

When he stepped onto the platform and ran his eyes over the crowd, he spotted a short, thick-bodied man with carrot-red hair. When their eyes met, the man broke into a smile and hurried toward him.

"Dr. McGuire," he said, extending his hand. "Weldon Kurtz."

It felt good to hear the 'doctor' adjoined to his name. Hunter knew it would take awhile to get used to it.

As they shook hands, Kurtz said, "You look exactly like the daguerreotype you sent with your application. Couldn't have missed you. Dr. Aaron and I have certainly been looking forward to your working with us at the clinic."

"Not as much as I've been looking forward to it," Hunter said with a grin.

"I assume you have more luggage."

"Yes. There's a trunk in the baggage coach."

"Well, let's go get it."

The doctors had acquired a nice room for Hunter at one of Lexington's best boarding houses. Dr. Kurtz got him settled there, then took him in his buggy to a restaurant where they were to meet Dr. Bryce Aaron for supper.

Aaron was waiting for them, leaning against his buggy. Hunter knew it was him when he smiled and raised a hand in a friendly gesture. He was about Kurtz's height, but was quite slender and balding. Hunter climbed down, and the two men shook hands and introduced themselves.

After they had begun their meal, Dr. Aaron said, "Well, Dr.

McGuire, you've come to a very busy clinic. We have the only facility of its kind between Roanoke—fifty-five miles to the south—and Staunton—thirty-five miles to the north. I hope you've come expecting a lot of hard work. We're getting busier all the time."

"I welcome hard work, Doctor. I want to do my part while I'm interning here, and I want to learn as much as I can."

Kurtz winked at Aaron and said, "We were hoping you'd be the one to teach *us,* Doctor...being a graduate of Harvard and all."

"Especially a Harvard graduate who graduated in the top five of his class," Aaron said, and winked back.

Hunter's sand-colored eyebrows arched. "And just how did you learn that?"

Aaron took a sip of coffee. "Oh, we received a letter from a certain person who thought we ought to be aware that we've hired a genius."

Hunter tilted back his head and laughed heartily. "Okay, so my mom thinks I'm a genius. You know how mothers are."

"Yes," Aaron said with a chuckle, "we both have them."

"But seriously, Dr. McGuire," Kurtz said, "we're quite pleased to have you interning at our clinic."

"Thank you," Hunter said humbly. "The pleasure is mine."

Dr. Aaron looked at Hunter with a steady, pleasant expression. "In your application you said you were Virginia-born."

Hunter swallowed his bite of food. "Yes, sir. McCann's Run. It's in the western part of the commonwealth. Rural area. About halfway between Parkersburg and Clarksburg."

"You left there when you were pretty young, I recall."

"Yes, sir. I was five."

"Was your father practicing in that area up until that time?"

"No. It's a long story, but I'm a McGuire by adoption. My real father died when I was four, and my mother died a year later. Dr. Jason McGuire just happened to be in the area when my mother was dying, and he filled in for the family doctor. The McGuires adopted me and took me to Boston."

"You were the only child?" Kurtz asked, lifting his coffee cup to take a sip.

"I had a sister. Lizzie. Younger than me. Someone else adopted her. So how many employees do you have in the clinic?"

Both doctors took the hint and left the subject alone.

"Well, let's see," Aaron said. "We have three certified medical nurses on staff, and three nurses' aides. One of those aides is working toward her C.M.N. We have a janitor who comes in and cleans once a day, and a receptionist who works the day shift. She also does the filing work, takes care of the books, and does the banking. So we have eight employees."

"As you might guess," Kurtz said, "we work one C.M.N. and one aide on each of the three shifts. We have ten beds in one ward at the clinic, so the teams of two can pretty well handle it. Dr. Aaron and I normally work the day shift, but we both live close by, so if we're needed at any time during the other two shifts, we can easily be contacted."

Hunter nodded. "In our correspondence, you mentioned your plans to one day become a full-fledged hospital."

"Most assuredly," Kurtz said. "We figure we're maybe four years away from realizing that dream. But we'll make it by then, won't we, Doctor?"

"I have no doubt," Aaron said. "And it will be sorely needed by then, the way the population is growing around here."

The meal was soon finished and Dr. Aaron reminded his partner that they had a patient to check on before bedtime. Kurtz told him to go ahead, he would drive Dr. McGuire to the boarding house. Aaron bid McGuire good night; he would see him just before seven o'clock when the day shift started.

As Hunter rode with Dr. Kurtz through the dimly lit streets of Lexington, he said, "I've known for years that the Virginia Military Institute is here. I didn't notice it when the train pulled in."

"It's up on a hill that way," Kurtz said, pointing. "You can see it in daylight if you know where to look. See that cluster of lights up there?"

"Mm-hmm."

"That's it. You'll see the cadets around town a lot. Always in their uniforms. We treat one every now and then. Fine young men. Courteous and well disciplined."

Kurtz drove past the clinic so Hunter could see it, then headed toward the boarding house.

The next morning the sun was just above the tree-lined hills when Dr. Hunter McGuire left the boarding house and headed toward the clinic. The air was cool, and birds were singing in the trees.

A few of Lexington's citizens were on the streets as Hunter walked, and they responded warmly as he greeted them. When he reached the clinic, he entered the front door and found the reception area deserted. He moved past the reception desk, through a set of double doors, and into the hallway. A pretty lady in white was coming his way, carrying a bundle of sheets and pillowcases. She wore no cap, which identified her as the nurse's aide. When her glance fell on the tall young man, she stopped and smiled. "Good morning, Dr. McGuire. Welcome to the clinic, and to Lexington."

"Well, thank you, ma'am. But how do you know me?"

She giggled and said, "Us single girls have been studying your picture. The one you sent with your application."

Hunter blushed. "Oh. I didn't know the doctors had made it public."

The young woman set the bundle on a nearby table and extended her hand. "I'm Rita Watkins, nurse's aide."

Hunter gripped her hand lightly. "I'm happy to meet you, ma'am."

At that moment, a nurse appeared, coming from what appeared to be the ward at the end of the hall. Rita Watkins introduced Hunter to Molly Mulvane, who was in her early fifties. She explained they were about to go off duty when nurse Carolynn Atherton and nurse's aide May Godfrey came in. Both called the new intern by name before they were introduced. Again Hunter blushed, but found them to be charming ladies.

Then the doctors came in together, followed by young Doralee Chambers, the receptionist.

The day started off with Dr. Aaron giving Hunter a tour, acquainting him with the layout of the building and the normal routine of the day shift. Aaron explained that he and Dr. Kurtz wanted him to work the day shift for a month, the evening shift for the next month, and the night shift for a month after that. This schedule would give him a working knowledge of the differences in each shift.

The rest of the day was anything but dull. First Hunter was called upon to treat an elderly man who had fallen off a horse and broken his shoulder. Dr. Kurtz watched to see if Hunter could handle it and he passed with flying colors. Next was a teenage girl who had seriously cut her hand while learning to cut up chickens for canning. According to Dr. Aaron, Hunter did a perfect job of treating the cut, taking stitches, and bandaging.

Then a middle-aged man was brought in with heart failure, and Hunter worked side by side with Dr. Aaron for nearly four hours. In spite of their efforts, the man died, and Hunter had a first lesson in how to harness his compassion and grief and work with professional objectivity.

When three o'clock came, Hunter was worn out more from emotional strain than the hours he had put in. He was working with Dr. Kurtz on one of the elderly patients in the ward when Carolynn Atherton walked up and said that nurse Maude Edwards and aide Jodie Lockwood were in the building and she and May would be leaving for the day.

A few minutes later, a matronly woman in her early fifties came into the ward.

Dr. Kurtz looked up and said, "Maude, I want you to meet—"

"Dr. Hunter Newman McGuire," Maude finished for him, smiling at Hunter. "Glad to meet you, Doctor. Only I think you're better looking than Doralee was able to describe. She's not much with words."

Kurtz chuckled and said, "Maude, I think you're too old for him."

"I know that, Doctor, but I'm trying to help the single girls around this place find husbands."

"You count me out, Mrs. Edwards," Hunter said with a grin.

"Oh?"

"Yes, ma'am."

"And why's that? You a confirmed bachelor?"

"No, ma'am. But I—"

Maude turned around to see what had cut off the young doctor's words.

A petite young woman smiled at the small group and then fixed her attention on Hunter. "Hello, Dr. McGuire. I'm Jodie Lockwood, the nurse's aide for this shift."

Hunter McGuire was so struck with the young woman that he could hardly breathe. He guessed she was about eighteen. She had jet-black hair, deep-brown eyes, exquisitely noble features, and a blinding smile.

Jodie extended her hand and Hunter took it, returning her smile. "It's a pleasure to meet you Miss Lockwood. It is *Miss* Lockwood?"

"Yes."

"Jodie's the aide Dr. Aaron told you is working on her C.M.N. certificate," Kurtz said.

"Oh, yes. That's great, Miss Lockwood."

"How has your first day been?" she asked.

Hunter paused, thought on it, then said, "Well-l-l…it's

been...ah...educational, to say the least. But all in all, it's been enjoyable. And I'm sure excited about working here."

That night, Hunter had a hard time getting to sleep. The fascinating face of Jodie Lockwood wouldn't leave his mind. He told himself that if she wasn't a Christian, the first thing he would do was give her the gospel and do everything he could to lead her to the Lord.

He told God that he knew something completely different than anything he had ever experienced before had happened deep inside him the instant he laid eyes on Jodie. He had dated many young women in his church in Boston. Some were pleasant company, and he enjoyed being with them, but he had never felt anything like this.

Hunter finally fell asleep sometime after midnight. When he woke up the next morning, seeing Jodie was foremost on his mind.

Hunter chatted with Jodie at shift-change time on Friday and learned that she was seventeen. Even though she was a year younger than he had presumed, it made no difference. She was quite mature for her age. He was also thrilled to learn that she wasn't seeing anyone.

On Saturday, after an exhausting shift, Hunter and Carolynn Atherton were in the ward room attending an elderly woman when Jodie and Maude Edwards came in to start their shift.

Jodie came over to stand beside Hunter and looked at the patient, then glanced at Hunter. "Good afternoon, Dr. McGuire. What happened here?"

"Mrs. Caldwell fell out of bed a few moments ago," Hunter said. "I can't find anything broken, but she banged herself up some. And how are you this beautiful day?"

"Just fine. Hello, Carolynn."

"Hi, Jodie."

Jodie glanced at Hunter again and said, "Dr. McGuire, before you leave, I need to see you for a moment."

"All right. We're about through here. I'll come find you."

Ten minutes later, Hunter found Jodie by the reception area talking to Doctors Aaron and Kurtz. As he walked toward them, she broke off the conversation politely and said, "There you are."

Both doctors waited as Jodie said, "I'll only detain you a moment, Dr. McGuire."

I wish you'd detain me for the rest of my life, Hunter thought. Aloud, he said, "My time is yours, Miss Lockwood. Did you want to talk in private?"

"Oh, no. That won't be necessary."

Hunter felt a jab of disappointment.

The doctors were still standing there as Jodie said, "I just wanted to ask if you were planning to attend church services tomorrow."

"As a matter of fact, I am," he said. "I'm going to First Baptist."

Jodie's eyes lit up. "Well, that's exactly where I was going to ask you to come...as my guest. Will you? Come as my guest that is?"

"Well of course!"

The doctors moved closer. "Forgive me, Dr. McGuire," Dr. Kurtz said. "I was going to invite you to First Methodist Church, but just hadn't gotten around to it."

"And I was going to invite you to Oaklawn Presbyterian with me and my family tomorrow," Dr. Aaron said.

"No forgiveness necessary, gentlemen," Hunter said. "But since Jodie asked me first, I'll go as her guest."

"So you're a Baptist, eh?" Aaron said in mock dismay.

"Smart man," Jodie said with a giggle.

"Hah!" Kurtz said. "If he really had good sense, he'd be a Methodist!"

Everybody laughed, then Hunter said, "There isn't any

church going to take a person to heaven. Only Jesus can do that."

There was a twinkle in Jodie's eye as she said, "Even if being a Baptist isn't what takes a person to heaven, I figure as long as I'm going to make the trip, I might as well go first class!"

The three men laughed heartily.

"Dr. McGuire," Jodie said, "we have a lot of fun kidding each other around here, but let me say seriously, these two wonderful men are a joy to work for. You will come to love them dearly when you've been here awhile."

"I'm already getting quite attached to them," Hunter said.

"Will you need a ride to church in the morning?" she asked.

"No, thank you. My landlord said I could use one of his buggies anytime."

"And you know where the church is?"

"Yes. I saw it when Dr. Kurtz first took me to the boarding house."

"Well, Sunday school is at ten, and the preaching service is at eleven. The Sunday evening service starts at seven."

"Thank you, m'lady," Hunter said, bowing slightly.

Jodie curtsied.

Hunter bowed again, excused himself, and headed for home.

The Sunday morning church services were a joy and an inspiration to Hunter. He liked the pastor's preaching, and he liked the warm, friendly people. He was pleased to see a good number of cadets from the Virginia Military Institute in attendance.

Jodie introduced Hunter to Mr. and Mrs. Walter Blevins, who rented a room to Jodie in their home. The Blevinses invited Hunter to have Sunday dinner with them.

During the meal, Jodie offered to take Hunter on a tour of the town. Hunter accepted, saying they could use his landlord's horse and buggy.

The day couldn't have been more beautiful as Hunter and Jodie drove through the streets of Lexington and around its perimeter. How much better the birds sang since he had met Jodie Lockwood! The sun shone brighter and the air smelled sweeter.

As Jodie directed Hunter through the wealthy neighborhood, he ran his gaze over the fancy mansions with their high fences and superbly manicured yards, then looked at her and said, "It sure was a joy to find out you're a Christian, Miss Jodie."

"And for me to learn the same about you. And I'm glad you like the church."

"It's great."

As they left the wealthy section, Jodie pointed up the hill to the west and said, "There's V.M.I."

"Impressive."

"Mm-hmm. They call it the West Point of the South."

"Oh? I wasn't aware of that."

"Quite a setup, they have. On some days, you'll hear the cannons."

"Cannons?"

"They teach them cannoneering, along with the use of muskets and handguns. The cannon field is set up near the foothills of the Appalachian Mountains a few miles west of the Institute."

"That's interesting." Hunter paused, then said, "Have you dated any of the cadets?"

"A few. They're nice young men. Very polite and gentlemanly ...like yourself. I suppose you dated lots of young women in Boston."

"Some."

Hunter wanted to blurt out that he had never met a girl who so thrilled and captivated him as she did, but he kept it inside. They were now back in the center of the business district, where the tour had officially started.

"Well," Jodie said with a sigh, "that's about it. You've seen Lexington now. How do you like it?"

Hunter aimed the buggy toward the section of town where the Blevins lived.

"Fine. It's a real nice town." He wanted to add that the best thing about Lexington was that Jodie Lockwood lived there.

Jodie sighed again, and said, "I'm sure going to miss it."

Hunter wasn't sure he'd heard her correctly. "What did you say?"

"I said I'm sure going to miss Lexington."

"Y-you're leaving?"

"Yes. Next Friday. I'm moving to Baltimore."

CHAPTER SEVEN

Jodie's words were like a battering ram to Hunter's midsection. "Baltimore? How...how come?"

"Well, I've been with Dr. Kurtz and Dr. Aaron for the past fourteen months working toward my C.M.N. certificate. You probably know that means I'm halfway there. But my real desire is to also earn my C.S.A. certificate."

"Surgeon's assistant," Hunter said. "But that certificate can be earned only under a surgeon who is on the staff of a hospital approved by the American Medical Association."

"That's right. Have you heard of Dr. Benjamin Karr?"

"He's Baltimore's most prominent surgeon. One of the best in the whole country. Has his own clinic."

"He's also on staff of the hospital in Baltimore and the one in Washington, D. C. Both are approved by the AMA. So Dr. Kurtz, bless his heart, contacted Dr. Karr and asked if he would hire me and allow me to finish my C.M.N. training there while also gaining time and experience toward my C.S.A. certificate."

Jodie seemed so excited that Hunter put a smile on his face and managed to hide his disappointment.

Jodie's words came faster now. "The Lord had it all planned, Dr. McGuire. On the same day Dr. Karr received the letter, one of his potential C.S.A.s told him she was quitting in two weeks to get married. So...as of a week from tomorrow, I'll start to work for Dr. Karr! Isn't it wonderful?"

"Sure, that's great," he said. "I'm real happy for you." *Lord, forgive me for lying. I'm not happy about it at all.*

In the days that followed Jodie's announcement, Hunter hardly noticed the singing birds or sunshine or the smell of Virginia's fresh air. His heart was like a dead thing in his chest.

Each day when Jodie arrived for the evening shift, Hunter spent as much time with her as possible and had to act as if he were happy for this turn of events in her life. He desperately wanted to tell her he loved her, but it had to remain his secret for now.

At nine-thirty Friday morning, Jodie came into the clinic accompanied by Mr. and Mrs. Blevins, who were taking her to the depot to catch the train to Richmond. There she would board another train for Baltimore.

Hunter wished he could be with Jodie right up to the minute she boarded, but it was out of the question. He was on duty. And as far as Jodie and the others knew, they were just friends...barely acquainted.

Carolynn Atherton and May Godfrey came from the ward and joined the three doctors to tell Jodie good-bye. Carolynn and May embraced her and wished her the best, then excused themselves to get back to their patients.

Hunter looked on as tears misted Jodie's eyes when she moved close to Kurtz and Aaron and said, "I owe you two so much. Thank you for all you've done for me. She hugged them both as they expressed their wishes for her great success.

Then Jodie turned to Hunter and said, "It was a genuine pleasure to meet you, Dr. McGuire. I can see a wonderful future for you. God bless you."

"God bless you too, Miss Jodie," he managed to choke out. "I know you will do well as a surgeon's assistant."

Jodie smiled up at him and said, "If you're ever in Baltimore, look me up. It would be nice to see you again."

Hunter's smile felt painted on. "I'll do that."

Suddenly, she opened her arms. "I've hugged everyone else good-bye around here, do you mind if I do the same with you?"

The painful thudding of his heart seemed audible to Hunter as he felt Jodie's arms around him and he pressed his hands to her back.

Suddenly she was out of his arms and saying in a brisk tone, "Well, folks, we'd better get going."

The Blevinses moved out the door first, and Jodie followed while the doctors watched them walk to the surrey. Mr. Blevins took his wife's hand to help her aboard while Jodie waited.

Hunter saw his chance and hurried up to Jodie. "Here, Miss Jodie, allow me."

"Why, thank you, Dr. McGuire."

Hunter held on as she eased onto the seat.

Jodie smiled at him and said, "Good-bye, Doctor."

"Good-bye." Hunter wanted to cry out that he loved her, but all he did was stand and watch as the surrey pulled away and turned the corner. Jodie waved one more time before the surrey carried her from view. He felt as if she were taking his heart with her, and the pain wrung a groan from him.

When he returned to the clinic door, the doctors were still where he had left them. There was a sudden rumbling like thunder, and Hunter glanced up at the clear sky, then looked at the doctors as they chuckled.

"Cannons," Kurtz said.

"Oh, yes. Miss Jodie told me the Institute trains the cadets in cannoneering."

"It's been a couple of weeks since we've heard them," Aaron said. "You ever handle a gun, Dr. McGuire?"

"As a matter of fact, I do," Hunter said. "Or I should say I did. In my growing up years, my dad took me hunting in northern Massachusetts and southern New Hampshire. I got pretty good with a musket. Dad also taught me how to use a handgun."

"Well, remind me to stay on your good side," Kurtz said.

The three doctors laughed, then Aaron said, "Well, gentlemen, we've got work to do."

One night, about a week later, Hunter read his Bible, then doused the lantern and crawled into bed. Lying there with moonlight streaming through the window, he prayed, "Lord, I've got to be honest with You. I don't understand. Surely You didn't let me meet Jodie and fall in love with her just to tear my heart out? I've never felt about any girl like I feel about her. And I believe she would've fallen in love with me if we'd had enough time together.

"It just seems to me that it was Your hand that brought us together and that You mean for me to have Jodie for my wife, Lord Jesus. So I'm asking You to keep her from falling for someone else till I can tell her how I feel...and You can help her to love me, too."

On a rainy afternoon, when Jodie had been gone for over a month, Hunter arrived at the clinic for the evening shift just as a wagon marked "Virginia Military Institute" hauled up and came to a stop. A uniformed man was sitting in the bed of the wagon.

"Sir, are you one of the doctors here?" the man asked.

"Yes. I'm Dr. McGuire. May I help you?"

"Yes, Doctor. We have a very sick cadet here."

Hunter looked into the wagon bed and saw a ghostly pale young man, gritting his teeth and clutching his midsection.

"Let's get him inside," Hunter said.

"Doralee," Hunter said as he and the uniformed men entered the reception area, "this young man may have an acute attack of appendicitis. Would you find one of the doctors for me, please?"

Hunter hurried the cadet into the surgical room and onto the operating table.

"Have you been vomiting?" Hunter asked him.

"Three times...before we left the Institute," he said, and groaned.

"I'm going to probe in the lower abdominal area. It may hurt a little, but it's the only way I can find out what I need to know." To help keep the patient's mind off the pain, he asked, "What's your name?"

"Willie...Crane."

"How old are you?"

"Nn-n-n-ngh! Nineteen!"

"Where you from?"

"Rich...mond."

"So you're planning a military career?"

Suddenly Willie stiffened and let out a scream.

Nurse Maude Edwards came running just ahead of Dr. Aaron.

"What's going on?" Aaron said, plunging through the surgery door.

"Cadet Willie Crane here has appendicitis, Doctor," Hunter replied.

"Normal symptoms?"

"Yes, sir. The pain is right where it's supposed to be...and he vomited before they brought him here."

Aaron moved closer. "Let me check."

"Please do. If I'm wrong, I sure want to know it."

Aaron probed the painful area and made Willie scream again, then turned to McGuire. "It's appendicitis, all right. Nurse, prepare the patient for surgery. We'll go with chloroform."

Maude nodded and began to gather the needed materials.

"I'll have to ask you gentlemen to go to the waiting room," Aaron said to the two men who had brought Crane in. "It's just down the hall."

Both men headed for the door and disappeared.

Willie groaned and said, "Doctor, will I be all right?"

"I believe so, son," Hunter said. "But if we wait much longer, you might not be. The nurse is going to get you ready for surgery."

Dr. Aaron motioned for Hunter to move into the hallway. Once they were out of earshot from Willie Crane, Aaron said, "I want you to do the surgery."

Hunter's eyes bulged. "But, Doctor, I...the only appendectomies I've done were on cadavers. I observed several on live patients in medical school, but I think I should observe some more before I actually do it."

Aaron smiled. "Wasn't one of your reasons for choosing to intern here was that you would do surgery much sooner than in a hospital?"

"Well, yes, sir. But I didn't expect to do it *this* soon!"

"Can't learn to swim by watching someone else," Aaron said. "Got to hit the water yourself. Of course, I'll be right at your side to give any advice or instruction you may need."

"Whew! I thought you meant I'd be on my own."

Aaron laughed. "Only when you're completely ready for that."

During the surgery, Dr. Aaron stood by ready to offer assistance if needed. It wasn't. Hunter had performed the operation flawlessly.

*****

Late in the afternoon on the day after the operation, Hunter was on the opposite side of the ward from Willie Crane's bed, tending to another patient. His back was to the door and he didn't see the nurse's aide enter with a tall, dark-haired man in uniform.

Hunter heard Willie say weakly, "Hello, Major. It's nice to see you."

"I had to come and see how my number one cannoneer is doing," a voice replied.

Hunter finished his task and started toward the door. As he drew near Willie's bed, it struck him that there was something familiar about the dark-haired man. The major stood almost as tall as Hunter and was slender but muscular. He had an angular, craggy face and dark brown, close-cropped hair with short side whiskers. But it was the deep-set, blue-gray eyes and the way he stood that seemed most familiar to Hunter.

"Dr. McGuire," Willie Crane said. "I'd like you to meet my favorite professor at the Institute, Major Thomas Jackson."

"McGuire?" Jackson said, cocking his head and squinting as he took in Hunter's sandy-colored hair and sky-blue eyes. *"Doctor* McGuire? Not the adopted son of Dr. Jason McGuire of Boston?"

Hunter's skin tingled and his pulse quickened. "Tom? Tom Jackson of Jackson's Mill?"

The two men embraced and clapped each other on the shoulders. Willie watched and smiled, surprised to learn they were friends. The six other patients in the ward looked on with interest.

When the two men finally turned back to Willie, the major explained to him that he had not seen the doctor in fifteen years. In fact, Dr. McGuire had been only five years old.

Tom rested a hand on Hunter's shoulder and said, "I want to hear about your family, and all about you. Could we get together for an evening meal?"

"I'm on the evening shift for another three weeks, but how

about Sunday? You don't have school up there on the hill on Sunday, do you?"

"Sure don't. How about right after Sunday morning church services day after tomorrow?"

On Sunday the two old friends ate together and began to get acquainted all over again. They talked of times Hunter could recall, then he filled Tom in on his adoptive parents, his graduation from Harvard Medical School, and his internship at the Kurtz-Aaron Medical Clinic.

Tom had graduated from West Point in 1846 as a second lieutenant and was assigned to an artillery unit in the U.S. Army. The United States had just entered into war with Mexico, and he was sent immediately into that country to fight. He fought under the famous war hero, General Winfield Scott, and became fast friends with Captain Robert E. Lee, who was now making a name for himself in the U.S. Army as a full colonel. Hunter had heard of Lee and was impressed that Jackson knew him.

By the time the Mexican War had come to an end in July 1848, Tom had risen to the rank of major. Now he was professor of artillery tactics and philosophy of war at Virginia Military Institute.

Hunter smiled. "I've heard your cannons over there in the foothills."

"Some folks in these parts complain about the noise, but the only way to train men to fire the big guns is to have them fire the big guns."

Hunter smiled again and sipped his coffee. "How about marriage, Tom? Don't tell me you haven't been caught by some pretty lassie."

Sadness filled the major's eyes.

Hunter saw it and said, "Oh, Tom, I'm sorry. I—"

"No, no, no. Don't be. You would have no way of knowing. She had the same name as your adoptive mother."

"Ellie?"

"Ellie Junkin, oldest daughter of Dr. George Junkin. He's been a Presbyterian minister for several years, then became president of Washington College right here in Lexington."

"I've been by the campus many times."

"I met Ellie at church soon after coming here. We were married by her father at Oaklawn in 1853. Ellie died the next year, Hunter, giving birth to our first child, who was stillborn."

"Tom, I'm so sorry."

Tears misted Jackson's eyes. "I miss her something fierce. The Lord's given me peace, though. I know my Ellie is in a lot better world than you and I. Maybe someday the Lord will bring another mate along for me, Hunter. I don't know. That's in His hands."

Tom took a deep breath, let it out slowly, and said, "What about your little sister, Lizzie? How's she doing?"

It was Hunter's turn to look sad. His voice was heavy as he said, "I haven't seen her since the day the Catersons drove away from McCann's Run to go to North Carolina."

"What?"

"It's true. Within a month after my adoptive parents took me to Boston, Dad sent a letter to Bill and Bessie Caterson at Greensboro. The letter came back with a note on its face, saying there were no Catersons in or near Greensboro."

"How could that be?"

"Several months later, Dad made a trip to Greensboro and came upon the man who had hired Bill. The Catersons never showed up, and their prospective employer never heard anything afterward."

Jackson shook his head, frowning.

"Dad went to McCann's Run and asked if anyone there had heard from the Catersons. It was as if the three of them had disappeared off the face of the earth. Dad talked to the Ritchie County sheriff, and he said there was no way he could investigate the disappearance, and no other sheriff's department would, either. There's a lot of territory between McCann's Run and Greensboro. So, with no further avenues to pursue, Dad returned to Boston."

"And that's it? Nothing since then?"

"Nothing."

"What do you think happened?"

"I have no idea. It sounds like foul play, but I've never given up that Lizzie is still alive somewhere. God knows where she is. I've prayed daily that the Lord will bring us together again—as my birth mother would put it—'on the wings of the wind.'"

Jackson scrubbed a hand over his face. "Well, Hunter, with God all things are possible. You just keep praying, and don't give up."

As time passed, Tom and Hunter spent much time together and became close friends again. The major was known for loving to debate theological issues, and he and Hunter had a good time together doing so.

Hunter became acquainted with several young ladies at church, and even dated some, but there was a guard on his heart. He believed that somehow, in God's sovereign way, He would bring Jodie Lockwood back into his life. Several times a day, and especially at night, Hunter thought about her and prayed for her.

Many times Hunter came close to writing to her at the Karr Clinic in Baltimore, but he was afraid it would make him look as if he was trying to push himself on her.

He also contemplated asking for time off to make a trip to Baltimore. But when he recalled her parting words, he told himself it was an "if you're in the neighborhood" invitation. It would seem too bold on his part to go there just to see her.

CHAPTER EIGHT

By January 1856, Dr. Hunter Newman McGuire could stand it no longer. He would write a friendly but casual letter to Jodie. When she replied, it would give him an open door to write again and slowly build toward the lasting relationship he wanted with her.

He sent the letter to the clinic in Baltimore on January 10. Then he prayed and waited. When there was no reply by April 1, and the letter had not been returned by the postal service, his heart sank. He decided to try again.

Again there was no reply.

More than a year passed, and finally Hunter decided he would take some well-deserved time off and go to Baltimore. Whether it seemed bold or not, he had to tell Jodie he loved her.

Hunter arrived at Baltimore's Union Station on September 9, 1857. The row of horse-and-buggy rigs in front of the station made him think of Boston. He raised a hand and caught the first cabbie's attention. The cabbie snapped the reins, clucked to his horse, and pulled up beside Hunter.

"Welcome to Baltimore, sir. Where can I take you?"

"Do you know where the Benjamin Karr Clinic is?"

"Of course, sir. I can have you there in about twenty minutes."

Baltimore was sizzling in the heat, and Hunter fanned himself with his hat as the buggy carried him through the streets. They pulled up in front of the clinic and Hunter noted by his pocket watch that the trip had taken twenty-two minutes.

"Will you want me to wait, sir?"

"Won't be necessary," Hunter replied, alighting with bag in hand. He paid the cabbie, crossed the board sidewalk, and entered the clinic. It was an impressive building, with a large reception area painted in bright colors and decorated with fresh flowers. Several people were waiting. Hunter approached the receptionist, and she smiled pleasantly.

"May I help you, sir?"

"I hope so. I'm Dr. Hunter McGuire from Lexington, Virginia. "Would you know if Miss Jodie Lockwood is in? I'm a friend of hers."

The receptionist looked puzzled. "Are you asking if a Miss Jodie Lockwood works here, Doctor?"

"She came here over a year-and-a-half ago to finish her C.M.N. work and gain her C.S.A. certification."

"I see. Well, Doctor, the present staff—including myself—has been here only three months. Miss Lockwood was not here when we took over the clinic, I can tell you that."

"Took over the clinic?"

"Yes, sir. Dr. Jeremy Clayton bought the clinic from Dr. Karr."

"But it still says Benjamin Karr Clinic on the sign outside."

"Yes, sir, but— Oh! There's Dr. Clayton. He can answer your questions."

The receptionist intercepted the stout middle-aged man coming through the door and introduced him to Hunter, explaining that Hunter was looking for Jodie Lockwood.

Dr. Clayton invited Hunter to his office. When they were seated, Clayton explained that he bought the clinic from Dr. Benjamin Karr three months previously and brought in his own staff. Since Dr. Karr's name was so well known, he decided to leave the name of the clinic as it was, with Dr. Karr's permission. Dr. Karr had gone to Switzerland in semi-retirement and to do some teaching in a medical school in Zurich.

Dr. Karr's staff had scattered. He knew that all of them had left Baltimore but hadn't the slightest idea where any of them had gone.

"Dr. Clayton," Hunter said, "would there be a file around here that might have a record of Miss Lockwood? Something that might give me a clue as to her whereabouts?"

"Well, I don't know. Let's take a look."

McGuire followed Clayton into another office and waited while the man searched through folders in a file cabinet.

"Ah! Here's Miss Lockwood's file," Clayton said, lifting the folder and laying it on a nearby desk. He shuffled through the papers, pausing and read a little, then flipped pages and read some more. "Well, your Miss Lockwood finished the required time and Dr. Karr recommended her for the C.M.N. and C.S.A. certificates. According to this, she came here having completed fourteen months' work for the Kurtz-Aaron Medical Clinic in Lexington, Virginia."

"Yes, sir, I am aware of that. I'm doing my internship with Doctors Kurtz and Aaron."

"Oh, I see."

"That's where I met Miss Lockwood. Do you see anything there that would indicate where she went after receiving her certificates?"

Clayton looked through the folder again. "No, sir. All it says is that she received her certificates last April 27. There's no indication where she might have gone."

"Hmmm. Almost five months ago." Hunter felt keen disappointment. He thought for a moment, then said, "Dr. Clayton, do you have an address in Switzerland where I might contact Dr. Karr?"

"I have the address of the school where he's going to teach, but he won't start until a year from this fall. He and his wife were going to tour Europe for a year."

Hunter thanked Dr. Clayton and left the clinic. He rode back to the depot and raked his mind for a solution. If he only knew where her family lived, they could probably tell him where she had gone. Maybe Doctors Kurtz and Aaron could help. They probably had that information in their records.

Hunter arrived back in Lexington and explained to the doctors what had happened in Baltimore. When the doctors checked the file, they saw that Jodie had listed Athens, Tennessee, as the nearest town to her country home. They recalled that she had received a letter telling her that both her parents had drowned in a boating accident. By the time the letter arrived, her parents had already been buried. The doctors offered Jodie time off to go home, but she declined, saying there was no need since the funeral was already over.

That night, Hunter knelt beside his bed and prayed, "Lord Jesus, Your Bible says that the steps of a good man are ordered by You. How can I believe anything but that You ordered Jodie's steps *and* mine when You let us meet? You haven't taken my love for her out of my heart, and You know I can't get her out of my mind. Please bring whatever is needful into my life to lead me to her."

Hunter was now working the day shift at the clinic. Kurtz and Aaron had built an addition to the building, adding ten more beds. They hoped it wouldn't be long before they could convert the clinic into a full-fledged hospital.

Late in the afternoon on the day after he arrived back from Baltimore, Hunter left the clinic and started walking toward the boarding house. He looked up to see Tom Jackson in a buggy with Mary Anna Morrison beside him. Hunter smiled to himself. For the past four months, Tom had been courting Mary Anna, who, like his first wife, was the daughter of a Presbyterian minister.

Hunter liked Mary Anna. She had a pleasant way about her, and in the four months that Tom had been seeing her, she had brought a brightness to his eyes that Hunter had not seen since their boyhood days.

Tom brought the buggy to a halt. "Hello, Doc. Welcome back."

"Afternoon, Major. Miss Mary Anna."

"Doc, we meant to get to the clinic before your shift ended and offer you a ride home. I want to know about your Baltimore trip, and Mary Anna and I would like to talk to you."

"I'll take you up on it," Hunter said, climbing in beside Mary Anna.

Jackson clucked at the horse and headed for the boarding house. "Actually, Doc," Tom said, "we'd like to take you out for supper and do our talking."

Hunter laughed. "Well, far be it from me to turn down a free meal!"

"I figured you'd like to freshen up first. Right?"

"Yes. It's been a harrowing day."

"Well, I'll ask right off, then. Did you find Jodie?"

"No. She's no longer at the clinic, and no one there could tell me where she is."

Hunter explained the situation at the Karr Clinic in Baltimore and then what he had learned from Aaron and Kurtz.

Tom sighed as he looked past Mary Anna to his friend, and said, "Hunter, I can only offer you Tom Jackson's opinion..."

"I value your opinion."

"It seems to me that the Lord has other plans for you. Certainly if He wanted you to have Jodie for your wife, He would let you two get together. Just seems to me that the Lord must have someone else in mind for you to marry, and that's why you've hit this rock wall. Wouldn't you say?"

Hunter nodded slowly. "What you say is sensible, Tom, but I love that girl so much. Being without her is tearing me up."

"It wouldn't if you'd give your heart a chance to reach out to someone else."

"Easier said than done, ol' pal. You know I've dated several girls. Nice Christian girls. But when I'm with them, my mind is on Jodie."

"Hunter," Mary Anna said, "there are a lot of women who would give their eyeteeth to have a man who loved them like you love Jodie."

"Yes'm," Hunter said, sliding from the buggy. "Would you two like to come in and sit in the parlor while I freshen up?"

The Appalachian Café on Main Street was just beginning to fill up when Hunter, Tom, and Mary Anna arrived. Tom waited until the food was delivered to the table and he had thanked the Lord for it before saying what was on his mind.

"Well, Doc, you probably know what we want to talk to you about."

Hunter grinned. "I think I'm about to hear a wedding announcement."

Mary Anna laughed. "This doctor is awfully smart, Tom."

"Don't have to be very smart to see what's been going on between you two the last few months. And may I say I'm very happy for both of you. So when is the day?"

"Depends on you," Tom said.

"Me?"

"Yep. Will you be in town on Sunday afternoon, December 20?"

"I will if that's the day of your wedding."

"Good. It's hard for a fella to be best man at his friend's wedding if he's somewhere else," Tom said.

Hunter smiled and looked at Tom. "I'm deeply honored that you'd want me to be best man."

"We both want it, Hunter," Mary Anna said.

Tom Jackson and Mary Anna Morrison were wed at Oaklawn Presbyterian Church on Sunday afternoon, December 20, 1857.

Dr. Hunter McGuire—still dreaming of Jodie Lockwood—buried himself in his work.

When the new year came, serious trouble was brewing within the United States. The slavery question was becoming a heated issue. Twelve years previously—in 1846—the Northern states had outlawed the institution of slavery. The Southern states refused to follow suit because of the enormous impact it would have on the Southern economy.

One day in late January, things were unusually quiet at the clinic. Doctors Aaron and Kurtz were sitting in Kurtz's office after lunch, discussing the slavery issue when Hunter came in from a house call. He hung up his hat and coat in the hall and entered Kurtz's office carrying a rolled-up newspaper in one hand and his medical bag in the other.

"How's Mr. Benkleman?" Kurtz asked.

"Just a bad cold. He'll be all right. Have you gentlemen seen today's *Sentinel?*" Hunter unrolled the paper so they could see the front page.

"More about the slavery controversy?" Aaron asked.

"Yes. They're about to get into fistfights in Congress. A couple of Northern congressmen made speeches yesterday and just about had those politicians swinging at each other. The Northerners say we're immoral for embracing slavery, and they're going to force us to give it up. I really haven't paid a lot of attention to this issue, have you?"

"Well, Doctor," Aaron said, "we've never had much industry here in the agrarian South, and a high percentage of Southern money is tied up in plantation and cotton futures. To pay workers' wages for labor would break the plantation owners' backs financially."

Weldon Kurtz picked up where Aaron left off. "I don't know if you're aware of it or not, Dr. McGuire, but there's a growing demand for cotton in the U.S. and in Europe. The plantation owners see an opportunity to greatly strengthen the Southern economy because of this increasing demand."

"I've picked up on it now and then in the newspapers," Hunter said. "So now things are heating up because the Northerners are opposed to plantation owners using slave labor to accomplish their financial goals."

"That's it," Kurtz said with a nod. "So they accuse Southerners of being immoral to try to force them to abolish slavery. If this doesn't work, they'll turn to stronger measures."

"I'll guarantee you the people of the South will not bend to Northern pressure," Aaron said. "The Northerners will never be able to force abolition below the Mason-Dixon Line. We'll fight them first."

"From what I see in the paper, I think you're right," Hunter said.

"We're bowing our necks," Kurtz said, "not because we're all in favor of slavery, but because the Northerners are infringing on our states' rights. It's nobody's business up north to tell us how to run our economy."

"I agree," Hunter said, "but I can't say I agree with one human being making chattel of another."

Aaron nodded. "We both feel the same way, but we also understand that the South's economy would suffer a devastating blow if slavery was abolished. The main thing is, those folks up north need to keep their noses out of our business. We're not going to let them dictate abolition to us."

When another year had passed, the name of abolitionist John Brown showed up in the newspapers. By the spring of 1859, Brown had shed blood in Kansas and Missouri over slavery, then turned his attention to Virginia.

As the months passed, the violence grew worse. On October 17, 1859, Brown and a group of his followers seized the U.S. Armory at Harper's Ferry in defiance of the pro-slavery Southerners, killed five civilians, and took hostages. The U.S. Marines were called in, with Colonel Robert E. Lee in command. Brown refused to surrender, and the Marines attacked.

Eleven of Brown's men were killed, including two of his sons. The rest were captured. Brown was tried at Charleston for treason against the Commonwealth of Virginia and sentenced to hang. His execution was set for December 2, 1859.

Virginia governor Henry A. Wise called for the Virginia Military Institute's Corps of Cadets to stand guard in Charleston while the hanging was carried out. Major Thomas Jackson took his artillery attachment from the Institute to comply. Brown was hanged without intrusion by fellow abolitionists, and Jackson led his men back to Lexington.

War fever, however, was on the rise. Abolitionists in the North were angry over John Brown's execution. As the new decade dawned, the battle over states' rights grew hotter among political leaders. In the next several months there was verbal skirmishing between the Northerners and Southerners in Congress, and as the verbal battle spread to the people, the threat of violence became a reality.

When Abraham Lincoln was elected president of the United States on November 6, 1860, it was all the Southerners could take. In the four-month interval between Lincoln's election and his inauguration on March 1, 1861, South Carolina seceded from the Union, followed immediately by six other deep-south states, and together formed the Southern Confederacy.

On February 4, delegates from the seceding states convened at Montgomery, Alabama, to frame a constitution, establish a provincial government, provide for armed forces, and elect Jefferson Davis president of the Confederate States. Davis was a West Pointer and a Mexican War hero. He was also a former U.S. Senator, as well as former U.S. Secretary of War.

It was apparent that other Southern states would secede.

Two days after Lincoln's inauguration, Jefferson Davis, on authorization from the Confederate Congress, issued a call for 100,000 volunteers for military service. Thus the Confederate States Army was born.

The Confederate Army immediately went to work by seizing Federal property within Southern borders, including forts, arsenals, and customs houses.

At Charleston Harbor, South Carolina, Major Robert Anderson—the Federal commander of Fort Sumter—resisted the demands of Confederate authorities that he surrender the fort.

By dawn's early light at 4:30 A.M. on April 12, 1861, a ten-inch mortar shell whistled in a high arc from the Charleston shore and exploded inside Fort Sumter. The American Civil War had begun.

Confederate shore batteries commanded by General P. G. T. Beauregard bombarded Fort Sumter for forty hours before Anderson finally surrendered. More Southern states seceded, and the armies of the North and South drew up their war plans.

*****

On April 20, Major Jackson received orders from Confederate authorities to bring the entire student body from Virginia Military Institute to Richmond, where they would be inducted into the Confederate Army. They were to begin their march at 12:30 P.M. on Sunday, April 21.

Because this would not allow time to attend services at the local churches, Major Jackson set aside the hour between 6:30 and 7:30 that morning for cadets who wished to have their own time of prayer and Bible reading. He had also asked Hunter to come to his house before he and the cadets left for Richmond.

When Hunter arrived, he joined Tom and Mary Anna in the kitchen, and they prayed together.

Afterwards, Tom opened his Bible and said, "Both of you know that my faith is in the Lord Jesus Christ for my salvation. I have told Mary Anna, Hunter, that I had peace when I fought in the Mexican War, and I know I'll have the same peace in this one. If the Lord sees fit to take me to heaven from a bloody battlefield, I'm ready to go. My sins have been washed away in the precious blood of God's Lamb, and I do not fear dying."

Tom found the page he wanted. "Here. Second Corinthians five, verses one through four. 'For we know that if our earthly house of this tabernacle were dissolved, we have a building of God, an house not made with hands, eternal in the heavens. For in this we groan, earnestly desiring to be clothed upon with our house which is from heaven: If so be that being clothed we shall not be found naked. For we that are in this tabernacle do groan, being burdened: not for that we would be unclothed, but clothed upon, that mortality might be swallowed up of life.'"

By this time Mary Anna was wiping away tears.

"Mary Anna," Tom said, "you're my beloved wife. Hunter, you are my best friend in this world. I just wanted to leave you both with this Bible passage and for you to hear it read by my own mouth. Should the Lord see fit to take me Home, please remember that I went in perfect peace, my mortality being swallowed up of life."

While Mary Anna and Hunter walked with Tom to the spot where he and his men would begin their march to Richmond, Tom said, "Doc, if this war goes full-scale, which it could, the Confederate Army is going to need doctors. I'm asking you to consider being a volunteer if the need arises."

"We haven't talked about it, Tom," Hunter said, "but it bothers me to have my parents on one side of this conflict, and me on the other."

Jackson nodded. "There's going to be a whole lot of this kind of thing as the war progresses."

"Mom and Dad have been very understanding about my situation. They know I'm against human beings owning other human beings, but they also know that my allegiance belongs to the South. From what they've said, I know it's not going to divide us if I carry my medical skills to the Confederate battlefields. So if I'm needed, let me know."

CHAPTER NINE

On April 18, 1861, Lincoln was in the East Room of the White House, listening to eyewitness accounts of the bombardment of Fort Sumter, when there was a tap on the door.

Lincoln's young private secretary, John Hay, entered. Hay was a slight man, with dark curly hair and mustache. "You asked me to let you know if Senator Blair had been able to talk to Colonel Lee, sir."

"Yes?"

"He did, sir, and the Colonel has arrived."

Lincoln thanked the men for their reports and waited for them to exit the room before telling Hay to show Colonel Lee in.

Seconds later, Lincoln's craggy face crinkled in a smile as he moved toward the silver-haired man, his hand extended. At six feet four inches in height, Lincoln towered over most men, and Lee was no exception.

Colonel Robert Edward Lee had seen Lincoln only from a distance and was stunned to see how gaunt the president looked up close. As he shook Lincoln's hand, he drawled, "I am glad to make your acquaintance, Mr. President."

"Same here," Lincoln said, his deep-set eyes appraising the fifty-five-year-old army officer. "Come...sit down."

As Lee sat on a plush, overstuffed chair, Lincoln said, "Colonel, I'll get right to the point of my asking for this meeting."

"Yes, sir?"

"I've been going over your military record, and I like what I see. Since we are now at war with the Confederates, I'm searching for the right man to put in command of the Union Army. I believe you are that man. What would you say to that?"

Lee's countenance sagged, and he cleared his throat. "Mr. President," he said, in his soft Southern accent, "I am honored that you would see me capable of commanding the Union forces. However, I must tell you that just two days ago I drew up my letter of resignation from the United States Army. I was about to present it to the 'powers that be' when Senator Blair approached me, saying you would like to see me. In respect to you, I came immediately, planning to turn in my resignation later today."

Lincoln passed a lean hand over his mouth. "Then I must ask you to reconsider, Colonel. I am genuinely interested in making you the commander of the Union army."

"My decision to resign did not come easy, Mr. President. I am a man who has always loved his country, and if you have examined my military records, you know I served well in the Mexican War."

Lincoln nodded. "That's the reason you attracted my attention. I see military genius in you, Colonel. I would like to employ it for the Union cause."

Lee sighed. "Mr. President, I am a native-born Virginian, as you probably know. Virginia is a Southern commonwealth, and the Virginia Peace Convention passed an ordinance of secession yesterday. I cannot and I will not fight against my own people. I mean no disrespect, Mr. President, but I must decline your offer."

Lincoln's eyes clouded. There was a break in his voice as he said, "Colonel Lee, it disturbs me greatly to think of you as my enemy."

"I feel the same way about you, sir," Lee said, "but I guess that's the way it is."

There was a moment of awkward silence between them, then Lincoln rose to his feet. "I'm sorry it turned out this way, Colonel. Perhaps this war will be short-lived and we can soon be friends again."

Lee extended his hand. "You have my deepest respect, Mr. President. May God grant both you and President Davis the wisdom to make it short-lived. If you don't, this land we love will be a cauldron of blood."

Colonel Robert E. Lee's prediction began to come true the very next day when Federal troops from Massachusetts arrived in Baltimore, Maryland. They had to march from one depot to another to board a train for Washington. Angry Southern sympathizers, carrying Confederate flags, threw bricks and rocks at the soldiers. When the soldiers answered back with guns, the citizens started shooting too. By the time it was over, at least four soldiers and nine civilians were dead, and hundreds more were injured and wounded.

That same day, the U.S. Armory at Harper's Ferry, Virginia, was evacuated by the Federals when they learned that a swarm of Virginia troops were coming to take it by force.

On April 20, Colonel Lee sent a wire to President Jefferson Davis, offering his services, and was immediately appointed commander of the Confederate Army of Virginia. Lee went to work to build a strong fighting force.

On April 27, Major Thomas J. Jackson was promoted to colonel and was given eleven thousand men. On May 1, he was ordered to the armory at Harper's Ferry to guard it in case the Federals tried to take it back.

At the same time, Major General Joseph E. Johnston was

made commander of the Confederate Army of the Shenandoah. Brigadier General Pierre G. T. Beauregard had already been appointed commander of the Army of Northern Virginia.

During May and June, skirmishes took place in western Virginia, Missouri, and along the Potomac River in Maryland. On July 11, the first major battle took place at Rich Mountain, Virginia, with Major General George B. McClellan leading the Federals. Lieutenant Colonel John Pegram led the Confederates. Pegram's unit was put on the run by McClellan's troops, but not without leaving dead and wounded Yankee soldiers on the mountain.

Jefferson Davis knew heavy battles were imminent and he needed to strengthen the Army of the Shenandoah, especially. He had great confidence in Colonel Jackson. On July 12, he promoted him to Brigadier General and gave him command of the First Brigade, Army of the Shenandoah under General Johnston.

In the middle of the afternoon on July 15, a rider in a Confederate Army uniform galloped through Lexington and halted in front of the Kurtz-Aaron Medical Clinic. He pulled a sealed brown envelope from a saddlebag and headed for the door.

"Hello, Lieutenant, may I help you?" Doralee Chambers asked from the reception desk.

"Yes, ma'am. I'm Lieutenant Paul Morgan, First Brigade, Army of the Shenandoah. I have a very important message for Dr. Hunter McGuire. Is he in?"

"Yes. He's with a patient at the moment. I'll tell him you're here and see how long he thinks it might be."

Doralee returned in less than two minutes. "Dr. McGuire said to have a seat, Lieutenant. He will be with you shortly."

When Hunter entered the reception area in his white frock, Morgan rose to his feet. "Dr. McGuire? I'm a courier from Brigadier General Thomas Jackson, sir."

Hunter's eyes widened. *"Brigadier General* Jackson, eh? I learned only recently that he had been promoted to colonel."

"Well, he's now commander of First Brigade, Army of the Shenandoah."

"Oh? So he's not at Harper's Ferry any longer."

"That's correct, sir. He's camped with the brigade over by Manassas. General Johnston, commander of the Army of the Shenandoah, is on his way there with the rest of his troops. General Beauregard is leading his Army of Northern Virginia to the same place right now. This could be a real bloody battle, sir."

McGuire looked at the envelope in Morgan's hand. "And you have a message for me from General Jackson?"

"Yes, sir." Morgan placed the envelope in Hunter's hand. "He asked that you read it in my presence and respond. I'm to ride back immediately and give him your answer."

Hunter pulled out the letter, and read silently:

> Dear Hunter,
>
> You said to let you know when I needed you to come. We are about to engage in a furious fight with the enemy. There will be many men killed, and many wounded. I need you. The Confederate soldiers need you. Please give Lieutenant Paul Morgan your reply. I am anxiously waiting.
>
> Yours expectantly,
> Tom

At sunset on July 17, Brigadier General Thomas Jackson was sitting in Major General Johnston's tent on the bank of Bull Run Creek, near the town of Manassas.

"It's hard to say how many men McDowell will come with," Johnston said, "but we'll give them a fight they won't soon forget.

They'll know they've got a tiger by the tail when we get through with them. We'll—"

"General Johnston, sir," came a voice from outside the tent.

"Yes?"

"General Jackson's courier is here and wishes to see him."

Jackson sprang off his chair and went outside. Johnston followed. Jackson stepped out into the light of the setting sun and saw his old friend standing with Lieutenant Morgan. He was speechless for a few seconds, then said, "Hunter! I didn't expect you to come this soon!"

"I told Doctors Kurtz and Aaron that I would be volunteering my services to the army whenever you sent for me, Tom—er, excuse me...*General.* By the way, congratulations on your two promotions since I saw you last."

"Thank you," Tom said, and grinned.

"Anyway, Kurtz and Aaron were prepared for me to go. You probably don't know that since I finished my internship they made me a junior partner in the clinic. Plans are that when it becomes a hospital, I'll become a full-fledged partner."

"I didn't know, but congratulations."

Tom Jackson then introduced Hunter to General Johnston. As they shook hands, Johnston said, "Dr. McGuire, I've been hearing a lot about you from General Jackson. Welcome to the Army of the Shenandoah."

"Thank you, sir."

"I can't tell you what it means to have you volunteer your services. You do understand, though, that the Confederate government will pay you for this."

"Tom—there I go again—General Jackson advised me of it, sir."

"We know we aren't going to match financially what you receive in Lexington, but—"

"That's no problem, sir. My heart is with these men. I want to do my part in this war."

"Well, your part is very essential—saving lives."

"Every one I can, sir, even if it's a Yankee soldier."

Johnston grinned. "Your friend here told me that's how you feel. And I have nothing against that. He said something like this: 'An enemy is no longer an enemy when he is wounded and incapable of fighting against us.' Do I have that right, General?"

"Exactly," Jackson said.

"Doctor," Johnston said, "we hope to have this war over with soon. I want to see you go back to that clinic and make good with your career." He nodded solemnly and continued to speak. "Because of General Jackson's recommendation of you as a physician and surgeon, I am officially appointing you as Corps Medical Director under his direct command. We have other doctors coming, but most of them are less experienced than you. They will take orders from you. I'll let you and General Jackson work out the details. He'll show you what we have in the way of medical supplies."

There were many skirmishes between the Federals and the Confederates during the next five days. Then, on July 21, the two armies clashed head-on along the banks of Bull Run Creek. Thirty-five thousand Union troops led by Major General Irvin McDowell stormed against twenty-four thousand Confederate troops led by Brigadier General P. G. T. Beauregard, and eighty-five hundred troops led by Major General Joseph E. Johnston.

It was a hot, humid day as the two sides battled it out. Bodies were strewn on the bloody fields—some dead, some wounded—as cannons boomed, muskets flared, and powder smoke filled the heavy air.

Among the Confederate losses was Brigadier General Bernard Bee, commander of Third Brigade, Army of the Shenandoah. Bee was killed ten minutes after he gave Tom Jackson the nickname—Stonewall—that would stay with him for the rest of his life.

During the heat of the battle, Bee and his brigade were spread out on a hillside, firing at Union soldiers attempting to ascend the hill. On top of the hill, some fifty yards above Bee and his troops, was General Jackson's artillery, firing at enemy artillery positioned in a heavily-wooded area. The Union infantry below were trying to take out the Confederate cannoneers and their leader.

Jackson courageously stood erect amidst a hail of bullets so he could see where to direct his cannoneers to fire. General Bee shouted above the din, "Form! Form! There stands Jackson like a stone wall! Rally behind the Virginians!"

Only seconds after Bee was shot and killed, a cannonball exploded near Jackson. Shrapnel whistled on both sides of him, a molten fragment hitting his left hand, ripping into the middle finger, and another red-hot chunk catching the tail of his coat.

Jackson stuck his bleeding hand into his pocket and remained where he stood, just like a stone wall.

When there was a respite in the fighting, the general left a colonel in charge and rushed onto the back side of the hill where a hospital tent had been set up. There were already several wounded Confederate soldiers lying around it and inside on the tent floor. When Jackson entered the tent, a young doctor looked up and said, "I'll be with you in just a second, General."

Jackson nodded. "I don't believe I know you."

"I'm Dr. Bruce Dean, General."

"Where's Dr. McGuire?"

"He's on the field somewhere, doing what he can for the wounded who can't make it to the tent. Now, General, let me take a look at this. Well, you're out of this battle. This finger will have to come off immediately. I'll get some chloroform and—"

"You're not cutting this finger off, Doctor," Jackson said. "It isn't that bad."

"Oh, but it is, sir. If I don't amputate right away, it can very well result in your death."

"How much experience do you have with this kind of wound?"

"Well, not much, General, but I *am* a medical doctor, and—"

"Just wrap it up. I've got to get back to my post. I'll have Dr. McGuire look at it later."

Dean's mouth turned down. "If you insist. But I'm telling you, the finger has to come off."

As Jackson headed back, the Yankees started to come at the hill again. When the general's men saw him, they shouted, "Three cheers for General 'Stonewall' Jackson! Hip-hip-hooray! Hip-hip-hooray! Hip-hip-hooray!"

Further down the slope, General Bee's men—now commanded by Colonel Efram Smith—joined in and began shouting at Jackson, calling him "General Stonewall."

It was midafternoon when the Union troops found themselves outgunned and outmanned in spite of their greater numbers. They turned back toward Washington in hasty retreat.

By dusk, all was still along Bull Run Creek, except for exultant Confederates who rejoiced over their victory...and the wounded who moaned and cried out in pain.

At the hospital tent, Dr. Hunter McGuire and Dr. Bruce Dean labored over the wounded men. Darkness fell and they continued to work until two other doctors showed up from another brigade to help. While they worked by lantern light, they discussed the new nickname for General Jackson.

Jackson stepped up to the tent and overheard his old friend say, "Well, gentlemen, I'll tell you what. I've known the man as long as I can remember. We grew up in the same rural area. If there ever was a man who deserved to be called 'Stonewall' it's him. He—"

"Hello in the tent," came the familiar voice. "You have a wounded general out here."

Hunter stepped outside and noted his friend's bandaged left

hand. He examined the finger in the presence of Dean, who was embarrassed when Hunter pronounced that all it needed was some stitches. Hunter had Dean take the stitches, and Jackson alleviated some of Dean's embarrassment by commending him for doing a good job.

When Stonewall Jackson and the rest of the Confederates sent General McDowell and his battered troops retreating to Washington, the Northerners—who thought they would make short order of the ragtag Confederate armies—now recognized they had a genuine war on their hands.

Because of the rout at Bull Run Creek, President Lincoln relieved General McDowell of his command and replaced him with Major General George Brinton McClellan.

The following year there were hundreds of skirmishes between Union and Confederate troops, including some in Missouri and as far west as New Mexico.

In November 1861, Stonewall Jackson was made commander of the Army of the Shenandoah and promoted to major general.

While almost countless skirmishes were taking place east of the Mississippi River on Southern soil, General McClellan—after much prodding by President Lincoln—finally moved his army to the peninsula between the York and James Rivers in Virginia. His orders were to attack Richmond, which had become the Confederate capital in May 1861.

General McClellan had received improper information from Union intelligence, which reported that his army was vastly outnumbered by General Johnston's Army of Northern Virginia. McClellan moved at a snail's pace, taking two months to advance to the outskirts of the Confederate capital. He spent a third month sitting in front of the enemy's fortifications without launching an attack.

McClellan's reluctance to move on Richmond had President Lincoln furious.

During the same period, Stonewall Jackson was driving Union forces from the Shenandoah Valley. In late June 1862, Jackson brought his army back to the Richmond front to participate in the Seven Days' Battles, June 25 to July 1.

At the same time, General Johnston's new command attacked General McClellan's troops repeatedly and drove them all the way back to Harrison's Landing on the James River.

The Union forces were taking a sound beating. President Lincoln was frustrated that his top field commander seemed reluctant to carry the battle to the enemy. As Lincoln put it to General Henry W. Halleck, whom he made General-in-Chief over all Union land forces on July 11, "McClellan has the slows."

Lincoln was pleased with Major General John Pope's performance in the Peninsular Campaign, and ordered him to form the Union Army of Virginia, which would carry the battle to the Rebels in central and western Virginia. McClellan and his troops were ordered to stay close to Washington to stand guard. McClellan was furious that Pope would be sent to the field and he planted in one spot, but obeyed Lincoln's orders, remaining in charge of the Union Army of the Potomac.

Pope led his troops into battle at Manassas against Stonewall Jackson's Army of the Shenandoah August 29–September 1, which became known as the Second Battle of Bull Run.

When Lincoln learned of the fight going on at Manassas, he ordered McClellan's Union Army of the Potomac to rush to Pope's aid. McClellan was too late arriving, however, and the Confederates whipped Pope's army. The Second Bull Run victory resulted from the courage and masterful strategy of Stonewall Jackson, whose name was fast becoming a household word, not only in the South, but also in the North. Almost every day his name was on the front pages of newspapers reporting on the War.

In Washington, President Lincoln was sorely disappointed in Pope's performance at Manassas. He sat down with Halleck and vented his frustration. Halleck began bringing up names of other Union generals as possibilities to replace Pope.

Lincoln listened, but didn't respond.

When Halleck had exhausted his list, Lincoln said, "I have an idea, General. Since we're short on men who are capable and experienced enough to lead our military forces, I'm going to relieve General Pope of his command and merge his Army of Virginia with General McClellan's Army of the Potomac. General McClellan will be commander of the entire force."

"Mr. President," Halleck said, cautiously, "you have me in this position because you respect my military opinions."

"Of course. There's something you wish to say?"

"Yes, sir. My concern is not with the merging of the two armies into one. After the defeats we've been experiencing, I'm sure that would serve to unite our men in a big way. But McClellan, sir. Haven't we had enough of his reluctance? You said yourself, Mr. President, that he has the slows. Surely there's another general who could head up the newly formed Army of the Potomac."

Lincoln rubbed his tired eyes. To Halleck, the president's cheekbones seemed to protrude even more than they had the day before, and his eyes seemed to have sunken deeper.

"General, there's not a man you've listed who can lead men like McClellan can once he *does* take them into battle. You won't argue with that, will you?"

"No, sir. But what can we do to light a fire under him, so he'll move like we want him to?"

"Let's have a meeting with him," Lincoln replied. "I'll prod him hard."

CHAPTER TEN

On Monday, September 1, 1862, Major General George McClellan was called from the army camp just outside of Washington to meet with President Lincoln and General-in-Chief Henry Halleck in the east room of the White House.

Lincoln and Halleck were standing up when John Hay ushered McClellan into the room. McClellan was a small man, only five-feet-five. His men affectionately called him "Little Mac" outside of his presence. The president and Halleck shook hands with McClellan, then sat down at a table for their meeting.

"General," Lincoln said, "I called you here so the three of us could discuss the demoralized condition of our troops."

"It certainly concerns me, Mr. President," McClellan said. "The Confederates have fought like wildcats. It seems nothing we do discourages them, or even slows them down. They come into each battle with a vengeance, and even though they must be just as weary, worn, and hungry as our men, they seem to fight all day long as if they were more than human."

"It's all in the mental attitude, General McClellan," Halleck said. "My personal opinion is that neither you nor General Pope have instilled the proper mental attitude into your men. This is nothing less than a lack of leadership. Everything rises or falls on leadership. Certainly you will agree with that."

McClellan was nervous under Halleck's penetrating gaze. "It is the truth, General Halleck. I must agree with it."

Halleck looked at Lincoln, who seemed willing to let him continue. "With General Pope, in my opinion, it was a lack of military strategy. His men lost confidence in him in the Manassas battle. With you, General, I see something different. When you are in battle, you have a keen mind for strategy and a way of keeping your men fired up to fight. But the problem—and I know Mr. Lincoln agrees with me—is your lack of taking the fight to the enemy. To put it bluntly, General, you're too slow. Consequently, you allow the Confederates to outmaneuver you, and when you do, you lose the battle. This is what's demoralizing your men."

Abraham Lincoln fixed his deep-set eyes on McClellan and waited for a reply.

McClellan squirmed a bit and cleared his throat. "Mr. President, General Halleck, what appears to be slow moving to you is simply my style of military strategy. Rushing into a battle without proper preparation can prove devastating."

"So can waiting too long," Halleck said.

The discussion continued for some two hours. Finally McClellan agreed to take another look at his tactics and make the necessary adjustments.

Halleck was not satisfied and was about to say so, when Lincoln said, "All right, General McClellan, that's good enough for me. Now, let me explain what I have in mind."

The president laid out his plan to relieve General Pope of his command over the Union Army of Virginia and merge that army into the Union Army of the Potomac. McClellan would retain his position as commander.

Little Mac was pleased, and agreed that it was a smart move.

Henry Halleck was dismayed that McClellan would be the

top man of the newly merged force, but kept it to himself.

"All right, General," Lincoln said. "You are the chief field commander of the combined forces. I'm depending on you to reorganize the demoralized army and to rally it into the fighting force that it no doubt can be. You must lead them to victory by crushing General Lee's armies and bring this war to a swift end."

"I'll give it my best, Mr. President...my very best."

On Tuesday, September 2, General Lee met with Generals Jackson and Longstreet. The Confederate Army of the Shenandoah was still camped outside of Manassas.

"Gentlemen," Lee drawled, "there will never be a better time than right now to take advantage of the low morale of the Union troops."

"Can't argue with that, sir," Longstreet said. "We've got them with their tails between their legs."

"So what do you have in mind, General?" Jackson asked.

Lee paused a moment, then said with a slight grin, "March our troops onto Northern soil and launch an attack."

Both men showed surprise.

"Too bold, you're thinking?"

"Well...no, sir," Jackson said. "I think it's a great idea. That would shake them even more. Just where do you have in mind to make the attack, sir?"

"Maryland," Lee replied. "At least start there. Maybe carry it into Pennsylvania. I think we need to strike while the iron's hot. In my mind, putting our footprints on Union land would further demoralize them. They've brought the war onto Southern soil, let's hand it back to them."

"I like it!" Longstreet said.

Jackson was a little less exuberant. "How soon, sir?"

"Right away. Next few days."

"But our men are tired, sir," Jackson said. "They need shoes. And they could use new uniforms. Some of them are in pretty bad shape. Shouldn't we let the men rest up for a while before we march into Maryland? We're a little low on ammunition and supplies, not to mention food."

"We can't wait," Lee said. "Yankee morale is at an all-time low. I'm aware that our men are tired, but they've got heart, General. They can do it. And like I said, we've got to strike while the iron's hot."

"I understand," Jackson said, "and I agree, sir. Our men have heart like no soldiers I've ever seen. Just what are your objectives?"

Lee smiled. "Well, let me make it clear that I'm not interested in occupying Union territory. I just want to harass them and take the spirit out of them. As for ammunition and supplies, we can lay our hands on some pretty quickly from Richmond. And we can feed the troops from the fields of the Maryland farmers. Lincoln's troops are doing that to our farmers every day.

"Not only that, but the invasion would lure most of the Federal forces away from Washington, thus preventing another enemy march on Richmond when they decide they're ready to fight again."

"Good thinking," Jackson said, grinning.

"So, gentlemen, the opportunity to level a powerful blow to Billy Yank's breadbasket is at our fingertips. We've got to move quickly."

"Have you discussed this with President Davis?" Longstreet asked.

"Not yet. I wanted to get your reaction before I moved ahead with the plan. Since you now see the importance of striking quickly, I will write President Davis a letter and send it with a courier tomorrow."

"How many troops are you planning to take into Maryland, sir?" Longstreet asked.

"Fifty thousand."

"Exactly *which* troops?"

"Let me answer that question by explaining a big change I have in mind."

Lee shared with the two generals his plan to merge Jackson's army with the Confederate Army of Northern Virginia. He would then divide the combined armies into two corps of five divisions each. Jackson would head up one corps, and Longstreet—whom Lee called the "Old Warhorse"—the other. The fifth division in Jackson's corps would be the army's cavalry, under the command of Major General James E. B. (Jeb) Stuart.

"It would be my pleasure to have General Stuart's cavalry a part of my corps, sir," Jackson said.

"Then you're in agreement with my entire plan, General Jackson?"

"Indeed, sir. Let's hit those Yankees where it hurts most—at home."

Lee turned to Longstreet. "And you, General?"

"One hundred percent, sir. Let's deal Billy Yank some real misery."

On September 3, General Lee wrote a long letter to President Davis, outlining his plan as he had spoken it to Jackson and Longstreet, and sent it by courier that very day. He admitted that his men were in tattered uniforms and needed shoes, but expressed his confidence that they would fight with everything in them. He closed the letter by affirming this would be the South's most powerful move since the Civil War began.

Next, Lee merged the two armies, then divided them into two corps of five divisions each. The weary soldiers were exuberantly in favor of their leader's plan.

*****

On September 4, as the Confederates prepared to march toward the Potomac, General Jackson moved his troops to the camp just outside Leesburg, Virginia, where the rest of Lee's army was collecting. Wagons were coming in from Richmond, loaded with ammunition and supplies.

As his men set up tents for their brief stay, Jackson moved among them, speaking words of encouragement.

Presently, General Lee appeared and explained to Jackson that in the re-formation of the Confederate army, he was placing Major General Ambrose Powell Hill as commander of Jackson's Second Division. There would be five brigades under Hill. Four of the brigades were already in the camp. The one Lee had designated as First Brigade was on its way from North Carolina under the command of Brigadier General O'Brien Branch. Lee had actually sent for Branch's brigade three days before the second Bull Run battle. Now they would make a strong addition to I Corps' Second Division.

Lee then handed Jackson a description of the makeup of his entire I Corps, giving him the names of all the commanding officers and their units. The official count of all officers and fighting men under Jackson and Longstreet was 49,981.

A slow grin spread across Jackson's face. "Well, General, you still owe us nineteen men. Didn't you say we'd go across the Potomac with fifty thousand?"

Lee chuckled. "You're a real stickler," he said, and walked away.

Jackson called a meeting of his division commanders, Generals A. R. Lawson, Ambrose P. Hill, John R. Jones, Daniel H. Hill, and Jeb Stuart. When the meeting was over, the sun was low in the western sky. The generals scattered to pass on the information to their unit leaders.

When General Hill returned to his division encampment, he found that his First Brigade had arrived. Its commander, Brigadier

General Branch, was waiting for him. After shaking hands, Hill told Branch the information from General Jackson that he was about to pass on to his brigade commanders.

"Quite a hero General Jackson's turned out to be, sir," Branch said. "I like that name Stonewall."

"It fits him, that's for sure."

"You're going to have this meeting with your brigade commanders right now, sir?"

"Yes."

"Could I have about half a minute? Then I'll go with you."

"Sure. I can wait."

"Thank you, sir." Branch glanced toward the spot where the First Brigade was pitching tents. "Corporal Stedham! Will you send Major Dayton over here right away?"

The corporal nodded and dashed in the other direction.

To Hill, Branch said, "Major Dayton studied under General Jackson at Virginia Military Institute, sir, and was wondering if the general was on the grounds. He'd really like to see him again."

The young man hurrying toward them was tall and ruggedly handsome. As he drew up, Branch said, "General Ambrose Hill, I want you to meet Major Rance Dayton."

Dayton extended his hand and expressed pleasure over making his division leader's acquaintance.

"Major Dayton," Branch said, "General Hill was just in a meeting with General Jackson, so he is indeed on the grounds."

"Oh! I've got to see him. Do you think it would be all right to look for him, General Hill?"

"I don't know why not," Hill said, pointing across the camp to the west. "That's his tent over there. The larger one."

Stonewall Jackson was talking with Hunter McGuire when his aide called through the tent flap, "There's someone here to see you, General. You said it was all right to interrupt."

"Certainly," Jackson said, rising from his chair. "You don't have to go yet, do you, Hunter? Come on out while I see who this is and what he wants."

"Might be Abraham Lincoln, Tom," Hunter said, and chuckled. "Maybe he wants some advice on how to whip hardheaded Southerners."

What the general saw was a familiar face grinning at him. "Well, I'll be! Rance Dayton! How are you, you scalawag?"

"I'm sorry for interrupting you and this gentleman, sir, but I just had to see you. I arrived about an hour ago with the First Brigade to serve in General Hill's division."

Jackson suddenly noticed Dayton's uniform. "And you're a major already!"

"Yes, sir. And commander of the Eighteenth North Carolina Infantry Regiment."

"Well, Major Dayton, I want you to meet the closest friend I have in this world, Dr. Hunter McGuire. Dr. McGuire is Corps Medical Director. He and I have known each other since we were boys."

As McGuire and Dayton shook hands, Jackson explained to Hunter that Dayton had studied at V.M.I.

"Let's see, Rance—I mean Major," Jackson said. "What year was it you graduated? About '57 or '58?"

"June 4, 1858, sir."

"So what did you do after graduation?"

"Returned to my home in Fayetteville, North Carolina. I decided to go into law enforcement and was hired as deputy sheriff of Cumberland County by Sheriff Tucker."

"So you left your deputy job to get into the War, is that it?"

"Not quite, sir. Sheriff Tucker retired early in 1860, and even though I was pretty young, I ran for sheriff and got elected. Of course, when the War broke out last year, I felt it was my duty to get into it, especially since I'd graduated from V.M.I."

"You plan to stay in the military when the War is over?"

"No, sir. I'm going back into law enforcement. Thought I might go out west and take up marshaling one of those tough cattle towns."

"You're not married, I take it."

"Ah...no, sir. Had one on the line, but she decided she didn't want to marry a man who wore a badge. So she married—pardon me, Dr. McGuire—she married a doctor."

Hunter grinned. "Some women just have good sense."

Rance noticed five young soldiers from his regiment crowding close, eyeing Stonewall Jackson with looks of admiration.

"Hello, guys," he said with a chuckle. "I know what you're here for." To Jackson, he said, "General, these men are part of my regiment, and you're their hero. I've told them all about my V.M.I. days, studying under you, and they've read about you in the papers down in Fayetteville, where we all grew up together. They've been almost as excited as I have since learning we'd be assigned to your corps, and they want to meet you."

Jackson greeted the five men warmly and then introduced them to Hunter.

"You men better treat Dr. McGuire real good," Jackson said, "because one of these days he could be treating *you!*"

Hunter watched the five young soldiers walk away and noted how new their uniforms looked compared to some of the other men's. He turned to Jackson and said, "I'm concerned that so many of our men need shoes. I've been treating sore feet ever since we got here."

"I know, Hunter, but I don't know what can be done. General Lee wants to cross the Potomac and take the fight to the Federals right away. There's no time to get shoes shipped in."

"General," Rance Dayton said, "I happen to know that our regiment brought along about a dozen extra pair of shoes. I can let you have those."

"We'll take them," Jackson said with a smile.

"And be very thankful for them," Hunter said. "A dozen fewer men with sore feet is significant."

"I'll get them to you right away, Doctor. Do you want them delivered to you?"

"Yes. I'll pick the men with the sorest feet and see if we can get them fitted."

Hunter shook Dayton's hand again and excused himself.

"Rance, come on into the tent and sit down," Jackson said. "Let's talk about old times at V.M.I."

"You sure you have time, sir?"

"A few minutes, anyway. Come on in."

They sat on straight-backed wooden chairs next to a frail table that served as Jackson's desk.

"Sir, I have to tell you, when I saw in one of the Southern newspapers that you had been dubbed 'Stonewall' at First Bull Run, I thought to myself, 'Fits my favorite professor perfectly.'"

Jackson let a smile tug at his lips. "You think so, eh?"

"I know so, sir. When I sat in your classes and watched you on the artillery practice field, I saw a rare strength in you. If I had to go into battle, I knew I'd want you to be my leader."

"Rance, I appreciate your kind remarks, but let me say that whatever is in me that makes me like a stone wall comes from the Lord."

Dayton grinned. "That sounds like you, sir."

"Then you do remember the times I talked to you about your need to open your heart to Jesus and let Him save you, Rance." Jackson's eyes were full of compassion. "Have you done so?"

"Well, sir...no, I...I haven't. General, I know what you're saying is right. And I will think about it."

"You don't need to think about it, Rance. You need to do it. Just tell Jesus you're a sinner in need of salvation. Tell Him you believe He died for you on Calvary and rose from the grave so He could save you. You once told me you believed it. Do you still?"

"Yes, sir."

"Then act upon your head belief and make it heart belief, Rance. You can settle it right this minute, if you will."

Rance cleared his throat. "I'll sure think on it, sir. And... thank you for caring about me." Rance stood up and shook the general's hand. "I really will think about it."

"Just don't die while you're thinking about it," Jackson said.

"Yes, sir. I must get back to my men now. God bless you, sir."

Jackson watched his former student walk away in the dull light of dusk. "Keep him pressured, Lord. I want to see him saved."

CHAPTER ELEVEN

The Army of Northern Virginia, led by General Robert E. Lee on his white horse Traveler, marched north through Leesburg. It was a sunny, clear morning for the long procession of men, horses, mules, wagons, caissons, and cannons on wheels. Stonewall Jackson and James Longstreet, sitting straight-backed and proud in their saddles, rode on either side of the general.

The bands of both Corps marched in one unit, playing D. D. Emmett's song, "Dixie," as the Confederate army marched along Leesburg's main thoroughfare. Hundreds of cheering spectators lined both sides of the street. People stepped up and handed food to the soldiers and spoke encouraging words about their move onto Maryland soil.

One stout woman shouted from a balcony, "The Lord bless your dirty ragged souls! Show Billy Yank that fancy pressed uniforms aren't everything!"

Many of the soldiers raised their muskets and shouted back that they would do that very thing.

Hunter McGuire rode in a medical supply wagon driven by Corporal Lanny Dixon not far behind the three generals. There were four other medical supply wagons belonging to I Corps further back in the line, each manned by a doctor who was under Hunter's authority as Corps Medical Director. General Longstreet's II Corps also had four medical supply wagons, a Corps Medical Director, and four doctors.

All eight wagons had received supplies from Richmond, and some supplies had been donated by doctors in Leesburg. Hunter was grateful his new medical kit had arrived—he was sure he would need it once they invaded Northern territory.

"They tell me you know General Stonewall quite well, Doctor," Corporal Dixon said to Hunter.

"Since I was a small child. He's eleven years older than I am. He was my hero then and he's my hero now."

"Mine, too. The thing I admire most about General Stonewall is his courage to stand up for the Lord."

"He's no coward, I'll guarantee you that. And he's sure not ashamed to let it be known that he loves Jesus."

"I passed by his tent late the other night on my way to sentry duty and heard him praying for his men. Really touched my heart."

"He cares about his men, Lanny, not only their lives and limbs, but their souls. Too bad there aren't more generals like him."

When General Lee was two miles outside of Leesburg, he twisted around and looked back along the line of nearly fifty thousand men, animals, and equipment on wheels. The tail end of the line was just leaving the outskirts of the town. There was a new light in his men's eyes. This march and what it meant—taking the War to the Federals on their own soil—had energized them.

Lee veered his army eastward toward the Potomac River, planning to cross at White's Ford about five miles from Leesburg. The

Potomac was a half-mile wide at the ford, and as usual for early September, about five feet deep. The river was fringed by lofty trees in full foliage and the banks were flower-strewn and green with grass.

It would take considerable time to get his entire army across—at least a full day. The wagons, cannons, and caissons would take the most time and effort. They would have to cross single file because the ford was narrow and the river bottom grew deeper just a few feet on both sides of it.

Lee called a halt as he and Jackson and Longstreet reached the west bank of the Potomac just before noon. When the entire army had collected, Lee explained that he wanted to move as much of the army as possible onto the Maryland side before dark.

The first troops stepped in with their muskets held carefully out of the cool water, which felt good to their sore and blistered feet. The rest of the army cheered, excited to be taking the offensive against the enemy who had stepped onto Southern land well over a year ago.

At dusk, with the larger part of his army still on the Virginia side, General Lee settled his men down for the night.

The next day, as one of General Jackson's units was crossing the broad river, a team of balky mules hitched to one of the caissons stopped about forty yards out and refused to budge. Jackson shouted to the driver that he was holding up progress. The driver shouted back that he had tried everything he knew, but this was the most stubborn team of mules he had ever seen.

"Major Harmon," Jackson said to one of the men near him, "ride out there and help that driver get those mules moving."

"Yes, sir." Harmon snapped a salute and gouged his horse's sides, splashing into the Potomac and forcing his mount past the tangle of halted wagons. When he reached the mules, he leaned over and grasped the bridle of the nearest one and jerked it hard, letting loose a blast of profanity. It took less than half a minute for the mules to respond to the major's tirade and surge forward. Harmon touched his hat brim and smiled when the driver thanked him. As Harmon rode back, he glanced toward General Jackson and noticed the displeasure on his face.

"The ford is clear now, General. There's only one language that'll make stubborn old army mules understand on a hot day that they must get out of the water."

Jackson continued to scowl as he said, "Just because some foul-mouthed soldiers in this army use that kind of language to make mules obey doesn't mean it's necessary, Major. The tone of your voice is what they respond to. You could shout 'Rhubarb!' in the same tone of voice and they'd respond."

Harmon looked chagrined. "Sorry for the profanity, sir."

"Apology accepted, Major, but that doesn't clean out my ears."

"Excuse me, General," Harmon mumbled. "I...I need to go check on some of the wagons in my unit before they reach the water."

It took a day and a half to get the entire army and its equipment onto the Maryland side. The sun was going down on Saturday, September 6, as the band members crossed over, holding their instruments above their heads.

Lee was sure that by now his crossing onto Northern soil had reached even the ears of Abraham Lincoln.

On Friday afternoon, September 5, news of the Confederate crossing of the Potomac hit Washington like an artillery shell.

Ever since the previous Sunday, when reports of the debacle at Bull Run had come in, panic had prevailed among the federal officials, including President Lincoln and his General-in-Chief,

Henry Halleck. The crossing of the Potomac suggested that the Confederates were about to move on Baltimore, which would be only a prelude to an attack on Washington.

Word of the Confederate invasion spread fast among the Union troops and stirred their ire. In the past few days, since their beloved "Little Mac" had been appointed commander of all Federal troops around Washington, morale had begun to lift. Lincoln had no man among his military leaders who could come near the degree of popularity McClellan enjoyed with the troops.

Lincoln told McClellan that he was expecting him to bring the men out of their depression over so many lost battles and to turn them into a crack fighting unit as they had once been.

Spurred by Lincoln's trust in him and by Lee's brazen crossing of the Potomac, McClellan began marching the bulk of his restructured army northwest toward Maryland on Saturday, September 6. He took six corps with him—eighty-four thousand troops—leaving two corps behind to defend Washington.

It was eleven o'clock on Sunday, September 7 when General Lee led his army of nearly fifty thousand men to a spot about two miles south of Frederick, Maryland. They would make camp there after they marched through the town. There were Marylanders among Lee's troops, and he wanted to see what kind of reception his army would receive. Not only did Lee want to test the degree of Southern sentiment as reported by the newspapers, he also wanted to impress the Marylanders with the size of his army.

By noon, the long column was marching into Frederick with Confederate flags snapping in a hot, stiff wind that had been building since early morning. The double-sized band played "Maryland, My Maryland," and people of all ages began to line Main Street. Church services were letting out, and the crowd began to swell by the hundreds. Soon there was a combination of jeers by pro-Union people and cheers by those who favored the South.

As the procession moved slowly through town, the boos and hisses seemed louder than the cheers, and Lee realized the newspapers were guilty of either false or mistaken reporting.

Just as he and his two main generals passed Frederick's First Baptist Church, angry pro-Union men began throwing rocks and bricks. The band stopped playing, trying to protect themselves and their instruments.

Lee didn't want a confrontation with civilians. He called for his adjutant, Colonel Robert Chilton, and told him to ride back along the column and tell the men to protect themselves as best they could, but not to retaliate.

A brick sailed through the air and bounced off the side of Hunter McGuire's wagon, striking a small boy who had just come out of the church ahead of his parents. Hunter saw the boy go down. He leaped from the wagon and knelt beside the unconscious child. The rock-throwing stopped, and the army procession kept moving.

"I'm a doctor," Hunter said to the well-dressed men and women who pressed close. "Do any of you people know this boy's parents?"

McGuire heard someone close by shout, "Nurse Lockwood! Nurse Lockwood, Timmy Jones is hurt!"

Hunter's head jerked up as he rose to his feet, lifting the small, limp form in his arms, and looked toward the church.

"Timmy's parents are over there on the porch," someone said.

Hunter peered over their heads and saw a woman bound off the porch of the church building, a young couple on her heels. She hoisted her skirt slightly and lost her hat to the stiff wind as she ran toward him.

When Jodie Lockwood saw the tall, sandy-haired man who was cradling Timmy, her face blanched.

"Dr. McGuire!" she said. "I...I'm so glad to see you!"

Hunter's throat felt tight.

The boy's parents closed in, frozen with fear. "Oh, Timmy! Howard, he's dead! He's not breathing!"

"He's breathing, ma'am," Hunter said, his own emotions stirring like a whirlwind within him. "But he's unconscious. I'm a doctor. Is there a doctor's office near?"

"Mr. and Mrs. Jones," Jodie said, "this is Dr. Hunter McGuire. I recommend him without reservation. Let's get Timmy to Dr. Roberts's office."

"May I carry him, Doctor?" the boy's father asked.

"It's best that I do, Mr. Jones. I need to keep pressure against the head wound until we can get him to the doctor's office."

The man nodded and took his wife by the hand. "Come on, Lillian. Timmy's going to be all right."

General Jackson suddenly appeared on foot. "I saw the boy go down, Doc. How is he?"

"Hard to say. I'll know more when I can examine him. I suspect he has a concussion. Miss Lockwood, here, is a nurse, and she's about to take us to the doctor's office."

"We'll set up camp at that spot south of town," Jackson said. "Meet us there when you can."

"Will do. Let's go, Miss Jodie."

Jackson's eyes widened. *Jodie Lockwood?*

The crowd looked on as Hunter and the Joneses followed Jodie down the street.

Without breaking stride, Jodie turned to Hunter and said, "I'm Dr. Harvey Roberts's nurse at the Frederick Medical Clinic. It's just in the next block. Dr. Roberts was called out of bed in the middle of the night by a rider from Sharpsburg. There's no way to know when he'll be back."

"I'll do everything I can for Timmy, if the parents will give me permission," Hunter said.

"Miss Jodie's word is good enough for us, Doctor," Howard

Jones said. "We trust you. Do whatever you have to for our son."

"Here we are," Jodie said, as they arrived at the clinic. "I dropped my purse when I jumped off the church porch, but there's a key hidden around back. I'll use it to go through the back and open the front door."

The Joneses remained in the waiting area while doctor and nurse took Timmy into the back room. Ten minutes later, Jodie opened the door and stuck her head out. "Timmy's going to be fine. Dr. McGuire is taking stitches in the gash, and we'll be through in just a few minutes."

"Thank you, Lord," Timmy's mother said on an exhaled breath.

When the door opened again, Hunter emerged with Timmy in his arms. The boy's eyes were a bit glazed, but he recognized his parents and reached for them. Lillian Jones talked in low tones to her son as he lay in her arms, his bandaged head on her shoulder.

"He's going to be all right, then, Doctor?" Howard Jones asked.

"Yes," Hunter said, smiling. "He's got a concussion, but it will clear up. Took eight stitches to close the gash. Timmy should rest for a few days...not do the things active boys his age usually do. Have Dr. Roberts check him by Wednesday. He'll know when to take the stitches out."

Both parents nodded.

"Timmy will be drowsy for a while, but keep him awake till bedtime this evening. If he becomes nauseated, alert Nurse Lockwood. I'll be at the Confederate camp just south of town, at least for this evening. Call on me if you need me."

"We will, Doctor," Lillian said. "Thank you so much."

"What do we owe you, Doctor?" Howard asked, reaching for his wallet.

"Not a thing. It was my pleasure." Hunter winked. "Of course if you'd like to add a little extra to the offering plate in this evening's service..."

"I'll do it!" Howard said, as they left.

When the door clicked shut, Hunter and Jodie slowly turned to face each other.

CHAPTER TWELVE

"I can't tell you how nice it is to see you again, Doctor." A sweet smile lighted Jodie's face.

Hunter caught himself just short of making a fool of himself. "It's wonderful to see you again, Miss Jodie. I...I've thought about you many times since we met—how long has it been?"

What do you mean, McGuire? It's been exactly seven years and three months. And you've thought about her millions of times.

"So you've been working for Dr. Roberts since you finished at the Karr Clinic?"

"Aren't you amazing? You even remember where I was going when I left Lexington!"

"Some things I guess we never forget," Hunter said. Even as he spoke, he could hardly believe he had found Jodie after all these years.

Jodie told Hunter about earning her C.M.N. and C.S.A. certificates at the Benjamin Karr Clinic, and then getting hired by Dr. Roberts. Hunter thanked God for bringing them together again.

"So what about your career?" Jodie asked. "How long have you been an army doctor?"

"Since July 17 of last year. When I finished my internship almost five years ago, Kurtz and Aaron made me a junior partner. And they plan to take me in as a full-fledged partner when the clinic converts to a hospital. Of course, everything is on hold until this war is over."

"So you've been there for some battles."

"Yes...the two at Bull Run Creek have been the bloodiest, but we don't know what's to come."

"Oh, I hope it doesn't last much longer! Today was my first glimpse of General Lee. He looks quite distinguished, doesn't he? And if I remember the newspaper pictures correctly, I think the man who came to ask about Timmy was Stonewall Jackson."

"That's him, all right. Tom—General Jackson and I are old friends. We knew each other as boys."

"Well, I'm impressed, Doctor. It isn't everybody who can say they're old friends with the now-famous Stonewall Jackson."

"No, I guess not. He's the one who asked me to volunteer my services, and he coerced General Johnston into appointing me Corps Medical Director."

Jodie laughed. "I'm sure there had to be coercion." She studied him closely for a moment, then said, "Dr. McGuire, have you married?"

"No. No I haven't. And I'm surprised that you're still *Miss* Jodie Lockwood. Surely you've had many proposals?"

Jodie turned toward a pair of straight-backed wooden chairs nearby. "Do you have time to sit down, Doctor, or do you need to get to the camp?"

"I have time," he said, adjusting the chairs so they faced each other. "Here, allow me." Hunter seated Jodie, then took the other.

Jodie smiled. "To respond about the 'many proposals,' Doctor, I have met several fine Christian men over these years, both in Baltimore and here in Frederick. And...well, there have been a few marriage proposals. But in each case, I just couldn't accept."

"I see. Go on."

"I couldn't accept for two reasons. Number one, in each case I had no peace from the Lord about it. That would be enough right there to keep me from accepting a proposal. The second reason was that I didn't feel the kind of love for any of the men that goes with deciding to get married."

"That's important," Hunter said. "Marriage is a lifetime proposition. Certainly both people should have a deep and abiding love for each other."

"Dr. McGuire, may I ask why you haven't married?"

Hunter chose his words carefully. "Well, Miss Jodie, several years ago I fell head-over-heels in love with a very special young lady. Beautiful inside and out, and a devoted Christian. But she went far away, not knowing how I felt about her. I tried to find her so I could tell her of my love, but it was as if she had vanished off the face of the earth."

"Oh, I'm so sorry," Jodie said. "You...you still don't know where she is?"

Hunter had prayed for this moment, longed for it seven years and three months. "I haven't known where she was until about an hour ago."

It took two or three seconds for Hunter's words to register in Jodie's mind. Suddenly her heart seemed to stop and she felt a blush start at the back of her neck and envelop her body. Tears filled her eyes.

"Miss Jodie, I'm sorry. I didn't mean to upset you. I—"

Jodie shook her head and finally spoke. "You haven't upset me, Hunter. I...I mean, Doctor. It's not that at all. I don't know how to say this except to just come out with it. Within a few days after I left Lexington, I found myself thinking of you constantly. Soon I realized I had fallen in love with you, but I had no way of knowing how you felt about me.

"I wanted to write to you in the worst way and say that I loved you, but it would not be proper to speak first, so I prayed and asked the Lord that if He had chosen you for me, He would bring us together in His own time and His own way. I couldn't believe He would let me meet you and fall in love if He hadn't given you the same kind of love for me. I—"

"Oh Jodie..." Hunter dropped to his knees in front of her. "God was keeping us for each other all along. I love you, Jodie! I love you!"

Jodie threw her arms around Hunter's neck. Their tears mingled as their lips met softly, sweetly. He held her for a long time, then rose to his feet. "Jodie, I feel like I'm dreaming," he said.

Jodie looked up at Hunter with shining eyes. "I almost gave up," she said. "As time passed, and the Lord hadn't brought you back into my life, I began to think it wasn't God's will for us to be together."

Hunter took her in his arms again and spoke softly. "I prayed so hard, and sometimes horrid thoughts pierced my mind—thoughts that you had already married. Somehow I just couldn't accept those thoughts. Somehow I knew in my heart that the Lord had let you come into my life long enough for me to fall in love with you, and someday He would bring us together and let you learn to love me, too."

"I don't have to learn, darling," Jodie said. "I've been loving you for seven years."

They stood in each others' embrace, savoring the sweetness of it, then Hunter said, "Jodie, I sent you two letters while you were still at the Karr clinic. I guess you never got them."

"No, Hunter. I'd have been the happiest woman in the world if I'd received them."

"But they never came back. I wonder what happened to them."

Jodie was silent a moment, then said, "I think I know what happened. We had a receptionist at the clinic who handled all the mail. She was an atheist. She became quite angry when I witnessed to her about Jesus and told her the Bible says those who say there is no God are fools. From that time on she made life as miserable for me as she could. Dr. Karr finally fired her not long before he sold the clinic. I'm sure she intercepted your letters."

"I know about Dr. Karr selling the clinic to Dr. Clayton."

"You do?"

"I couldn't stand not seeing you, so I took a few days off to go to Baltimore. When I arrived at the clinic, no one knew you. Dr. Clayton found your records, but there was nothing to indicate where you might have gone. And now, on a windy Sunday, the Lord has brought you to me, as my mother would say, 'on the wings of the wind.' That's from—"

"Psalm 104:3. It's one of my favorite verses!"

"It was one of Mom's, too. She used it a lot. Before she died she said she was going to heaven to be with Dad, but that one day Jesus would come walking on the wings of the wind and bring us all back together—Lizzie, Mom, Dad, and me."

"Lizzie? Your sister?"

Hunter nodded, sadness capturing his eyes. "My father had been dead a year when Mom died. Lizzie and I were adopted by different families. I was adopted by a doctor and his wife from Boston. That's where I grew up. Lizzie was adopted by a family in McCann's Run, Virginia, where we were born. She was only two years old. They left for North Carolina right after the adoption but never got there. They just disappeared without a trace."

"Oh, Hunter, that's awful."

"I guess I never asked you where you're from, Jodie. Your family, and all that."

"Well, I was born and raised in the South. Southeast Tennessee, just outside of Athens."

"In the country, eh? A real Tennessee plow girl."

Jodie grinned. "I guess. Well, anyway, I wasn't raised in a Christian home. Neither of my parents were Christians. They both drowned while boating on Lake Chicamauga after I had moved to Lexington. My roommate in Lexington, who was like a sister to me, took me to First Baptist Church, and that's where I came to know the Lord."

"Bless her heart," Hunter said. "Do you have any siblings?"

"No. I wish I did. Would've been easier if I'd had brothers or sisters to help share the grief when my parents died. What about you, Hunter? You probably still think about Lizzie a lot."

"Every day."

The clock on the wall caught Hunter's attention. "Guess I'd better get back to the camp. It's nearly three-thirty. Tom—I mean, General Jackson is going to wonder what's happened to me."

Some of the light went out of Jodie's eyes. "How long will General Lee stay camped out there?" she asked.

"Probably not long. I don't really know what he's got in mind. All I know is that he's brought his army here to harass the Yankees."

"When will I see you again, Hunter?"

"I'd love to say I'll be here tonight for the church services, but since I don't know what's being planned, I'd better say look for me when you see me coming."

As he spoke, Hunter rose from his chair, lifting Jodie's hand. Without hesitation she moved close and put her arms around him. Hunter smiled and folded her close. "If I'm dreaming, Jodie, I don't want to wake up."

They kissed lingeringly and then Jodie lay her head against Hunter's chest. "So we don't know when we'll see each other again," she said.

"I'm afraid there's no way to tell. We may march a long way tomorrow. But I know where to find you now, and I'll be back just as soon as I can. And..."

"Yes?" she said, leaning back to look into his face.

"If you move elsewhere, tell *everybody* in town where I can find you."

She laughed. "I'm not planning to move, but you have my word on it. I won't be so hard to find again."

"Before I go, let's thank the Lord for bringing us together." Hunter took Jodie's small hands in his own and closed his eyes.

"Dear Lord," he began, "I must ask You to forgive me for all the times I doubted You, even when I prayed so hard that You would bring Jodie to me. We both thank You from the depths of our souls for guiding our lives and for bringing us together in Your own time and Your own way. We don't know when this awful war will be over, but You do. Please protect Jodie. Keep her, I pray, in the hollow of Your mighty hand, and let us be together again very soon. In the precious name of Jesus, we pray. Amen."

Hunter held Jodie close as she wept. When she had gained some composure, she blinked against her tears and said, "I'll show you the boarding house where I live. It's on the way south out of town."

As they walked along Main Street, Hunter kept an arm around Jodie's shoulders. Soon they were at the outskirts of Frederick. Grassy meadows and fenced farm fields spread out before them, and they could see the white tents of the Confederate camp some two miles in the distance, beneath tall trees.

"Jodie, if it's at all possible, I'll come into town and see you before we break camp and move out. If I don't come, you'll know I just couldn't do it. But know this much for sure...you'll see me the first opportunity I get."

"Then I will live for that moment, darling," she said, softly.

Hunter headed down the road and looked back after walking about thirty yards. Jodie remained where he had left her, and he could see tears glistening her cheeks.

When he was almost out of sight from her, he paused and looked back again. She stood in the golden light of the late afternoon sun, waving at him. As he waved back, his heart seemed to swell with love for her. "Lord," he said, "I love Jodie more now than ever."

*****

General Lee's adjutant, Colonel Chilton, met Hunter as he approached the camp.

"Yes, Colonel?" Hunter said, as they drew abreast.

"General Lee asked that you stop by his tent, Doctor. He's located beneath those tall elms."

Hunter thanked the adjutant and started for the general's tent, greeting soldiers as he went. General Lee was outside, talking with Stonewall Jackson, when Hunter walked up.

"You wanted to see me, sir?"

"Yes, Doctor. Both General Jackson and I are concerned about the boy. Is he all right?"

"Yes, sir. He has a concussion and needed some stitches to close up the gash on his head. But he'll be fine."

"That's good news." Lee turned back to Jackson. "You and General Longstreet meet with me first thing in the morning. Right after breakfast."

"We'll be here, sir," Jackson said, and started to head back to his Corps. Hunter bid General Lee good evening and walked away beside his old friend.

When they were out of earshot from any of the soldiers, Jackson said, "Hunter, unless I misunderstood what I heard in town today, that was your Jodie Lockwood, wasn't it?"

Hunter's face was beaming. "It was, Tom. God brought Jodie to me right there in the middle of Main Street!"

"And?"

"Tom, you won't believe it."

"Try me."

"She's been in love with me all this time. Said she knew it only days after arriving in Baltimore, but didn't think it proper to write to me, not knowing my feelings. She just prayed like I've been doing all these years. She's had opportunities to marry, but God picked her for me, Tom…and He saved her for me!"

Jackson halted abruptly.

"What's wrong?" Hunter asked.

"You *did* ask her to marry you, didn't you?"

"Well, no. I...I didn't take it that far today. But when I see her again, I sure will. Fellow has to use a little discretion, Tom."

"But you have no doubt she'll say yes?"

"None whatsoever."

A wide grin spread over Jackson's face. "Well, my friend, let me say that I sure am glad I was wrong. It looks like the Lord did have Jodie picked out for you. I hope the two of you will have a marriage as good as Mary Anna's and mine."

When Hunter looked at all the men in I Corps whose sore feet needed his attention, he knew he wouldn't be able to see Jodie again that evening.

After finally climbing into his bedroll just before midnight, he could hardly sleep for thinking about her. He'd found her, and she was in love with him.

At the boarding house in Frederick, Jodie stared up at the dark ceiling, marveling at the miracle of meeting Hunter again. The Lord had brought him to her, just as she had prayed He would. Hunter hadn't brought up marriage, of course. But when he did, she had her answer ready.

At his tent in the Confederate camp, General Lee was wide awake. Just before darkness fell, he had received an intelligence report from Jeb Stuart's scouts that the Union Army of the

Potomac had left Washington on Saturday, led by Major General George B. McClellan. "Little Mac" was headed on a straight line for Frederick with eighty-five thousand to ninety thousand troops.

CHAPTER THIRTEEN

Daylight came across the Maryland sky in changing sheets of color. Sunday's wind had died down to a moderate cool breeze, but would grow hot again as the day progressed.

Generals Jackson and Longstreet finished breakfast and started for their commander's tent. General Lee was seated with a map before him.

"Good morning, sir," Jackson said. "You look tired."

Lee sighed. "Please sit down, gentlemen. I didn't sleep at all. Too much to do. After you two were in your bedrolls last night, General Stuart's scouts rode into camp. They estimate that at least eighty-five thousand men left Washington Saturday and are headed this direction."

"Are you surprised, sir?" Longstreet asked.

"Not that they're coming...only the number. It doesn't deter me from harassing the stuffing out of the Federals, but it does change the way we're going to do it."

Jackson and Longstreet noted the map on the table, folded to focus on Washington, D. C., and the states of Virginia, Maryland, and Pennsylvania.

"As you gentlemen know," Lee said, "it's been in the back of my mind that if all went well in our invasion, we might drive our troops as far north as Pennsylvania."

He picked up a small twig and pointed at Frederick on the map. "My thinking is this: From Frederick we could move part of our army northwest across Catoctin Mountain—right here—and South Mountain—here—to Hagerstown, Maryland. From where we sit to Hagerstown is approximately twenty-seven miles."

Lee moved the twig's tip as he spoke. "Right here is the path of the Cumberland Valley Railroad. By moving our army northwest, as I just indicated, we would be shielded on our right flank by these mountains. We would follow the path of the Cumberland Valley Railroad, which curves seventy miles northeast from this point to Harrisburg—Pennsylvania's capital."

"And I think I see what you've got in mind," Jackson said. "Just west of Harrisburg lies the Susquehanna River and the key bridge of the Pennsylvania Railroad. You're after the bridge."

Lee smiled and rubbed his tired eyes. "You get a good grade in class today, Thomas J."

"Sure!" Longstreet said. "That bridge is vital to McClellan's supply line."

"That's correct," Lee said. "The destruction of the bridge would sever a vital Union supply route between east and west and weaken McClellan considerably.

"Now, to implement my plan, we'll have to safeguard our own lines of communication and supply against Union cavalry raids. Here's what I've come up with: We can shift our lines westward into the Shenandoah Valley behind the protection afforded here by the Blue Ridge Mountains. But first we'll have to deal with two Federal outposts that stand virtually astride my intended supply route in the Valley."

Jackson was ahead of his commander again. "You're speaking of Harper's Ferry and Martinsburg, sir?"

"Yes. I'm kicking myself for not keeping troops at Harper's Ferry when I brought you away from there, General. Now we've got to take the place from the Federals again. They've got twelve thousand troops camped there. Fifteen miles northwest of there—right up here—is Martinsburg, where the Federals have a twenty-five-hundred-man garrison. In order to eliminate these two threats, we'll have to temporarily split our army in two. General Longstreet, you will take three of your divisions—Hood's, Walker's, and Jones's—and begin the first leg of the movement into Pennsylvania. You will cross South Mountain to Boonsboro, halfway to Hagerstown. I will go with you.

"Meanwhile, General Jackson, you will take the other two divisions of II Corps—McLaw's and Anderson's—and all of your own I Corps and take over the Union garrisons at Harper's Ferry and Martinsburg. When you've accomplished that, our entire army will converge on the banks of the Susquehanna right at this point. We'll destroy the bridge at Harrisburg, then cut south, fortify ourselves, and clash head-on with McClellan's under-supplied army."

James Longstreet shifted his big frame on the chair and shook his head. His words had a slight biting edge to them. "General, I don't like dividing our forces."

Lee blinked, and Jackson's head came up. Longstreet was known for speaking his mind, but this bold statement surprised the other two men.

"I don't like it because it weakens us," Longstreet said. "I think whatever we do, we need to keep our forces together."

"In this situation, General," Lee said, "it's the only sensible thing to do—blow up the bridge at Harrisburg, cutting off Union supplies from McClellan's army, and neutralize Harper's Ferry and Martinsburg to keep our own supplies coming unhindered. My plan will work because there's no way the Yankees at those two outposts can stand against the numbers we'll throw at them."

"But what if McClellan gets past the point you indicated on the map where we'd cut south to meet him?" Longstreet asked. "Then we'd have to chase him down, which would give him time to fortify. We've got to remember, General, that if General Stuart's scouts are accurate in their estimation, McClellan has us heavily outnumbered."

"But you're forgetting something—McClellan's temperament."

"Sir?"

"The man is slower than the seven-year itch. He's an able military leader, I'll give him that, but he's a very cautious one. Believe me, we'll easily have time to come south from Pennsylvania and wait for him when he reaches this point, right here. Big surprise for McClellan! By that time, we'll have all his supply sources cut off. Since we're outnumbered, it's the only way we can come out the victors."

Longstreet darted his eyes to Jackson. Stonewall grinned at him. "I believe our esteemed leader is on target here, General."

Longstreet stared at the map in silence, his face rigid.

After a few moments, Lee said, "Well, Old Warhorse, are you with me?"

Longstreet's face muscles relaxed. "Of course, sir, but reluctantly. I just don't hanker to split our forces. However, you are the boss of this outfit, so I'll comply."

Lee glanced at Jackson, grinned, looked back at Longstreet, and said, "You're a good man, and I appreciate the fact that you aren't bashful about expressing your opinions."

Longstreet smiled slightly. "Bashful, sir, I am not."

Lee rose from his chair. "Well, gentlemen, I'll put this plan into writing and make it an order. Then I'll have Colonel Chilton make a copy for the head officer of each division."

"You haven't said when we'll split the army and move out, General," Jackson said.

"Well, it's going to take Colonel Chilton several hours to make all the copies once I get the original into his hands. I'd say we should plan to move out at sunrise on Wednesday."

Longstreet masked his surprise. He had expected they would

move out tomorrow. Waiting until Wednesday would give McClellan another day to march his troops westward.

The sun had set that evening when Jodie Lockwood finished drying the last supper dish and placed it in the cupboard. She removed her apron, hung it on a wall peg in the small kitchen, and picked up the lantern.

When the knock came at the door, her first thought was that Dr. Roberts needed her to help with a medical emergency.

It was Hunter, with a bouquet of wildflowers in his hand.

Jodie's face glowed as she greeted him. "Oh, I'm so glad you're here! And those flowers...they're beautiful!"

"Not as beautiful as you. When God made you, He did His most excellent piece of work."

"Aren't you the flatterer." She raised up on tiptoe and kissed Hunter softly. "Come in, darling. I'll put these flowers in water."

Jodie wore a simple cotton print dress, but to Hunter it was royal attire. He followed her to the kitchen and lifted the dipper from the water bucket while Jodie took a small vase off the cupboard shelf and extended it toward him.

"Only about a third, Dr. McGuire."

He poured the water carefully and grinned. "Yes, Nurse Lockwood."

Jodie slipped the stems into the vase and set it on the cupboard. Then turning to Hunter's embrace, she declared, "I'll never throw them away. When they begin to wither, I'll press them in a book and keep them always."

Hunter looked into her eyes, the amber glow of the lantern playing on their faces. "I love you, sweet Jodie."

"And I love you, my darling Hunter."

After his tender kiss she stayed within his arms.

"Hunter, I'm so glad you didn't have to leave. Do you know

yet when General Lee will be moving his army out?"

"Word is it'll be Wednesday morning at daylight."

"Then can you come a little earlier tomorrow night and let me fix you a nice meal?"

"I can arrange that. What time?"

"How about six o'clock?"

"Six o'clock it is. I'll look forward to it."

"I've been told I'm a good cook. I hope you will agree."

"If it's you cooking it, it has to be good."

"Dr. McGuire, you are what is known as a diplomat."

"Well, since yesterday just about noon, I've been known as the happiest man on earth. If that makes me good at diplomacy, so be it. How about going for a walk? There's a half-moon up there in God's big starry sky."

"I'd love it."

Windows glowed with lantern light as Jodie and Hunter strolled hand-in-hand beneath a canopy of stars and listened to the seemingly millions of crickets playing their nightly music.

"Isn't God's creation wonderful?" Jodie said. "Everything around us is so beautiful."

Hunter squeezed Jodie's hand. "If it were only as peaceful as it looks tonight," he said.

Soon they were at the town's south edge and they could see the winking fires in the army camp.

"I hate to think of the coming battle," Jodie said, her voice low. "This war is so senseless."

"War is always senseless. I don't know why people can't just live and let live."

"Because Jesus said there would be wars and rumors of wars all the way up to the end time. But I'll sure be glad when this one is over."

"It would be a lot easier for a married physician and surgeon to have a normal life than following these armies around," he said.

Jodie looked up, trying to see Hunter's expression in the pale silver light. "Just any married physician and surgeon, or one that I know personally?"

"The one who is so in love with you that sometimes he thinks his heart is going to burst right through his chest. Will you marry me, Jodie?"

Jodie had practiced her answer, but now it came out totally different. "Oh, darling, I…I…What am I stammering for? Of course I'll marry you!"

Hunter took her in his arms and kissed her long and tenderly. He felt her warm tears on his face. He held her against him and pressed the side of her head to his chest. They stayed that way for a long time with only the sound of the night breeze in the nearby trees and the music of the crickets.

Hunter broke the silence. "Let's talk about our engagement. We want to be right and proper in it. Do you think four or five months is long enough? I mean, it's not like we're fresh out of high school."

"I'm sure four or five months would be proper," Jodie said. "And maybe by that time the War will be over."

"I hope so. But even if it's not, we'll get married anyway. That is, if you don't mind being married to an army doctor who follows the battles."

"I don't mind."

"I knew you'd say that. We can set the exact date later, but for now we'll say January or February."

They had turned back toward town when Jodie stopped abruptly and pulled at Hunter's hand. "Hunter—"

"Hmm?"

"You will be careful, won't you? I know you're not right out in the middle of the battlefields, but bullets and cannon shells can travel a long way."

"I'll do my best to keep this engaged man alive, sweetheart."

"You do that."

*****

On Tuesday morning, September 9, Colonel Chilton stood over General Lee as the Confederate Army leader signed the copies of his plan. At the head of each page were the words *Special Orders Number 191.*

When he had signed the last order, Lee looked up at Chilton. "Colonel, I ask you to personally deliver these to each division commander."

"Yes, sir."

"Tell each man that the orders pinpoint our movements over the next several days, and they are to guard the papers with care."

"I understand, sir."

"Since I talked this plan over with Generals Jackson and Longstreet this morning, I've had a change of mind. I'm putting Major General Daniel Hill's division with General Longstreet's three divisions into Pennsylvania. If either General Jackson or General Longstreet questions this change, tell him to come and see me at once."

"Yes, sir."

Stonewall Jackson and Hunter McGuire stood talking outside Jackson's tent when the general suddenly chuckled. "So she's going to give you a sample of her cooking, is she? What are you going to do if it's bad?"

"It won't be. That sweet petunia couldn't do *anything* bad."

Jackson shook his head. "Son, the love bug has bitten you with real sharp teeth."

"General Jackson, sir," came a voice from behind them.

Jackson pivoted as Colonel Chilton approached. "Good morning, Colonel."

"Good morning, sir. And good morning to you, Dr. McGuire."

Chilton took some folded papers from the stack he was carrying and extended them toward Jackson. "This is General Lee's Special Order, sir. You know about it. He said to tell you that he made a change after he talked with you and General Longstreet. If you have any questions, you are to see him immediately."

"All right. Thank you."

When Chilton was gone, Jackson smiled at Hunter. "Well, my friend, I guess I'd better read this over. You and Jodie have a good time this evening. The fact that you're going to get a home-cooked supper makes me miss my Mary Anna even more."

"Well, I'd invite you along, Tom, but—"

Jackson laughed. "Sure you would! Now get out of here! I've got important work to do."

Hunter walked away, a broad smile on his face.

Jackson entered his tent to read the special orders. When he saw that General Lee was taking one of I Corps' divisions with him into Pennsylvania, he sat down to write a note to General Hill.

Jackson copied the orders word-for-word on a fresh piece of paper and added a note at the bottom to make sure Hill understood that he was in agreement with Lee's last-minute change.

He signed the note, folded the paper, and stepped outside to scan the men milling about camp. He spotted Lieutenant Garth Mallory walking in his direction.

"Lieutenant!" Jackson called.

Mallory's head lifted and he hurried to Jackson. "Yes, General?"

"I need this very important paper delivered to General Daniel Hill. Would you see that he gets it right away?"

"Certainly, sir." Mallory accepted the folded paper, and Jackson thanked him then returned to his tent.

As Mallory threaded his way among the tents, he spotted a corporal who was in Hill's division. He hailed the corporal and explained that General Jackson had given him a note to deliver to

General Hill. Would the corporal do it for him…he had some other things to tend to.

The corporal took the note, pulled three cigars from his shirt pocket, and carefully wrapped the note around them. He placed the small bundle back in his pocket and told Mallory he would deliver the note to General Hill.

That evening Jodie answered Hunter's knock wearing a two-piece dress of cobalt blue sateen. It had a pointed basque waist and a lace Byron collar and cuffs, and small silver buttons. Her mass of jet-black hair was elegantly upswept, with trailing curls.

Hunter was enchanted.

"Come in, darling," Jodie said. "Supper will be ready in a few minutes."

Hunter moved through the door, his eyes sweeping over her. "Jodie, you look gorgeous! I love your hair like that…and that dress—"

"I wanted to dress in a special way for you tonight. I hope it pleases you."

Hunter took her in his arms and kissed her.

Later, after they had given thanks for the food and begun to eat, Hunter told Jodie the army would be pulling out in the morning at dawn.

"Oh, Hunter. I'm going to miss having you so close."

"I'm going to miss being so close," Hunter said. "And I'm going to miss this scrumptious cooking. Couldn't we get married right now and just run away from all this?"

Jodie grinned. "I wish we could. Do you really like my cooking?"

"Couldn't be matched this side of heaven."

As the meal progressed, the happy couple talked of their wedding and the future that lay before them.

Later, when the dishes were done and the kitchen cleaned up, Hunter and Jodie took a walk in the moonlight, this time through town to the north. Since Hunter had no idea what would become of the Confederate invasion of Maryland—and he was sworn to secrecy concerning Lee's push into Pennsylvania—he couldn't tell Jodie when he would see her again.

When they returned to the boarding house, Jodie wept and clung to Hunter. He kissed her soundly, told her once again that he loved her, and walked away into the night.

At dawn on Wednesday morning, September 10, 1862, General Lee's army had finished breakfast and the men were hastily pulling down tents and loading wagons. The tattered soldiers, refreshed after four days' rest, were in a cheerful mood.

By the time the sun was up, Lee and his troops had begun their move. To further impress the citizens of Frederick, he marched his fifty thousand-strong army through town.

The combined bands played "The Girl I Left Behind Me" as people gawked from windows, while others stepped out onto porches and still others lined the street. Both Union and Confederate flags waved. There was booing and hissing mingled with cheers, but as Lee had figured, there were no rocks or bricks thrown.

Hunter sat on the wagon seat next to Corporal Lanny Dixon. As they drew near the clinic, Hunter looked for Jodie. Suddenly he spotted her, standing next to a distinguished-looking man he presumed was Dr. Roberts.

Hunter smiled and waved. Jodie pointed him out to Dr. Roberts, then blew him a kiss.

To conceal his real objective of heading southwest to Harper's Ferry, Jackson marched his troops north as if they were going with Lee. When they were out of sight from Frederick, he turned them around, veered west, and dropped down into a shallow valley.

CHAPTER FOURTEEN

General Lee's strategy was sound, but his estimate of McClellan's movements was in error. He was not aware of the pressure Abraham Lincoln had put on McClellan to step up the pace. The eighty-four thousand troops of the Union Army of the Potomac drew near Frederick from the south at midafternoon on Friday, September 12.

Major Generals Ambrose E. Burnside and Joseph Hooker flanked McClellan as they rode.

General Hooker let his ice-blue gaze roam the area ahead and said, "General McClellan, sir, that open area fringed by tall elms looks like a good place to make camp. Should be enough room for all of us there."

"Looks good to me," McClellan replied.

As they drew nearer, Hooker rose up in his stirrups. "Sir, there have been tents and a large number of men here."

"Lee!" McClellan said. "He camped here, and not long ago!"

Joe Hooker was the first to dismount and scan the area. "I'd say by the way the grass looks and by the depth of the footprints in the soft dirt, they left here two days ago, three at the most."

"Well, if this place was good enough for Bobby Lee, it's good enough for George B. McClellan. General Burnside, ride back along the column and tell them we're camping here."

"Yes, sir." The balding general with the muttonchop whiskers wheeled his horse about.

That night McClellan met with his Corps leaders. The major generals stood in a half circle, facing their leader. A large fire burned close by.

"Gentlemen," McClellan said, "I have not yet decided how long we will camp here. I'll make that decision after I send some scouts out in the morning. When they find Lee, we'll make our move. However, in the morning, we're going to march our entire column through Frederick. If I know Bobby Lee like I think I know Bobby Lee, he's already done that to impress the people. Well, George McClellan will not come behind Bobby Lee in anything."

At the same time McClellan was picking his camp site south of Frederick, Robert E. Lee was doing the same for his four divisions at the base of South Mountain, some fifteen miles northwest.

When Lee's tent was set up, he stepped inside and sat down, rubbing his chest. Colonel Chilton, who was carrying in the general's bedroll, noticed the grimace on Lee's face.

"General, sir, you're in pain. Shall I get one of the doctors?"

Lee took a deep breath and winced. "That won't be necessary, Colonel, thank you. I'm just having a little pleurisy. I've had it before."

"Sir, I really think I should go get Dr. McGuire."

"No, really," Lee said. "I'll be all right in a minute or two."

"Sir, at the risk of being hanged for disobeying my superior officer, I *am* going to fetch Dr. McGuire." With that, Chilton was out of the tent and gone.

Lee smiled, then winced again from a spasm of pain.

Five minutes later, Hunter was listening to Lee's heart with a stethoscope while Colonel Chilton stood by.

When Hunter had finished, he said, "General, it's not pleurisy. You have an irregular heartbeat. Has any doctor ever told you this?"

"No."

"Well, sir, this is going to sound impossible, but my advice to you is to try to relieve yourself of too much pressure."

Lee smiled. "I've got a war to fight."

Hunter reached into his black bag and pulled out a small white envelope. "I'm going to give you a sedative, General. I want you to take half of these powders right now and the other half in the morning. Hopefully, you'll feel better by then. I'll check on you again tomorrow."

Hunter was about to leave when rapid, pounding hooves were heard outside. Colonel Chilton stepped out and called back, as the horse skidded to a halt, "It's one of General Stuart's scouts, sir."

"Show him in," Lee said.

The scout introduced himself as Sergeant Harland Bailey, and told Lee that another scout had asked him to bring the message that a large unidentified part of McClellan's Union Army of the Potomac was marching south from Pennsylvania toward Hagerstown.

Lee's hand went back to his chest. "How has McClellan managed to do this? It hasn't been that long since he pulled out of Washington. There's no way he could have sent part of his army into Pennsylvania last Saturday and had them there already heading south toward Hagerstown!"

"All I know is what the scout told me, sir."

"Well, I've got to believe him. Colonel Chilton, go bring my division leaders, quick!"

Lee was shouldering into his shirt when Hunter stopped him. "Sir, we need to get this sedative into you now."

Moments later, General Lee, back in shirt and coat, met with his division leaders. Since Hagerstown was to be the springboard for Lee's invasion into Pennsylvania, he told the generals they would pack up immediately and ride through the night to get there. He would take three divisions, totaling sixteen thousand men, leaving Major General Hill's division of five thousand at South Mountain to guard the rear.

Hunter McGuire insisted on going with Lee to keep an eye on him. Lee did not argue.

At sundown in the Union camp, the tents had been pitched and the cooks were building fires to start supper. A delegation of Frederick businessmen, upon hearing that the Federals were making camp on the same spot where the Confederates had been, had come to the camp and now gathered in front of General McClellan's tent, talking to him.

McClellan's weary soldiers sat on the ground to rest, and some stretched out to catnap. Two soldiers—Sergeant Bloss and Corporal Mitchell of Burnside's IX Corps—sat under an elm, discussing where Lee might have taken his army.

"Maybe they got cold feet and circled back south," Mitchell said.

"That would be something," Bloss said. "Maybe this time they'll all drown in the Potomac."

"Yeah. Sure would make it easier on—"

Mitchell was staring at something in the tall grass a few feet away.

"See something?" Bloss asked.

Mitchell stood up and headed into the grass. "Some kind of package over here," he said.

Bloss watched Mitchell pick up something white and heard him say, "Well, whattaya know? Some dumb Rebel lost three cigars. They're wrapped in—" Mitchell slipped the paper off the cigars and suddenly tensed. "John, c'mere! Look at this!"

Bloss got to his feet and took the paper from Mitchell's fingers. As he scanned the message, his eyes widened. "Do you realize what this is?"

"Yeah! We need to get it to General McClellan!"

"Let's take it to General Burnside first. It'd be best if he took it to General McClellan."

Burnside's aide told them the general was in conference and could not be disturbed. Bloss and Mitchell headed for their own division leader, Brigadier General Samuel D. Sturgis.

General McClellan was still in conversation with the businessmen from Frederick when he noticed three soldiers hastening toward him. He recognized General Sturgis, who was carrying a white sheet of paper.

"General McClellan," Sturgis said, "Sergeant Bloss and Corporal Mitchell have found something you must see immediately."

McClellan excused himself to the businessmen and angled the paper toward the last rays of the sun. His grip on it tightened as he saw the heading: *Special Orders Number 191, Headquarters, Army of Northern Virginia, September 9, 1862.*

Soldiers began to gather as word went round the camp that something important was happening. McClellan lifted the paper over his head and shook it, laughing heartily. "Talk about a stroke of good fortune. This is more than I could ever have hoped for!"

"What is it, General?" asked one of the businessmen.

"A special order from Bobby Lee to his division leaders! He has split his army, sending Stonewall Jackson to Harper's Ferry and Martinsburg to capture our outposts there. Lee is with the rest of his army, headed toward Pennsylvania to blow up the Pennsylvania Railroad bridge at Harrisburg. We got 'em where we want 'em! Now we'll crush the Confederate army!"

McClellan then asked Bloss and Mitchell how and where they had found the paper. He commended Mitchell for his sharp eye, and told him he would be a sergeant when he woke up the next morning.

When McClellan turned back to the businessmen, he said, "I need to use the telegraph in town. Can you gentlemen—"

"I run the telegraph office, General," one of them said. "It's yours to use, free of charge."

"Thank you, sir. I need to wire President Lincoln and tell him the news."

McClellan hastened into town and sent a wire to Lincoln, saying he would send trophies of the victory when the Confederates were vanquished.

On his return to the camp, McClellan moved among the men, waving the lost order and stirring them up by shouting, "With this paper, I will whip Bobby Lee!"

Lee's three divisions—including Stuart's cavalry—arrived at Hagerstown at dawn on Saturday morning. Stuart sent two scouts north to see how close the Federal troops were.

The day passed while the men caught up on their sleep in shifts. Jeb Stuart insisted that General Lee get some sleep, saying he would awaken him when the scouts returned.

Lee slept for about three hours and was up again, waiting with Stuart at the edge of camp. It wasn't until sunset that the two scouts returned. When they saw Lee and Stuart, they drew rein.

"We couldn't find any Union troops anywhere," a scout said. "The reason we've been gone so long is because we wanted to make sure. We went several miles into Pennsylvania and covered broad swaths separately. The report you received, General Lee, was erroneous."

Lee was so relieved that he felt no anger toward the scout who had made the false report. He thanked the men, then turned to Jeb Stuart. "General, we'll camp here for the night and return to General Hill's division at South Mountain in the morning."

Four hours later, when all the men except the sentries were in their bedrolls asleep, General Lee was just slipping off his boots when he heard footsteps and a low voice. "General Lee, sir, I assume you're still awake."

"Yes."

"It's Corporal Tom Humphrey, sir—one of the pickets. There's a gentleman here from Frederick who would like to see you. He says it's important."

"Just a moment, Corporal."

Lee pulled on his boots, straightened his shirt and coat, and opened the tent flap. He could see two figures standing in the dark. "You rode all the way here, alone, from Frederick, sir?"

"Yes, General. My name is Stephen Cunningham. I own the Cunningham Hotel in Frederick."

Lee shook the man's hand and bid him sit on one of the wooden folding chairs inside the tent. Cunningham then said, "I'm afraid I'm a bearer of bad news, General, but somebody had to come and tell you."

Lee's brow furrowed. "Bad news?"

"Yes, sir. General McClellan and some eighty-four thousand troops arrived about noon today and are camped on the same spot where you were."

Lee's eyebrows arched. "Arrived today?"

"Yes, sir. Some of the pro-Union businessmen in town decided to go to the camp and talk with McClellan. I went along to see what I could learn. Although my wife and I have lived in Maryland for thirty years, we were born in Alabama, and our sympathies lie with the South."

"I'm glad to hear that, Mr. Cunningham. So the bad news is that McClellan is camped at Frederick?"

"Well, no, sir. The bad news is that one of McClellan's men

found a copy of an order you issued to your division commanders on September 9. It was numbered 191. McClellan now knows your plans to destroy the railroad bridge at Harrisburg, and he knows that General Jackson has been sent to capture the Union garrisons at Harper's Ferry and Martinsburg."

Lee felt the strength go out of him. He put a shaky hand to his forehead. "Well, Mr. Cunningham, this *is* bad news. I thank you for riding all the way here to let me know."

"I felt it was my duty as a loyal Southerner, General. I'll be heading back home now."

As Cunningham rode away, Lee turned to Humphrey. "Corporal, I need you to awaken General Longstreet. Tell him I must see him right away."

Suddenly Lee and Humphrey heard a stirring in the darkness to the south, then a horse blew and a voice came from the same direction.

"General Lee! Sergeant Rick Wells, sir. On picket duty. I have Lieutenant Charles Simeon from General Hill's division at South Mountain with a message for you."

Even as Wells spoke, Simeon handed him the reins and approached the general. "Sir, General Hill sent me to advise you that an enormous number of small campfires can be seen toward Frederick from the southern tip of South Mountain. He's sure it's the Yankees, sir. The fires are within about a mile and a half of our camp."

Lee spoke to Humphrey. "Corporal, I not only need General Longstreet, I need his division leaders."

Humphrey nodded and disappeared.

Lee then turned to Simeon. "Lieutenant, tell General Hill to move his division into Turner's Gap within South Mountain. He'll be best fortified there."

"Yes, sir."

"Tell him I scrutinized the gap as we passed through. It would be advantageous for him to get his artillery up on the west side.

The flat rock formations will allow plenty of room and a clear shot where the Yankees have to expose themselves to enter the gap from National Road. Got it?"

"Yes, sir."

"Tell General Hill he must hold the gap at all costs. We will begin our march from here at dawn and get there as soon as we can."

Four sleepy-eyed generals were heading toward Lee's tent, buttoning shirts and pulling up suspenders as Lieutenant Simeon galloped south out of the camp.

"Come in, gentlemen," Lee said. "I've got news for you, and we've got planning to do."

While his division leaders were digesting the new information, Lee told Jeb Stuart to send a courier immediately to Stonewall Jackson and inform him of the recent developments. Jackson was to hurry his capture of Harper's Ferry and Martinsburg, and then rush to South Mountain.

Lee discussed the situation with his division leaders, trying not to show discouragement. They would push hard for South Mountain at daybreak. Dan Hill was going to need all the help he could get.

It was about an hour before dawn when General Hill stood at the north edge of his encampment with his brigade leaders beside him. They were Brigadier Generals George B. Anderson, Alfred H. Colquitt, Samuel Garland, Roswell S. Ripley, and Robert Rodes.

National Road was barely visible at the point it plunged into the mountain. They talked in low tones about the coming battle, and periodically glanced toward the Yankee camp where only a few fires flickered now. Suddenly they heard the sound of thundering hoofbeats echoing out of the gap.

"He made good time," Colquitt said.

"That's why I sent him," Hill said evenly. "Simeon's a good horseman."

Lieutenant Simeon delivered his message, and Hill turned to his brigade leaders. "All right, gentlemen. You heard General Lee's orders. We've got to move out before dawn when Billy Yank will attack, sure as anything. We've got to be ready to meet them at Turner's Gap."

By the time the sun was coming up on Sunday morning, September 14, General Hill had his division positioned for battle at Turner's Gap in the heart of South Mountain.

Hill climbed to a high point where he could see the southern entrance of the gap. There were no Yankees on the road yet. He ran his gaze along National Road, noticing that there was good enough defensive ground around the defile where National Road crossed the mountain. Even a small force could make it hot for the attacking troops.

However, as he studied the entire area, he noticed that his division was vulnerable on both flanks. Two roads branched off National Road near the eastern base of the mountain. One was the Old Sharpsburg Road, which angled to the south and crossed the range at Fox's Gap, a little less than a mile from Turner's Gap. A rough farm road left the Sharpsburg road part way up the slope and made a loop farther to the south before turning back and continuing along the top of the ridge through Fox's Gap to Turner's.

The second branch, the Old Hagerstown Road, made a circuit to the north, rejoining National Road at the crest. From it, too, there ran a wide, looping farm road, presenting the Yankees with still another flanking route. Hill decided that to hold Turner's Gap at all costs meant spreading defenders across a good three miles to cover all five roads.

The terrain of South Mountain was irregular, pocked by ravines and hollows, and marked by rounded peaks. The slopes were heavily wooded and thick with undergrowth and tangles of mountain laurel. Where the ground leveled off near the crest, a number of farms had been carved from the forest, their fields and pastures bordered by split-rail fences and stone walls. It would be a difficult place to maneuver troops and direct a battle, but it had to be done.

General Hill hurried to where his troops were setting up their defenses and explained what to do to be able to hold the gap against a massive Union force.

He quickly dispatched Garland's and Colquitt's brigades toward the other four roads to cover them against enemy approach.

Every unit was in place by six o'clock. Thankful that the Federals had not attacked at dawn, General Hill climbed even higher than before and looked to the south. What he saw left him breathless. Spread across the valley were Federal troops in all their array.

Hill set his jaw as he headed down toward his men. Billy Yank was going to find out that Johnny Reb might be low in number, but he was high in fighting spirit.

CHAPTER FIFTEEN

Just before eight o'clock that Sunday morning, General McClellan was sitting at a folding table outside his tent, sipping hot coffee and talking to General Burnside.

Late the day before, McClellan had learned from his signal stations on hills south of Frederick that the Federal garrison at Martinsburg had been captured by Stonewall Jackson's forces and that Harper's Ferry was presently under siege. McClellan had spent Saturday afternoon developing his plan of attack. He intended to relieve Harper's Ferry and pounce on the scattered units of the Confederates.

To accomplish these goals, he would first have to get his massive army across the Catoctin Mountain, just west of Frederick, and the more formidable South Mountain a dozen miles beyond. McClellan had guessed that Lee would learn of his arrival at Frederick when Lee passed through Turner's Gap. He would know the Federals were on his trail, and fortify himself near the small town of Boonsboro, just north of South Mountain.

On Saturday night, McClellan had sent the bulk of his army to camp near the southern tip of South Mountain. They were then to move on to Boonsboro and wipe out Lee's forces. Once that was done, they would go after Jackson's I Corps, wipe them out, and take back Harper's Ferry and Martinsburg.

At Frederick, McClellan held in reserve twelve thousand men. These he would bring with him to Harper's Ferry to help the other sixty thousand finish off Stonewall Jackson's I Corps. The War would soon come to an end, and George B. McClellan would go down in history as the General who polished off Bobby Lee.

"General McClellan," Burnside said, "shouldn't I go ahead and take my Corps through Turner's Gap? That would give us more momentum when we go after Jackson at Harper's Ferry."

McClellan and Burnside were not friends. It was known by every man in the Union Army of the Potomac that they simply tolerated each other. Burnside had felt all along that McClellan was too slow to attack, as did President Lincoln and Henry Halleck. Burnside had been pleased that McClellan had actually hurried his army from Leesburg to Fredericksburg, but he was already seeing signs of the old "slows" returning.

His suspicions were confirmed when McClellan replied, "No, General, I want your Corps here in reserve."

"But, sir, General Franklin's twelve thousand will be enough reserve. I really think I should take my men and head over South Mountain, now."

McClellan's expression turned sour. "I'll be the judge of that, General. In my thinking, it's best that you remain here in reserve. Please don't argue with me. You'll move out when I—"

McClellan's words were cut off by the rapid pounding of hooves. A rider galloped toward them from the north, and seconds later they recognized a lieutenant from General Pleasonton's cavalry.

"General McClellan!" the lieutenant shouted, thundering to a stop. "Lee wasn't at Boonsboro. He was waiting for us at Turner's Gap, and we've got a hot battle going on! The Rebels have the advantage of high ground, and they're going to be hard to dislodge. We can't tell if it's all of Longstreet's Corps in the gap or just part of it, but General Pleasonton wanted you to know about the battle. He figured you might want to send more men."

McClellan brushed a hand across his face, smoothed his mustache, and said, "You ride back and tell General Pleasonton I'm sending General Burnside's Corps immediately."

Burnside felt a warm glow flow through him but showed no emotion. "I'll round up my men and we'll be on our way in a jiffy, sir," he said.

The battle at Turner's Gap was indeed a hot one. Although the Confederates had the advantage of high ground, the Federals had the advantage in numbers.

General Hill was perched on a high spot above Turner's Gap, his adjutant, Colonel Barry Hucklesby, at his side. They were standing in a rock cleft, peering south at the swarm of blue uniforms pressing in a V shape into the mouth of the gap.

From further out, the Union artillery was arcing shells onto the Confederates' first line. Suddenly a screaming shell came close to where Hill and Hucklesby were positioned and burst a few yards below them. They felt its hot, brutal breath as they ducked, then heard the hiss of flying pieces of rock and the whine of shrapnel all around.

Hucklesby's ears were ringing as he straightened up. "You all right, sir?"

"Fine," Hill said, quickly looking back toward the battle. Through the smoke he saw ghostly figures moving toward the mouth of the gap. The Yankees had plenty of men. No matter what the Rebels threw at them, they just kept coming.

A hot wind was beginning to blow, and soon the smoke parted, revealing the green fields to the south speckled with bodies in blue uniforms. The outnumbered Rebels were fighting hard, and their guns were taking a toll on the Yankees.

But Union artillery was doing the same to the Confederate

army. When the Union musket balls couldn't reach the enemy, they arced shells over the natural rock fortresses.

Hill could also see Brigadier General Samuel Garland moving amongst his men, shouting encouragement and directing them to fill in gaps in the lines when others went down.

Down the National Road at the mouth of the gap, the Confederates were facing assaults from the right, left, and front. Bullets buzzed all around, and cannon shells exploded, sending deadly hot canister whistling every direction.

Hill studied the whole scene and said to his aide, "Colonel, if Generals Lee and Longstreet don't get here soon, we're done for."

He put binoculars to his eyes and looked north, then used the binoculars to scan the scene below. "Colonel..."

"Yes, sir?"

"We need more men at Fox's Gap. Go down there and tell General Hood to take his brigade over there on the double. He's got to plug a hole the Yankees are opening in our lines."

Hucklesby had been gone no more than a minute when Hill saw General Garland take a bullet and go down. Hill watched two of Garland's men carry his body a few feet away and lay his hat over his face.

By one o'clock the Southerners were feeling the pressure of the overwhelming odds. To make matters worse, in the distance they saw long columns of Federals marching toward South Mountain from Frederick.

Twenty minutes later, as the columns drew near, the Union soldiers recognized their esteemed leader riding beside General Burnside. McClellan's presence excited his troops. When the front of the columns drew near the battle, McClellan veered his mount to the side of National Road and drew rein. The passing columns of men cheered him as they marched toward the mouth of the gap.

*****

By three o'clock, General Hill could see that his exhausted men were on the brink of collapse. The Yankees had enough men that they could fight in shifts. There were no such breaks for the Rebels.

Then, seemingly at the last moment, General Longstreet's troops came into view from the north. They were dusty and tired after their long march over rough terrain, but ready to join in the fight. Hill dashed down amongst his men, shouting that help had arrived.

As Longstreet's troops approached the base of the mountain, closing in to reinforce Hill's gallant troops, the weary men cheered at the sight of General Lee. His presence and the reinforcements put new life in their fight.

Now that Lee and Confederate reinforcements had arrived, McClellan studied a map of the South Mountain area and made his decision. Thus far, his troops had made no serious attempt to force Turner's Gap or flank it. At 4:00 P.M., McClellan sent General Joseph Hooker's entire I Corps, except for one brigade, to make a wide flanking movement to the north. The unit he held back was Brigadier General John Gibbon's "Black Hat Brigade." Gibbon and his men were ordered to rush the Confederates headon at Turner's Gap.

Although the addition of Longstreet's troops was a boon to Hill's meager force, the arrival of twelve thousand more Federals did much to offset it. Still the weary Confederates gallantly fought on.

By sunset, Gibbon's Black Hat Brigade still had not penetrated

Turner's Gap but were battling it out several hundred yards below the summit with General Colquitt's brigade.

Soon the Confederates on the north side of the gap were under heavy fire from the troops McClellan had sent to that side.

Brigadier General Robert Rodes of Hill's division, with 1,200 men in his 26th Alabama Brigade, plus 150 cavalrymen sent by General Jeb Stuart, had to cover a difficult spur of the mountain that extended north from National Road, dipping into a ravine, then rising to a commanding peak nearly a mile away.

Two divisions from Hooker's I Corps were coming at them with such a wide front that Rodes knew he was flanked by a half-mile on either side. He had to slow the Federals down.

He called to the leader of the 150 cavalrymen, a captain named Errol Taylor, and told him to lead the way on horseback with thundering guns as he sent four hundred skirmishers into the woods and fields at the base of the mountain.

Taylor led his men as directed by Rodes and indeed took a toll on the Union soldiers approaching the base of the mountain. The four hundred roaring guns of the skirmishers did their part as well, and dropped dozens of Yankees who would never rise again.

But the massive numbers of Yankees kept coming. On Rodes's right, the Federal division under Brigadier General John Hatch was advancing along the Old Hagerstown Road. A split-rail fence ran alongside a cornfield at the side of the road. Hatch and his men became engaged in a fierce contest at the fence with Rodes's men, including some thirty cavalrymen.

Hatch fell, severely wounded, and was immediately succeeded in command by Brigadier General Abner Doubleday. Rodes had lost several men in the first few minutes of fighting at the fence and pulled his men back to regroup and make a charge.

As a ruse, Doubleday ordered his men to lie down quietly behind the fence. Rodes and his men rushed forward, suddenly wondering where the Federals had gone.

The 26th Alabama Regiment met a sweeping volley from the

hidden Federals that sent them rushing backward, leaving their dead and wounded along the fence.

When the sun's rim was disappearing below the horizon, Robert E. Lee was with James Longstreet, observing the battle on an elevated rock ledge. It was obvious the Confederates were losing ground.

"General," Lee said, "we are simply too well outnumbered, and there's no sign yet of Jackson. As soon as it's dark, we'll withdraw from here. We don't have a chance."

"I agree, sir. I'll spread the word."

At dusk, as the Federals began to set up camp, small groups of men went out to pick up their wounded.

Captain Errol Taylor was concerned over his five men who had gone down at the fence. If they were alive, he wanted to bring them in. He approached General Jeb Stuart with his request. "Sir, I know that since we're pulling out after dark we can't do anything about our dead. But some of my men may still be alive. Is it all right if I take a couple of men and go see?"

"Of course," Stuart said. "But be careful. Those Yankees might decide to get themselves some more trophies. Take a half-dozen men with you. If you run into any Yankees, get out of there quick. Even if it's only a handful. Understand?"

"Yes, sir."

Taylor chose his six men and they rode hard in the fading light. They found the five cavalrymen at the fence, their horses standing close by, looking on with ears pricked.

Taylor slid from his saddle, and Lieutenant Dirk Melby followed. The others stayed on their horses, watching for any sign of the enemy.

When Taylor and Melby had examined the last man, Taylor looked back and said, "All dead. Let's take their horses and head back."

Suddenly one of the mounted men shouted, "Yankees!"

A swarm of infantrymen came out of the woods in the dusky light, raising their rifles. Taylor and Melby dashed to their horses and vaulted into their saddles as Yankee guns spit fire.

"Go, men!" Taylor shouted.

Lieutenant Melby and the others gouged their horses' sides, putting them to an instant gallop. As they thundered away, Melby expected to see Taylor pull up beside him, but the captain was still sitting in the saddle, looking back at the Yankee soldiers running toward him.

"Lieutenant Melby, what's he doing?" one of the other cavalrymen said. "Why didn't he come with us?"

"I don't know! But if we go back, we'll only be taken prisoners. Let's go tell General Stuart!"

The Union soldiers who dashed toward Captain Taylor were part of an infantry regiment led by Lieutenant Adam Welch. Welch held his service revolver on the Confederate officer astride his horse. The rest of the men had their rifles leveled on him as they drew up. Those who were closest could see by the insignias on his collar and sleeves that he was a captain.

Taylor's horse nickered and bobbed its head as Welch barked, "All right, Captain, off the horse! You're our prisoner! Drop that rifle!"

When the captain continued to look off in the distance, Welch got irritated. "I said off the horse, soldier! *Now!*"

Sergeant Phil Rowan squinted at Taylor's face. "Wait a minute, Lieutenant." Rowan reached up and waved a hand in front of Taylor's eyes.

"Lieutenant! He's *dead!*"

"What?"

"Never saw one any deader. There's a bullet hole in his temple."

Welch finally saw the dark hole in Taylor's temple. "So there is. But how's he staying in the saddle?"

Sergeant Wallace Ulrich stepped up and tried to take the rifle from Taylor's death grip.

"I can't get it loose, sir," Ulrich said.

Welch took hold of the reins and pulled, but Taylor's dead fingers held them fast. "We've got to take him down, men. Sergeant Rowan, steady his body while I pry the reins from his fingers."

When the men had lowered the body earthward, it preserved the same position as in the saddle.

"Lieutenant, I've never seen or heard of anything like this," Ulrich said.

"Nor have I," Welch replied.

"I read something about it once, Lieutenant," one of the infantrymen said. "Can't recall the medical term for it, but it's something about death form, or figure, or shape. I guess it's happened a few times, especially on battlefields."

"Well, it's a new one on me," Welch said. "Let's take him to General McClellan. This is one for the books."

A slender crescent moon hovered overhead, giving off its meager light as Generals Lee, Longstreet, and Stuart stood together, listening to Lieutenant Melby.

"It doesn't make sense, Lieutenant," General Lee said. "Why would he just sit there?"

"Sir, we have no explanation for it. Captain Taylor leaped into his saddle at the same time I did and said, 'Go, men!' When I looked back, he was still sitting there, just waiting for the Yankees to come to him."

"Well, if any of you are thinking deserter, you can forget it," Jeb Stuart said. "Not Errol Taylor. Something snapped in his mind. That's all there is to it."

At that moment Hunter McGuire approached. "General Lee, sir..."

"Yes, Doctor?"

"We've got the wounded in the wagons. They're awfully crowded, but we have no choice."

"Do you have many near death?"

"Yes, General. We'll probably lose several before we get to Sharpsburg."

Lee sighed. There was a long pause, then he said, "Well, let's move out."

Under cover of darkness, the remaining Confederate troops slipped away down the western slope of South Mountain with the silver-haired commander in the lead. Lee had sent a courier to Stonewall Jackson, explaining what had happened at South Mountain, and that he was leading his troops to Sharpsburg, Maryland, along the banks of Antietam Creek. Jackson was to bring his I Corps there as soon as the military posts at Martinsburg and Harper's Ferry were secured.

As Lee rode beneath the night sky, he moved his lips in prayer, asking God not to allow Jackson to fall into a Union trap, too. A deep-settled peace came over him as he prayed.

The defense of South Mountain had proven costly. Lee could only estimate at that point, but he feared he had lost over two thousand men in the battle, and he had not yet asked Dr. McGuire how many were wounded.

Lee was considering letting his men rest at Sharpsburg until Jackson arrived. Then he would take his battered army back into Virginia and put an end to his invasion scheme.

*****

When morning came, General McClellan was not surprised to learn that the Confederates had pulled out. He gathered his six Corps leaders at his tent and said, "Gentlemen, we've put Bobby Lee on the run like a dog with his tail between his legs. As you know, I have scouts already trailing him. It wouldn't surprise me if he's headed for the Potomac. I've a feeling he's licking his wounds, and he'd like to lick them on home ground. Well, good enough.

"So, our next move is to head for Harper's Ferry and Martinsburg and lick Tommy Jackson the same way. Only we'll just go ahead and annihilate him." He glanced toward the horizon and added, "Let's be ready to pull out in thirty minutes."

Ten minutes later, a courier galloped into the Union camp and slid from his saddle where McClellan stood with Generals Porter and Hooker.

McClellan recognized him as being from his signal corps near Harper's Ferry. "You have news for me, Corporal?"

"Yes, sir. I'm sorry it has to be bad news."

"Well, let's hear it."

"Our garrisons at Martinsburg and Harper's Ferry are both in Confederate hands, sir. They have surrendered and are prisoners."

McClellan's face turned crimson. He looked at his generals with fire in his eyes. "Well, this throws a different light on things. We'll go after Bobby Lee and wipe him out first. As soon as the scouts return, we'll find out just where he's heading to cross the Potomac. Maybe we'll catch up in time to drown them before they can step on Virginia soil."

McClellan's scouts returned at ten o'clock and told him that Lee was not heading for the Potomac, but rather seemed to be on a beeline for Sharpsburg. McClellan made a quick decision. He would follow Lee and wipe him out on Maryland soil.

Because of his superior number of troops, McClellan did not hurry the men as they began the march westward.

CHAPTER SIXTEEN

Dawn came gray and dismal on Monday morning, with a soft rain falling. Jodie Lockwood awakened, stretched her arms, and said, "Good morning, Lord. We needed this rain, but you surprised me with it."

She padded to the dresser and leaned close, smiling at her reflection. "You fortunate woman! Hunter McGuire loves you. Just think of it. In a few months, you'll walk down the aisle and become Mrs. Doctor Hunter McGuire."

She wheeled about and hurried to the small table beside her bed where her Bible lay. She picked it up and held it to her breast, closing her eyes

"Thank You, Lord," she said aloud. "You've been so good to me. Thank You for keeping Hunter from falling in love with some other woman. He's mine, all mine, and You gave him to me. Thank You, oh, thank You!"

The rain was a gentle drizzle as Jodie walked to the clinic, humming a nameless happy tune.

Inside, she folded her umbrella and deposited it in the closet just as Dr. Roberts came from the back room. His face was somber as he bid her good morning

"You look sad, Doctor. Is something wrong?"

"You haven't heard."

A knot started to form in Jodie's stomach. "Heard what?"

"There was a big battle at South Mountain yesterday."

"Not good for our side?"

"No. Just the Southern grapevine, but folks in that area said Lee's troops were vastly outnumbered. Lots of bodies in the fields and on National Highway leading in and out of the gaps when the sun went down yesterday. Most of them were in gray uniforms."

The kindly physician moved close to Jodie and touched her shoulder. "I know what you're thinking. I won't say army doctors aren't in danger on those battlefields, but you can be thankful your young man is in medicine and not in a uniform."

"I am, Doctor, but with bullets and shrapnel flying all around—"

"Jodie, didn't you tell me God had kept Hunter for you for seven years?"

"Yes, sir," she said, fighting tears.

"Well, then, I believe He isn't going to let anything happen to him now. Sounds to me like the Lord's got it all worked out. Just trust Him."

"I do, Doctor, but—"

"No buts, dear. Either you trust the Lord's mighty hand in your life and Hunter's, or you don't. Which is it?"

"You'd have made a good preacher, Dr. Roberts," she said with a slight smile. "Maybe you missed your calling."

Roberts chuckled. "No. I'm doing what I'm supposed to. And speaking of such, my nurse is supposed to be preparing the examining room for Mrs. Ballard, who is due here in about five minutes."

"Oh, yes! I'll get right to it."

All day long, as patients came into the clinic, they talked about the battle at South Mountain. Jodie wished she knew where Hunter was, but so far the Southern grapevine had not supplied that information. It was the last patient of the day, a pro-Union man, who told them. While Jodie and Dr. Roberts worked on him, he bragged that the Confederates got whipped at South Mountain, and expressed his curiosity as to why Robert E. Lee had moved his army to the banks of Antietam Creek near Sharpsburg.

Word was, the man said, that General McClellan was on their trail. Some people were saying that part of Lee's army was elsewhere with Stonewall Jackson. If Jackson was on his way to Sharpsburg, and McClellan was headed for the same place, and Lee was already there, a whopper of a battle was coming.

The rain had stopped late in the afternoon, but dark clouds still covered the sky as Jodie walked home. She thought of Sharpsburg, just sixteen miles west. Was Hunter there with Lee? Or was he with Jackson? Most likely he was with Jackson. She thought of asking for time off to take a ride to Sharpsburg, but dismissed it, telling herself Hunter was Jackson's Corps Medical Director. Certainly he would be with his old friend.

But where was Stonewall Jackson?

It was noon on Monday when Lee's wet and bedraggled troops plodded through mud to the banks of Antietam Creek. They were less than a quarter of a mile from Sharpsburg when they made camp and set up their tents in the rain.

Lee and his officers were heavy-hearted. They had left their dead lying in the fields, the woods, on the rocks in Turner's Gap, and on National Road. But it was imperative they pull out when they did, or there would have been more dead men to grieve over.

Eight wounded men had died on the journey from South Mountain, and graves were hastily dug along the creek's edge. Before the dead were in the ground, two more men had died.

Hunter and the other Corps physicians labored without rest all day long, amputating shattered limbs, removing bullets and shrapnel, stitching up wounds, and doing what they could to relieve the pain and suffering.

Generals Lee, Longstreet, and Hill were in Lee's tent with the rain pattering softly on the canvas roof. They were discussing Lee's planned retreat into Virginia once Stonewall Jackson and his Corps arrived.

Lee was very discouraged, and he blamed himself for the defeat at South Mountain.

"General, sir," Dan Hill said, "it certainly wasn't your fault that your order got lost. Some soldier was just downright careless."

"That's for sure," Longstreet said. "I think we need to find out who he was and put him under discipline."

Lee raised a palm, shaking his head. "No, gentlemen. What's done is done, and if I had not insisted on putting the order in writing, none of this would have happened. The blame is on me. I should have had a meeting with all the division commanders and given it to them orally, making them memorize it."

"General Lee!" a voice called from outside. "Messenger here from General Jackson, sir!"

Longstreet opened the flap and let the man in.

"Yes, Sergeant?" Lee said.

"General Jackson wants you to know that all is secured at Martinsburg and Harper's Ferry. He is leaving General A. P. Hill's division to hold the prisoners, sir. There are 14,500 of them. General Jackson is leading the rest of his Corps toward Sharpsburg at this moment. They were to leave about ten o'clock this morning."

Lee gripped the man's upper arm and said, "That is good

news, Sergeant." He took a step back. "You're soaked to the skin, son. I'll fix it so you can use a tent to dry out."

"Thank you, sir, but there isn't time. General Jackson wants me to meet up with him and advise him of any plans you have."

Lee rubbed his bearded chin, looked at both Longstreet and Hill, who knew he was planning to retreat back into Virginia, and replied, "Sergeant, you tell General Jackson we're going to make a stand right here and have it out with McClellan. Tell him to come as quickly as he can."

Thirty minutes later, Lee stood in his crowded tent, looking into the faces of Major General Longstreet and his five division leaders, and Major General Hill, who was actually part of Stonewall Jackson's I Corps.

"Gentlemen," Lee said, "I had in mind to lead this army back into Virginia as soon as General Jackson arrived. But I've changed my mind. McClellan is on his way here, and we're going to show him how Southerners can fight."

They all nodded their agreement. The generals were not of a mind to retreat.

"Now, gentlemen, I know we saw General McClellan move with speed when he came to South Mountain, but I doubt he will do that again. And I have no doubt that General Jackson will be here quickly. All right, gentlemen. Let's make ready for Little Napoleon."

Stonewall Jackson and his troops arrived at the Confederate camp on Antietam Creek on Tuesday morning, September 16, just before ten o'clock. Longstreet's troops cheered their arrival, and General Lee was there to welcome them.

Jackson had brought 27,500 men with him, leaving General A. P. Hill and four of his six brigades at Martinsburg and Harper's Ferry—a total of 1,500 men.

There was no sign yet of McClellan.

Lee told General Longstreet to meet with all division leaders of I Corps and fill them in on the plans. He then took Jackson to his tent.

Lee motioned to a chair. "Sit down, General."

"If it's all the same to you, sir, I'll stand. I've been in that saddle a long time."

"Oh, certainly. Sorry...I didn't think about that."

"It's all right, sir. Since we're going to fight McClellan here, what do I need to know?"

"I'll fill you in after I hear the details of your capture of Martinsburg and Harper's Ferry," Lee said.

Jackson filled his commander in on the story, making sure his men received the credit due them. Lee smiled as he listened, nodding his approval.

At last Jackson said, "General, there were six men of the Eighteenth North Carolina Regiment who voluntarily went above and beyond the call of duty. In the dead of night, while trooper Everett Nichols was on sentry duty, he discovered that some two dozen prisoners were missing. Somehow they had managed to escape from a small shed.

"Nichols awakened his regiment commander, Major Rance Dayton, who roused the other four, and Nichols got a man from the regiment to fill in for him on sentry duty. They caught the escapees at dawn and brought them back."

Lee's brow furrowed. "How did they ever track them down in the dark?"

"That, sir, I cannot answer. Major Dayton was a student of

mine at V.M.I., so I know him well. He's exceptionally intelligent and resourceful."

"Well, that was fine work, to say the least. Dayton and those men are to be commended."

"I'd like for you to say that in person, if you don't mind, General. That kind of soldiering needs to be encouraged."

"I'll be glad to."

Five minutes later, Jackson led the six men into Lee's tent and introduced them to their supreme commander.

"Major Rance Dayton," Lee said, "you and troopers Billy Dean Baxter, Chuck Carney, Hank Upchurch, Everett Nichols, and Buford Hall have my highest admiration for what you did. I want to commend you for a job well done. Those Yankees who escaped could have caused all kinds of problems had they been able to get to some part of the Union army. I want you to know that I'm very grateful for men like you. God bless you."

Major Dayton took a half-step forward, back straight, shoulders squared. "General Lee, let me say for these men and for myself that it is a privilege to fight under your command. We are honored, sir. And if called upon to go beyond the call of duty again, we will gladly do so."

When Rance Dayton and his men were gone, Lee gave Jackson the details of his battle plan for meeting McClellan's army.

"I'm aware that it went bad for you at South Mountain, General," Jackson said. "What were our losses?"

"As of this morning, the best we can tell, the number of our men killed or missing is about twenty-seven hundred. The wounded we brought with us were about five hundred. Dr. McGuire and his staff have worked extremely hard to save as many lives as possible, but we've had twenty-seven more die since leaving South Mountain. A burial detail is digging more graves downstream right now. Dr. McGuire sent his staff to bed at four this morning. They slept maybe three hours, then went back to work. I believe Dr. McGuire is sleeping right now."

"Good. He'll need to get some rest. There'll be a lot more work for him when we engage McClellan."

Lee was doing some mental calculations. "With our losses and General A. P. Hill's division absent from us, we'll have about forty-five thousand men to face McClellan. I have no way of knowing his losses at South Mountain, but I'm sure they were nothing like ours."

"We'll be ready for them, sir," Jackson said. "Anything else we need to discuss right now?"

"No...just one thing to say, though."

"Yes, sir?"

"I'm sure glad you're here."

"Thank you, sir. I am, too."

"Let's give those blue-bellies a fight they won't forget."

Robert E. Lee had shaken his discouragement and still had hopes of gaining a victory on Northern soil. As his division commanders took their positions, the forty-five-thousand-man force in tattered uniforms were spread over an area of four miles.

The ground Lee chose for battle promised strong defensive positions, though hardly impregnable ones. Its most prominent feature was the tree-lined Antietam, which flowed in a north-south course a short distance east of Sharpsburg before joining the Potomac three miles south of the town.

The Confederates were situated all the way from the bend of the Potomac, which enclosed the little farming community, along high ground behind the swift-running Antietam Creek. Both of Lee's flank troops rested on the banks of the muddy Potomac, and the undulating of the Sharpsburg ridge afforded his men good concealment from any Union artillery which might be placed to the front.

The four-mile-long position was well strengthened by farms, stone walls, split-rail fences, waist-high outcroppings of limestone, and little hollows and swales. Northeast of town there was an old sunken road so deeply worn down by wagon wheels that it offered a good spot for riflemen to lay low and snipe at enemy troops. There were also several clusters of woods, each covering about an acre of ground. Amid all of these natural concealments were open fields.

Although the Confederate line would be stretched thin, Lee took advantage of another geographical feature. Just west of the long ridge was a major north-south road—the turnpike connecting Hagerstown, Sharpsburg, and Harper's Ferry. It would provide a perfect route for shifting troops back and forth rapidly.

Lee had chosen a heavily wooded area midway between his flanks to set up the hospital tents and place medical supply wagons. Open fields lay on three sides of the wooded area, and the creek on the other.

Antietam Creek was a defense barrier of sorts. It ranged in width between sixty and one hundred feet, and was fordable in only a few places. There were three bridges, however, that crossed the creek within the battle area, each about a mile apart. Lee saw to it that the lower bridge, a mile southeast of Sharpsburg, was directly beneath strong Confederate positions on the bluffs overlooking the creek.

The middle bridge, on the road to Boonsboro, was subject to Confederate artillery fire from the heights near Sharpsburg. The upper bridge, some two miles east of the Confederate artillery, was more difficult to cover. Lee would have to leave that bridge vulnerable to Union use.

*****

As Lee had predicted, McClellan came after them slowly. Two Federal divisions McClellan had sent ahead arrived in the area just after dark on Monday night. They pitched camp some five miles east of Antietam Creek. Their orders were to wait for the rest of the army and not engage in hostilities unless forced to do so.

Midafternoon on Tuesday, General McClellan rode at the head of his troops as they approached the Sharpsburg area. He was in high spirits. He had failed to save Harper's Ferry, but at South Mountain he had won what he described to his men as "a glorious victory." And if the letter he had received that day by courier from the White House was any indication, he was back in the good graces of his president.

McClellan reached into his coat pocket to read the message for the third time since the courier had ridden away. It said: "God bless you and all with you. Destroy the Rebel army, if possible. A. Lincoln."

McClellan's scouts had given him a full report of how Lee was setting up his defenses. They had estimated the Confederate force to be around forty thousand.

McClellan felt jubilant. He had the Confederates more than doubled in troops and pushed up against the Potomac.

He took a small unit of cavalrymen close to where the Confederates were positioned along Antietam Creek and scanned the area with his binoculars, then rode back to the camp and called a meeting with his division commanders.

As he stood in the long shadows of the tall trees, he drew a map of the Confederate stronghold in the dirt. After explaining how Lee had positioned his troops, he used the tree limb as a pointer and said, "My plan, gentlemen, is to make the main attack on the enemy's left. My decision to do so is dictated largely by the Confederate defenses at the two bridges that span the creek. We'll come at them with the bulk of our army from this third bridge, which they're not protecting.

"Now, while we're putting this major effort on Johnny Reb's left, we'll launch a diversionary attack against his right with a separate Corps. I'll watch how both attacks go. If either shows good success, we'll strike the center with reserves."

McClellan spoke to his generals one by one and laid out their particular positions. The key division would be that of "Fighting Joe" Hooker. He would lead the attack on Lee's left.

General Hooker was to move his division west toward Sharpsburg to a point where a country lane called Smoketown Road joined the turnpike. To the west, just across the turnpike, was a landmark by which Hooker would guide his advance: a one-story whitewashed brick building that stood out sharply against the green backdrop of the woods. The building was often taken for a schoolhouse, but it was the house of worship for a congregation of German Baptist Brethren, referred to by the locals as the Dunker church.

The Dunker church marked the southern boundary of the field where the first attack would be launched against the Rebels. The field of battle was rectangular-shaped, about a mile long and half as wide, and flanked by woods on the east, west, and north.

Even as McClellan was giving the other division commanders their battle orders, people of the community were leaving the area along the turnpike on foot and in wagons and carriages. Others were moving across the fields.

Sharpsburg and its quiet countryside had been settled mainly by people of German and Dutch descent. They had been untouched by the Civil War until Lee's invasion.

Many of Sharpsburg's thirteen hundred citizens refused to leave their homes, taking refuge in their cellars. A few hundred townspeople and farmers sought shelter in a large cave near the Potomac River. Before leaving for the cave, the farmers over whose ground the battle would rage did what they could to safeguard their livestock by closing them up in barns and sheds.

One farmer hid his team of horses in his cellar and muffled their hooves in gunny sacks.

Rain came with the darkness.

In a wooded area along the west bank of Antietam Creek, Dr. Hunter McGuire and his staff labored in four hospital tents to care for the men wounded at South Mountain. Six more had died since noon.

Hunter was on his knees, tending a soldier whose arm he had amputated three hours earlier. The young sergeant was barely conscious, but was moaning incoherently.

Hunter did all he could to bring the man's fever down. While he bathed the wounded man with cool water from the creek, he heard footsteps at the tent opening and turned to see his old friend Tom Jackson enter.

"Hello, Doc."

"Hello, General."

Jackson's eyes roamed the interior of the fifteen-by-twenty-five-foot tent, observing the men who lay on its grassy floor. Most were either unconscious or sleeping. Two of them looked up at him with languid eyes.

"Where you going to put all your patients by this time tomorrow, Doc?"

"It's going to be a big one, isn't it?"

"'Fraid so."

Hunter sighed. "I don't know what we'll do with the wounded tomorrow. The other two tents are as packed as this one. Guess we'll have to lay them on the ground outside the tent. I wish we had a hundred doctors and two hundred nurses."

Stonewall was quiet for a moment as Hunter continued to bathe the fevered sergeant. Then he said, "If you could choose just one nurse to be by your side, do I have to guess who it would be?"

Hunter looked over his shoulder and grinned. "If you had to guess, I'd say you either don't know me like I think you know me, or you've lost your mind."

CHAPTER SEVENTEEN

The rain continued to fall until about an hour after midnight. Few men in either camp slept well. Stretched nerves grew more taut with every noise. Jumpy pickets punctuated the night with bursts of gunfire, waking those few men who were fortunate enough to have dropped off to sleep.

Near the upper bridge, a soldier of the 103rd New York Regiment nearly set off a panic in the Federal line when he stumbled into a stack of muskets and knocked them down.

Even the animals seemed to feel the tension.

In both camps, whispers of a great battle to be fought grew louder, and men shuddered at the prospect of the wounds and death that awaited them.

Inside his tent, Stonewall Jackson could hear the sibilant whispers of the men in their bedrolls. He too was sleepless and rose from his cot to turn up the lantern wick. He reached for his Bible and silently read from Psalm 91:

> He that dwelleth in the secret place of the most High shall abide under the shadow of the Almighty. I will say of the LORD, He is my refuge and my fortress: my God;

> in him will I trust. Surely he shall deliver thee from the snare of the fowler, and from the noisome pestilence. He shall cover thee with his feathers, and under his wings shalt thou trust: his truth shall be thy shield and buckler.
>
> Thou shalt not be afraid for the terror by night; nor for the arrow that flieth by day; nor for the pestilence that walketh in darkness; nor for the destruction that wasteth at noonday. A thousand shall fall at thy side, and ten thousand at thy right hand; but it shall not come nigh thee.

"General Jackson, sir…" The voice came from outside.

Jackson laid his Bible on the small folding table and pushed aside the tent flap. He squinted into the darkness and saw a young soldier, perhaps no older than seventeen.

"Yes, soldier?"

"Sir, I…I need to talk to you. I hate to bother you but… would you have a moment?"

"Sure. Come in. What's your name, soldier?"

"Bradley Akins, sir. I'm from General McLaw's division, General Kershaw's brigade."

Jackson indicated the extra chair beside the table. "Sit down, Bradley. What can I do for you, son?"

"Well, sir, I know you're a man of faith. And…well, sir, to tell you the truth, I'm scared. Really scared. I saw plenty of blood and death at South Mountain on Sunday. It was my first battle. That was enough to really put the fear into me."

"Fear of being wounded?"

"Well, nobody likes to think of having his body ripped up, General. But it's more the fear of dying. I'm a Christian, sir…I think. But—"

"Wait a minute. You're a Christian you *think?*"

"Yes, sir, I—"

"If a man's really a Christian, Bradley, he knows it. Being saved isn't something God wants you to wonder about. Tell me why you think you might be a Christian."

"I was christened when I was a baby, sir. My parents said that means I'm a Christian."

Jackson leaned forward and looked into the young soldier's eyes. "Bradley, with all due respect to your parents, nobody goes to heaven because of any kind of religious ceremony. What makes you a Christian, according to God's Word, is faith in the Lord Jesus Christ as your personal Saviour.

"Like the rest of the human race, Bradley, you came into the world with a sinful nature that goes in the wrong direction—away from God. We have to turn from the direction we're going, acknowledge to Him that we are guilty, hell-deserving sinners, and receive Him into our hearts."

Young Akins nodded, the truth sinking in.

"Jesus went to the cross and died for us because there is no other way of salvation, son. You do believe He shed His blood on the cross and died for you, don't you?"

"Yes, sir."

Jackson flipped the pages of his Bible to Romans 10:9. "Here, read that to me," he said.

Young Akins cleared his throat. "That if thou shalt confess with thy mouth the Lord Jesus, and shalt believe in thine heart that God hath raised him from the dead, thou shalt be saved."

"Where does it say you must believe it, Bradley?"

"In my heart."

"That's right. You can believe the facts of Calvary in your mind, Bradley, but that won't save you. Believing in your heart is when you call on Him yourself. Look at verse 13 and read it to me."

Bradley cleared his throat again. "For whosoever shall call upon the name of the Lord shall be saved."

"Understand?"

"Yes, sir."

"Then, since you believe everything a man has to believe to

be saved, what do you have to do to settle it?"

Without hesitation Bradley said, "Call on Jesus in repentance of my sin and receive Him into my heart as my Saviour. And I'm going to do that right now, sir."

After Bradley Akins had opened his heart to the Lord, Stonewall Jackson showed him a few verses of assurance, then said, "Bradley, none of us know whether we'll be alive after the battle tomorrow. But whether it's me or you or both of us who is taken out of this life, we'll meet in heaven one day. God bless you, son."

The Federals had seven hospital tents set up along the east side of the creek in a forest of oak and walnut trees. Dr. Bernard Vanderkieft was in charge, assisted by Doctors William Child and William Ely, as well as several other war surgeons who were busy preparing for the battle.

Vanderkieft, Child, and Ely were in the main hospital tent, discussing the use of anesthetics, when Brigadier General George Meade, commander of Third Division, I Corps, appeared at the wide opening. A young woman, her dark hair parted in the middle and swept back into a bun, was with him.

"Gentlemen," Meade said, "you don't know this lady by sight, but you do know her name."

"Don't tell me!" Dr. Child said. "Is this Miss Clara Barton?"

Clara smiled as Meade said, "Your guess is correct, Doctor.

"And how did you know?" the lady asked.

"You've been at other battles to nurse the wounded, and I just had a feeling you might show up here. Thank you for coming."

Meade introduced the doctors to Miss Barton, saying she had already seen General McClellan. Clara then said with a smile, "Gentlemen, you will also be glad to know that before sundown I did a little recruiting in Sharpsburg. I have eight women who will come here at sunrise to help. They are not trained nurses, but they will be a tremendous help when the wounded are brought in."

Dr. Vanderkieft was a tall, dignified man of sixty. "Miss Barton," he said, "I want to add to Dr. Child's thanks, and tell you how much your being here is appreciated. And so is your recruiting work. I know those ladies will be a wonderful boon to us."

"Thank you, Doctor. I will be sleeping in the home of one of the women who will help us tomorrow. I came tonight because I wanted to know how you have things set up."

"Well, let me show you," Vanderkieft said.

As the first hint of dawn lighted the cloudless Maryland sky on Wednesday, September 17, 1862, ground fog hugged the hollows and moved on the surface of Antietam Creek. Countless misty tendrils danced over the fields, driven by a slight breeze.

On both sides, men rose from their bedrolls and prepared for battle.

Even the birds seemed to know what was coming. Instead of the usual dawn chirping and chattering and flitting from tree to tree, there was silence.

Hunter McGuire and his staff of surgeons ate a breakfast of hardtack, beef jerky, and water, then saw to their patients.

Hunter made his patients as comfortable as possible, then stepped outside. The morning light came slowly, putting an ominous spectral glow on the mists that enshrouded the towering trees.

Hunter had expected the Federals to attack at first light, but all was still. He looked at his pocket watch—5:51. He walked out onto the dew-laden, grassy field until he could see the creek winding its way toward the Potomac and the open fields toward Sharpsburg and the turnpike.

There was a sudden roar, like a clap of thunder. Seconds passed, and there was another roar, followed by two more, widely spaced. Hunter couldn't see anything yet. Then there was a long silence.

He looked back toward the hospital tents nestled with the medical supply wagons in the trees. All of his doctors and some of the wounded men were standing in a tight cluster, looking at him. He pointed eastward, where the cannon shots and shell explosions had come from, then shrugged his shoulders. White clouds of smoke now drifted skyward near the upper bridge almost two miles away.

The silence was suddenly broken with the crash of musketry and the roll of cannons. In fields much closer than the upper bridge, Hunter saw thousands of Federals fanning out as they came his direction like a blue river spreading across the land.

Abruptly, a gray wave came from the forest to Hunter's right. Muskets barked, cannons boomed, and the Union soldiers shouted. But the high-pitched, bloodcurdling Rebel yell transcended it all as the two opposing forces swept toward each other in a race of death and destruction.

Hunter looked on, fascinated and horrified by the sight. Through blue-white wispy smoke and yellow streaks of the rising sun, he saw the two armies collide.

The Battle of Antietam had begun.

Suddenly, both armies' artilleries blasted away, shaking the very ground where Hunter stood. He wheeled and ran toward the men who stood within the shelter of the trees. A cannon shell burst in the air near the hospital tents. The concussion of it popped McGuire's ears as another shell exploded near the first one, blasting a tree into smithereens and raining fragments of bark and shredded wet leaves.

"I thought we were safe here, Dr. McGuire!" Dr. Wesley Jensen shouted.

"Only safer, Doctor," Hunter said. He looked back to the spot where he had been standing. "That field right there will be full of soldiers and guns before long."

As the battle spread wider along the four-mile stretch of creek bank, the Confederate artillery, firing from elevated positions, blasted Union soldiers with one shell after another. Bodies were blown twenty and thirty feet from where they had stood.

General Stuart had assembled eight cannons from his own horse artillery and a dozen of Stonewall Jackson's guns on high ground across the turnpike from the Dunker church.

General Hooker's nine batteries opened up on them from a ridge on a nearby farm.

In Sharpsburg, the citizens crouched in their cellars, listening to the growing sounds of the battle—sudden roars, mysterious hums, then shrieking shells followed by explosions. Their cellars shook, raining dirt on them as they huddled and prayed.

At the upper bridge, which was out of Confederate artillery range, McClellan had four brigades swarming over it to gain better positions against the enemy.

Lee, however, had his eye on the area from his lofty position behind Antietam Creek. His troops were ready. As soon as the blue uniforms began running across the bridge, they were met with a long line of gray-clad infantry, charging at them and shouting the Rebel yell.

Men in blue toppled off the bridge into the creek, while the hail of fire ripping into the Confederate lines was devastating. But the Rebels' conduct was worthy of their leader's trust—they continued to run over the rough and stony field with their comrades dropping all around them.

The outnumbered Rebels fought with a tenacity seldom seen on a battlefield. Within minutes, the Federals were off the bridge and the Rebels waved their muskets in the air and jeered. They had won the first round.

There were three heavily wooded areas north of Sharpsburg that both armies wanted to possess. The East and West Woods were directly parallel with a half mile of open fields and the Hagerstown Turnpike between them. The North Woods made a natural border for the open fields about a quarter-mile from the end of the other two woods, and was bisected by the turnpike. The battle was barely more than an hour old when heavy fighting broke out in all three wooded areas.

The Dunker church sat next to the turnpike with the West Woods just behind it. Along the eastern edge of the turnpike, between the woods, was a twenty-acre cornfield owned by farmer David Miller. Southeast of the Dunker church, about two miles, was the Sunken Road, which lay between two fields of battle.

The Dunker church became the eye of the storm. McClellan, with his huge army spreading north, west, and south, concentrated his heaviest forces on Lee's troops set to defend the area around the church.

Joseph Hooker's I Corps infantry came in a long row, firing on the run. Stonewall Jackson's troops formed a line with John Bell Hood's brigade positioned in the center, Jubal Early's brigade on the left, and Daniel Hill's entire division on the right.

James Longstreet's II Corps was spread south and west of Sharpsburg to meet Federals coming by the thousands against them.

The hot pulse of battle sent quivering waves over the countryside, each cannon shot and shell explosion sending ear-splitting concussions over the land. Musket fire added to the din, and amidst it all were the repeated Rebel yells and Yankee shouts...and now the wailing, crying, and moaning of the wounded.

Clouds of powder smoke thickened and at times blotted out the sun. As men were cut down by the hundreds, fresh troops took their places.

Stretcher-bearers on both sides were already leg-weary from carrying wounded men to the hospital tents. East of Antietam, Clara Barton labored to keep some kind of order as men were brought in by the hundreds. Her eight female companions proved to be of great value to the Union doctors and to Miss Barton herself.

At the Confederate medical facility, Dr. Hunter McGuire and his staff of doctors labored to keep up with the numbers of wounded being brought in. The men wounded at South Mountain were moved outside to make room. Soon the tents were full, and even the newly wounded had to lie on the ground outside and wait until the doctors could get to them.

Hunter was digging shrapnel out of a young lieutenant when a Union shell struck the creek bank directly behind the tents. It splintered tree limbs, raining branches and dirt clods on the roof.

Hunter glanced up and saw that one tree limb was pressing deeply into the canvas. There was no one to remove it but Dr. Jensen.

When Jensen returned, McGuire shook his head despairingly. "I sure wish we had some help."

"I guess we could ask General Jackson to take some men off the fields to give us a hand," Jensen said.

Hunter shook his head. "They need every able-bodied man out there in the battle."

A hundred and fifty yards from the Confederate tents, a South Carolina battery was moving to a new position when a Union shell hit a caisson loaded with gunpowder.

The caisson blew apart as the doctors turned to look, and they could see nothing but torn and lifeless bodies where once the battery stood. "None of those men will need our attention," Hunter said in a tight voice.

He finished working on the young lieutenant and Jensen carried him outside.

The next patient was a private whose left arm was seriously damaged at the shoulder. Hunter went to the man's head, leaving his feet for Jensen. Very carefully, Hunter gripped the man's shirt by the right sleeve and collar and hoisted him onto the table.

"This one probably won't need much chloroform," Hunter said. "He's pretty well out of it."

"I hope he stays that way," Jensen said. "You want me to handle him...take off the arm?"

"Let me get a closer look before we decide to amputate," Hunter said, as he picked up a pair of scissors.

As he cut away the blood-soaked shirt, Hunter said, "I'm a little slower to amputate than most army doctors. When it's plain to see there's no use to try resection, I'll proceed in a hurry. But if I feel there's any chance I can save a limb, I'll do the resection."

Hunter sleeved sweat from his face and carefully examined the shoulder.

"I think I can save it," he said. "A resection it is."

When he was finished with the surgery, a young private with a damaged leg was laid on the table. Jensen was putting him under with chloroform while Hunter examined the leg.

"What do you think?" Jensen asked.

"I've saved a few legs with resection, but many more arms. Can't save this one."

While Hunter waited for the chloroform to take full effect on the soldier, he stepped to the tent opening and ran his gaze over the mounting number of wounded men on the ground. He wished he had a force of surgeons ten times larger than the one he had. And nurses, too.

He lifted his eyes to the battlefield and saw riderless horses, and some lying dead on the ground. Exploding shells scattered men in every direction. Long lines of infantry—gray and blue—swayed to and fro, with puffs of blue-white smoke rising from their muskets.

The roar of it all was more than noise. It was a savage, continual thunder that resounded over the fields and hills—a death knell for thousands of gallant men.

CHAPTER EIGHTEEN

More troops entered the fray a few dozen yards west of the Confederate hospital tents. A double tide of blue and gray swept onto the blood-soaked field, guns blazing, bayonets fixed. There was no flinching or dropping to the rear. Both sides fought heroically under murderous fire.

Hunter had just finished amputating the soldier's leg and needed a breath of air. He asked two stretcher-bearers who had recently come in to carry the man outside. Now he followed them and watched as they eased the soldier down among the other wounded men.

"Dr. McGuire," one of the stretcher-bearers said, "I think those two men over there are dead."

Hunter followed the private's glance and moved among the men to kneel down. "You're right, Private. What's your name?"

"Rick Acheson, Doctor. My partner here is Randy Williams."

Hunter nodded. "Would you men mind while you're here removing those two bodies?"

"Be glad to, Doctor," Acheson asked. "We'll put 'em back here among the trees where we've already laid a good number."

Hunter glanced at Wes Jensen, who stood in the opening of

the tent, mopping his brow. "Want me to do the next two or three, Doctor?" Jensen asked.

"What do we have in there?"

"Well, we had another probable amputation, but he just died. Next one is the one brought in about an hour ago with a chunk of shrapnel in his chest."

"Okay. We'll have Rick and Randy carry the dead man out. Let's get the next one on the table and—"

Hunter stopped speaking as he saw a man—a Union officer—not more than fifty yards out on the battlefield, stumbling blindly in wide circles. Even at that distance he could see blood streaming down the man's face blackened by gunpowder. The man was groping with extended hands as bullets buzzed around him.

"Be right back!" Hunter called over his shoulder.

Bullets zipped and thudded on all sides of Hunter as he ran in a zig-zag pattern toward the man. He felt a bullet pluck at his shirtsleeve and another buzz by his head like an angry hornet. He could now see the insignias on the Union man's collar and shoulders that indicated he was a major.

Hunter brought the man down with a flying tackle. The major swung blindly, trying to lay hold on whoever had attacked him.

"Listen to me, Major!" Hunter shouted. "I'm a Confederate doctor. You've wandered close to our hospital tents. If we don't get out of here fast, we'll both die! Do you understand what I'm saying?"

"My eyes! I can't see!"

"I know, sir. I'll do my best to get you to safety if you'll let me."

"Yes! Please!"

"All right. Now, I want you to relax. Don't stiffen on me. I'm going to drape you over my shoulder and run for cover as fast as I can."

"Why would a Rebel doctor do this for a Union soldier?"

"I'll answer that later. Here we go!"

Hunter lifted the tall, lanky major onto his shoulder while he was still on his knees. "Lord," he said, as he rose to his feet, "only You can make those bullets miss the two of us."

Hunter had just started to run when a shell struck behind him. The concussion knocked him down, and the major rolled eight or ten feet. Hunter saw two Union officers coming toward him on the run. They opened fire with their revolvers, cursing him.

"I'm a doctor!" Hunter shouted.

The men kept firing and didn't even break stride. Hunter made a dive for the major's belt and whipped the revolver from his holster. He hadn't fired a handgun for years, but it felt as if it had been only yesterday. He dropped the hammer and the nearest soldier went down. The other soldier fired again, his bullet plowing sod within a foot of Hunter. The doctor fired a second time, and the charging Union officer hit the ground and lay still.

Hunter was breathing hard as he picked up the major and made a dash for the trees and the tents. The angry zip and hiss of bullets did not let up.

Hunter recognized two of his other Corps doctors standing with Jensen and the two stretcher-bearers. There was someone else standing next to Jensen—a dark-haired young woman in a light-blue cotton dress with white pinafore.

Jodie!

Hunter's breath came in short gasps as he drew near the Confederate tents. Jodie met him as he staggered in with the Union major on his shoulder.

"Hello, Jodie," he gasped. "Busy day."

"Oh, Hunter! You took an awful chance!"

"Had to keep this man from getting himself killed. But speaking of taking chances, what are you doing here?"

"I came to help."

Hunter turned to the other doctors. "See what you can do for this man, while I catch my breath."

"He's unconscious, Doctor," Jensen said, lifting the man from Hunter's shoulder.

Randy Williams stepped in. "Let me help you, Dr. Jensen."

Jodie walked to a water barrel that hung on the side of a nearby medical supply wagon, filled a tin cup, and handed it to Hunter. When Hunter put the cup to his lips, Jodie noticed the rip in his shirtsleeve.

"Hunter, was this sleeve torn before you went out there?"

"I don't know. I don't think so."

"Then it must've been a bullet. Hunter, you nearly got shot!"

Private Rick Acheson looked at Hunter and said, "Why didn't you leave him, Doctor? A bullet would've ended it for him sooner or later. Then there'd be one less blue-belly officer."

Jodie looked at Acheson with piercing eyes as Hunter regarded him steadily and said, "When I became a medical doctor, I took an oath to do all in my power to relieve human suffering and preserve life. I saw a human being out there, blinded and dazed, with death hissing all around him. I did what I said I would do when I took that oath."

"But he's our enemy," Acheson said. "He's killed our men, and he'll do it again if he gets the chance."

"A wounded and helpless enemy is not our foe, Private. And this man will never fight in another battle. His eyes are gone."

Hunter handed the cup back to Jodie and turned to see about the Union major. Doctors Jensen and Paymer were bent over him.

"What do you think?" Hunter asked.

"The eyeballs are burned out," Paymer said, "but he should live. The bleeding has almost stopped. It's strange how the powder could strike him square in the face but no shrapnel hit him."

"Stranger things have happened," Hunter said. "I know you and Dr. Bowman have plenty to do in your tents. You'd better get on back. I'll have Jodie clean him up, then see what I can do for him."

"Sure," Paymer said, rising to his feet. "We saw you out there with bullets buzzing all around you and had to see if you made it back."

"Well, thank the Lord I did. And I appreciate your concern."

"Don't want to lose our boss man," Bowman said.

"Tell you what, fellows. I can let Dr. Jensen come and help you and the other surgeons, since I have Jodie now. Oh, I didn't introduce you."

"It's all right," Jensen said. "We introduced ourselves. She told us the two of you are engaged."

Hunter glanced at Jodie and smiled. "That we are."

As the three physicians headed toward the other tents, Jensen called over his shoulder, "Holler if you need me."

"Will do."

Hunter turned to look at Jodie. "Well, sweetheart, the next patient has shrapnel in his shoulder. Let's get it out."

Private Williams tapped his partner on the shoulder. "C'mon, Rick. There are more wounded men out there."

"Just a minute," Acheson said, lifting a hand. "Doctor..."

"Yes, Private?"

"Sir, I...I was out of line. I shouldn't have talked to you the way I did. I just saw that man as the enemy and...well, my nerves are a little uptight and—"

"It's all right, soldier. I understand. This war has us all uptight."

"Thank you, sir."

Hunter cuffed him playfully. "Go bring in some more of our wounded men, Private."

"Yes, sir."

When the stretcher-bearers were gone, Hunter lifted the next patient onto the table. The soldier was conscious but made no cry, in spite of his pain. "We'll get you fixed up, soldier," Hunter said. Then to Jodie, "The chloroform is on that small table. If you'll put him under, I'll go to work."

It took only two minutes for the chloroform to take effect. Above the sounds of battle, a cry for water was heard from outside.

"Can you take care of him, Jodie? Our man here is pretty well under."

"Of course."

"Tell you what, Jodie. They all need water. Take care of several, come back in and pour some more chloroform on the cloth, then take water to a few more. Okay?"

At the shriek of a cannon shell, Hunter dropped his scalpel and grabbed Jodie, pushing her to the grassy floor of the tent. The explosion rocked the ground and shook the tent, sending bits of hot shrapnel hissing through the canvas wall on the north side.

Hunter helped Jodie up, then turned to the other men who lay waiting for his attention. "Any of you fellows get hit?" Hunter asked.

The men shook their heads. Hunter quickly checked those who were unconscious and found they had not been hit either. He turned back to the operating table and discovered that the man was dead. Hunter sighed and lifted the dead soldier, cradling him in his arms. He stepped outside and saw Dr. Jensen running toward him, an expression of horror on his face.

"Doctor, that last shell nearly tore our tent apart! Dr. Paymer took a load of shrapnel in the chest. It's awfully close to his heart. We all agree we need your capable hands."

Jodie had come to stand by Hunter and heard what Jensen said. Hunter glanced down at her. "I'll need your help...

"You've got it," she said.

Hunter looked back at Jensen. "Okay, Doctor. Jodie will show you who's next in our tent. The one after that is a Sergeant Hector Tannen. Part of his jaw is gone."

"What about the Union major?"

"He's been in and out of consciousness, Doctor," Jodie said. "He isn't bleeding any more, so you can leave him until the men in worse shape are tended to."

Jensen nodded. "You two know where to find me."

"Wish you had somebody to assist you," Hunter said. "I'd let Jodie stay with you but—"

"You just do everything you can for Doc Paymer."

The clouds of powder smoke above the valley allowed sunshine through only when a gust of wind parted it. Dead men sprawled over the ground from the Potomac to the Antietam, and to the east for a mile. Some were crumpled in hollows, and a few lay draped over a waist-high stone wall or split-rail fence.

The acrid odor of burnt gunpowder, hot metal, and spilled blood filled the air. The smell of burnt and splintered trees and blasted earth only intensified the stench of death.

There was wreckage everywhere. Fences torn apart, farm buildings destroyed, heaps of human limbs outside hospital tents, cornfields trampled, army horses and domestic farm animals lying lifeless among thousands of dead and dying soldiers, and naked tree stumps where unmerciful artillery had wreaked havoc.

It was only noon.

Across a half-mile of battlefield around the Dunker church, everything seemed to be happening at once. The fighting had died down and almost come to a halt as both sides reloaded their weapons. The silence lasted for nearly five minutes, punctuated with the cries and moans of the wounded.

Then, simultaneously, the hostile battle lines opened up a tremendous fire upon each other. Just north of the church a long line of men in gray charged toward Union infantrymen situated behind a split-rail fence. McClellan had sent reinforcements to that spot, and Federal fire ripped through the oncoming ranks of Confederates.

Rebels went down in heaps, but those who survived the first volley pushed on, loading and firing and shouting as they advanced. These were Stonewall Jackson's men, and there was something in them of hysterical excitement—an eagerness to take the battle to the enemy with a reckless disregard for everything but victory.

Those who reached the fence vaulted it with bayonets flashing.

In an open field just west of the church, which stood thirty feet away, Union troops charged Confederates. Empty muskets brought bayonets into play. Soon there were more Rebels lying on the ground than standing on their feet. Their lieutenant called for retreat, and they began to pull back.

The Federals refused to let up. They came on with a vengeance, taking time to reload and shoot most of the fleeing Rebels before they could reach the relative safety of the trees near the church.

Across the Hagerstown Turnpike, at the north end of a ten-acre pasture, the Confederates had rushed a unit of Union artillery and captured a cannon. The Union captain in charge shouted for his five other cannons to swing about and fire their big guns loaded with canister at the nearly two dozen Rebels.

The Confederates, rejoicing in the capture of the Federal cannon, suddenly realized what they had gotten themselves into. They tried to find shelter when they saw the five black muzzles aimed their direction and the gunners yanking the lanyards.

When the smoke blew away, the bodies of the Rebels had been shredded beyond recognition.

*****

Just south of the Dunker church, General Jackson had watched the battle turn into a nightmare. Two of his divisions had come across the turnpike from the fields to the east, only to meet a swarm of Federals.

His solid lines began to come apart as they crossed the turnpike under heavy artillery and musket fire, breaking into scattered clots with a few flags still upright. As the hail of bullets and grapeshot assailed them, the flags began to disappear.

Jackson sent for Brigadier General John Bell Hood's division, which was resting in a wooded draw three hundred yards to the west. They had been outnumbered better than two-to-one, and what had been a division of thirty-five hundred was now down to twenty-three hundred.

Still astride his horse, Jackson waited for Hood's troops to emerge from the draw. Soon he saw a rider galloping toward him from the northwest where Jeb Stuart's cavalry was fighting.

The rider pulled up, sweat streaming down his face, and gasped, "General Jackson, sir! General Stuart asks that you send at least a brigade to the fields west of the West Woods! We're being whittled down!"

"Tell him I'll send reinforcements as soon as possible, Sergeant. That's going to be awhile. Our forces are being whittled down everywhere. He'll have to hold on till I can send help. But I've got to find them, first."

As the sergeant galloped away on his foam-flecked horse, Stonewall Jackson felt a coldness settle in his bones.

CHAPTER NINETEEN

General Lee had stayed near the battle front earlier in the day, but as afternoon came on, he moved to an abandoned barn in a wooded patch a quarter-mile west of Sharpsburg.

By two o'clock, the battle was breaking into four sections—the West Woods, the Miller cornfield across the turnpike, the Sunken Road northeast of town, and the lower bridge a mile south of the Sunken Road.

Lee called his two Corps leaders to the old barn. He assigned Jackson to the West Woods and Miller cornfield areas, and Longstreet was to concentrate his forces at the Sunken Road and the lower bridge, known as Rohrback's Bridge.

General McClellan had set up headquarters at a farmhouse on a hill more than a mile east of the fighting. He kept Major General Fitz-John Porter with him.

The generals had telescopes strapped atop stakes in the ground. While McClellan sent orders to his division leaders,

Porter studied the field with unrelenting attention and had something new to tell McClellan every time the chief commander turned back to him.

At the Confederate medical facility, Hunter McGuire finished his delicate task of extracting chunks of shrapnel out of Paymer's chest. Paymer was breathing steadily when the last stitch was taken. "You did a beautiful job, Doctor," Jodie said. "I'm proud of you."

"I'm just thankful you were here to help me." He picked up a towel, wiping blood from his hands, and moved toward her. "I sure could use one good solid kiss."

"I think that could be arranged."

"Oh, excuse me!" the couple heard Dr. Jensen say.

Hunter released Jodie and turned.

"I just wanted to see how you were doing with Doc Paymer," Jensen continued.

"Just finished. Look for yourself."

Jensen moved close to the operating table and looked at the unconscious man's features. "He's going to be okay?"

"Far as I can tell. The shrapnel was dangerously close to his heart but didn't touch it. How are things going at tent number one?"

"Good and bad. Did well with the man with the severed ear. The sergeant with the ripped-off jaw will live, but he's going to be disfigured for the rest of his life. Had two others die on the table, I'm sorry to say. Have one I'd like you to look at. Maybe you'll want to do the surgery."

"All right. How about the Union major?"

"Haven't gotten to him yet. I gave him some laudanum about half an hour ago. He's in quite a bit of pain."

Hunter turned to Jodie. "Honey, why don't you take a little rest?"

"No time for that, dear Doctor," she said. "Let's go see about those men."

Stonewall Jackson was positioned on a brush-covered knoll in the West Woods with one of his aides, Private Henry Kyd Douglas, at his side. His troops were situated in the woods with artillery along the edge of the trees and infantry spaced intermittently between the cannons.

McClellan's infantry came across the open fields in seemingly interminable columns of blue flanked by artillery batteries. Jackson's artillery cut loose and the infantry followed suit. Cannon and musket belched their volleys with telling accuracy. Casualties in the Union ranks were appalling, but on they came with a flash of bayonets and flutter of flags, halting the lines only long enough to readjust themselves.

Stonewall Jackson stood fearlessly on the very edge of the terrible battle, observing it through his binoculars. The enemy was showing himself to be indomitable. No matter how many the Confederate guns cut down, there were always more to take their places. Not so with the men in gray. They started short in number and were becoming fewer.

There was one bit of encouragement. When Jackson had left Major General A. P. Hill's division in charge of the Union prisoners at Harper's Ferry and Martinsburg, he had told Hill to secure the prisoners so he could leave two brigades with them and bring the other two to Sharpsburg.

Hill and his two brigades had arrived at the Antietam battle at midmorning. Jackson had placed them with the Branch and Gregg brigades, letting Hill resume charge over them. They were now part of the fighting forces in the Miller cornfield.

Jackson swung his binoculars from the battle at the West Woods to see what was happening there.

*****

General Hooker's compact columns of infantry had swept into the cornfield with the crushing weight of a landslide. The outmanned Rebels were pushed back at first, but fought back tenaciously.

Even as Jackson observed the battle from his lofty position, great patches of corn were blasted by artillery, and most of the field looked as if it had been struck by a storm of bloody hail.

At the north end of the cornfield, in the heat of the action, was the 18th North Carolina Infantry Regiment, commanded by Major Rance Dayton. Dayton had his regiment hunkered down in the corn, where some of it still stood seven feet tall. They had met a fierce onslaught from the enemy infantry and repulsed it with musketry fire so rapid and well-aimed that the Federals had backed off to regroup.

Now the Federals were coming again.

Dayton looked around at his weary, hollow-eyed men. They had fought for over nine hours. Since their meager breakfast, they'd had nothing to eat but the corn they were munching on now, while their dead and wounded comrades lay around them.

A sergeant appeared from the rear and knelt beside Dayton. "Major, we're runnin' mighty low on ammunition."

The blazing sun beat down mercilessly, and Dayton licked his parched lips. "Get to General Branch and tell him we need more."

"That's where I just came from, sir. He said there isn't much more left in the caissons."

"Then we'll have to throw rocks till they close in, then we'll go to bayonets, fists, and teeth," Dayton said. "Has General Branch sent word to General Jackson that we're low?"

"I don't know, sir."

"Go find out."

When the sergeant had disappeared, Dayton ran his gaze over the dirty faces of his men. "We're low on ammunition, boys.

Gather the cartridge boxes off the dead and wounded. We're going to need all we can get!"

In a few minutes, the heavy lines of Union troops were closing in again. "All right, men, listen to me!" Dayton called. "Hold your fire until I give the word! I want them so close you can tell the color of their eyes!"

When the first line of Federals drew close enough, Dayton took a deep breath and shouted, *"Fire!"*

Muskets roared and flamed in the Federals' faces like a blaze of lightning. The entire front line, with few exceptions, went down. Those who were not hit wheeled and ran back toward the next wave, which halted under their commander's orders.

While the Federals regrouped, Dayton shouted, "Take the guns and ammunition off those dead Yankees, boys!"

As Dayton's men scurried to gather the guns and ammunition, he saw a fresh horde of Yankees. McClellan had sent reinforcements.

"Get ready, men! This'll be a big one! Don't fire till I say so!"

While the major waited, his mind flashed back to his latest talk with Stonewall Jackson about life, death, heaven, and hell. Jackson's words echoed in his mind: *Are you ready to die?*

No, he was not ready to die and face God. He had never come to Jesus in repentance of sin and asked Him for salvation. He watched the Federals close in, shouting curses.

"Fire!"

The whole world seemed to explode as guns on both sides belched flame. The air filled with dust and smoke and the cries of wounded men. Dayton saw the Yankee leader go down—a young major.

The wall of fire thrown up by the Confederates and the heaps of blue-uniformed bodies on the ground had the Yankees in disarray. They pulled back, looking for their leader. When they couldn't find him, they pivoted and headed back across the field.

"After 'em, men!" Dayton shouted, and led the charge.

They were about two hundred yards out from the cornfield, firing at the retreating Federals, when Dayton saw Yankee reinforcements forming at the far end of the field.

"Back!" Dayton shouted. "Back to the cornfield! Re-form the lines!"

As the 18th North Carolina wheeled at their leader's command, the retreating Yankees stopped to allow reinforcements to pass them. When the space between blue and gray widened, Union artillery opened up fire.

Cannon shells shrieked their high-pitched song of death, exploding in yellow flame. The roar was deafening as shell after shell rained down. The double shriek of a pair of Union shells sounded close behind.

"Get down!" Dayton shouted.

The men dropped, hugging the ground as tightly as possible. As soon as shrapnel stopped hissing through the air, Dayton looked up and saw that his men in the front had taken a direct hit.

"Get up and run!" he shouted, scrambling to his feet. "The cornfield will be out of their range!"

It was every man for himself. Dayton bolted with them, but when he drew near the men who had been hit, he saw movement. It was Sergeant Buster Camden.

Dayton halted and knelt by the wounded man. "I'll carry you, Buster."

Camden's face was a mass of blood. "No, Major. Go on. I'm done for anyway."

"No way I'm leaving you here." Dayton heard the whine of another shell and felt something tug at his pantleg. "Okay," he said, running his hands under Camden's body, "here we go."

When he stood, his leg gave way. He cushioned Buster from falling and looked down to see torn flesh and a piece of jagged black metal embedded in his thigh. His pantleg was soaked in blood.

"Major, go on! They're coming!"

Dayton looked over his shoulder. The Union infantry was coming like a deluge. He gritted his teeth against the pain and struggled to lift Camden.

"Can't leave you, Buster."

The men of the Eighteenth staggered to a halt at the edge of the cornfield and looked back for the first time.

Billy Dean Baxter was the first to speak. "It's the major and—I can't tell who the other man is! The major's been hit, too!"

"I'm going after them!" Everett Nichols shouted, and broke into a run. "Cover me!"

Four more men ran after him—Billy Dean Baxter, Buford Hall, Hank Upchurch, and Chuck Carney.

"Cover us!" they yelled.

Captain Jack Fleming, who was next in command, gave the order. "Load up, men! We'll have to run out there a ways to be effective! Shoot around the men and over their heads! They'll stay low!"

Rance Dayton saw his five friends running toward him, and he glanced back at the oncoming horde of blue uniforms.

"Back! Go back!" he shouted. "There's no chance!"

The fearless five came on. Billy Dean and Everett lifted Dayton. The other three hoisted Camden and took off running as fast as they could. The Federals were now within range, and bullets began to zip and whistle around the rescuers.

Billy Dean grunted and went down, and Everett stumbled. The other three men paused.

"Go on!" Dayton shouted, gritting his teeth in pain.

"Billy Dean's dead, Major," Everett said.

"So's Buster," Hank said.

"You guys carry the major," Chuck Carney said. "I'll be a shield."

The other three men quickly had the major off the ground and were running toward their comrades. Suddenly the meaning of Carney's words sunk into Dayton's brain. Carney had positioned himself to take any bullets!

"Look over there!" Carney shouted with a whoop. Rebels were charging the Federals, taking them by surprise. The Federals left off their pursuit of Dayton and his gallant men, and braced themselves for the fresh onslaught.

It was Stonewall Jackson's doing. When he had seen what was happening in the cornfield, he'd sent two regiments of General Early's brigade to intervene for the Eighteenth North Carolina.

Jodie watched Hunter lift his latest patient off the operating table and carry him outside. She glanced through the tent opening and could see bodies strewn so thickly on the field that there was hardly a place for the stretcher-bearers to walk. The moans and cries of wounded men could be heard above the nearby sounds of battle.

As Hunter re-entered the tent and laid the blinded Union man on the table, Jodie moved up next to him. Hunter glanced at her, and a warmth reached out from her dark-brown eyes and touched him. He silently mouthed, *I love you.*

Jodie set a pan of fresh water on the table next to the operating table, picked up a clean cloth, and began to gently wash the major's face. The major was conscious, though laudanum had eased his pain. A slight smile curved his lips. "I thought I heard a woman's voice from out there. Those are female hands, aren't they?"

"You're very perceptive, Major," Hunter said. "What you don't know is that those hands and that voice belong to the most beautiful woman in the world. Her name is Jodie Lockwood. She's a Certified Medical Nurse and Surgeon's Assistant. But even more important, she's my fiancée."

The major was about to say that Jodie had to be the second most beautiful woman in the world, when it struck him that he would never again look upon the face of his wife. He kept his reply to himself, and said instead, "I think your last name is McGuire, Doctor. Correct?"

"Yes. *Hunter* McGuire. And we don't know your name, Major."

"Jim Halstead, II Corps, Third Division, under Brigadier General William French."

"Yes, sir."

"How can I ever thank you for what you did? You risked your life to save mine. I remember asking you why you would do such a thing. You said you'd tell me later."

"I did it, Major Halstead, on impulse. I saw another human being about to get killed, and I ran out there to try to save his life."

"But did you stop to think the effort might cost you your own life?"

"It crossed my mind, but I couldn't let it stop me. Besides, I've taken an oath as a medical doctor to save lives. But there was a stronger force than my oath. I'm a Christian, Major. My faith is in the Lord Jesus Christ for the forgiveness of my sins and the salvation of my soul. When I saw you stumbling about out there, I didn't see an enemy in a blue uniform. I saw another human being on the edge of death. I had to save your life if I could."

A wan smile spread over the blind man's lips. "Well, bless the Lord! I'm a born-again, blood-washed man myself. It's wonderful to know I'm in the hands of a Christian doctor."

"Major, we can fellowship and talk a little later, but right now I've got to work on those eye sockets. There are burnt powder crystals in there that can cause infection. Jodie's going to put you under with chloroform. It'll take awhile, and I don't want you in any more pain than necessary."

"Thank you—both of you," Halstead said.

The sounds of battle were still thundering across the valley when Hunter and Jodie finished their work on Major Halstead.

Shuffling footsteps outside caught their attention, and they turned to see two exhausted, panting men carrying Major Rance Dayton. Hunter focused on Dayton's pale features, then recognized the two men as Everett Nichols and Chuck Carney. Hunter noted the makeshift tourniquet on Dayton's leg. "Looks like you took a bullet, my friend," he said.

"Shrapnel," Dayton replied.

"He asked us to bring him to you, Dr. McGuire," Carney said.

"All right. I've got some other men in worse shape, Major, but I'll get to you as quick as I can."

"That's fine, Doctor. I'll wait."

"This is Nurse Jodie Lockwood, Major. She'll check the tourniquet and give you some laudanum."

It wasn't until sunset that Hunter was free to work on Rance Dayton's leg. Rance told Hunter how his five friends had saved his life, risking their own to do so, and how Billy Dean Baxter had been killed while doing his part.

Jodie smiled at Hunter, who had shown the same kind of bravery that day. But she knew there would be no medals for saving the life of an enemy officer.

The battle raged on at the West Woods, the Miller cornfield, and Sunken Road.

Major General Ambrose E. Burnside's four divisions made a heroic stand at Rohrback's Bridge. Though they lost hundreds of men, they held onto the bridge. By dusk, the weary men on both sides were giving up the fight in sheer exhaustion, and the surviving men of IX Corps were calling it "Burnside's Bridge."

Generals Lee, Jackson, and Longstreet were glad for the Union army's weariness, for their own ammunition was almost gone.

CHAPTER TWENTY

As the sun buried itself below the western horizon, George McClellan withdrew his army across Antietam Creek to the east, and Robert E. Lee's army collected on the west side.

Battle-jaded men on both sides looked out over the smoldering fields where tiny flames still licked the bark of trees and the evening breeze carried wisps of smoke across the valley. After twelve horrible hours, the battle was over.

Bodies were everywhere...buckled, crumpled, sprawled, and in many places, heaped. The movement of the wounded in their torment gave the field a crawling effect.

Truce flags were raised to allow the long, tedious job of picking up the wounded. Night, when it came in its fullness, carried a mournful chorus of misery and suffering from the pitch-black hollows, woods, and fields. It would be days before doctors on both sides would be able to care for all the wounded. Many would die while waiting. Hundreds more would die from their wounds in the days and weeks to come.

*****

Generals Jackson and Longstreet were busy with their division leaders, doing what they could to encourage and comfort them.

General Lee sat alone in his tent, his head bent low. Depression, like the hot wind that had blown through the valley that afternoon, descended on his mind. He had led his men into a horrendous battle they could not have won.

The odds were against them at the start, but he had felt there was a slim chance to chalk up a victory on Northern soil, and his men had willingly followed him.

Now, thousands of faithful soldiers were dead. Other thousands would be crippled and maimed for the rest of their lives.

Tears flowed down the general's cheeks as he prayed for God to take the moans of the men from inside his head.

Hunter and Jodie worked as fast as possible to care for as many wounded men as they could.

It was nearly midnight when Jodie asked, "Did you bring enough medical supplies? I mean, from what the stretcher-bearers are saying, we've got several thousand wounded men still lying out there."

"I don't think we've got nearly enough supplies. When this battle is over, I'll cross the creek and talk to the Union medical director over there. Maybe he'll give us what we need."

Jodie's eyes widened. "You mean they might start fighting again in the morning?"

Hunter was about to nod when a familiar voice came from the tent opening, "It's not likely, Miss Jodie."

Hunter looked over his shoulder. "Hello, Tom. I inquired about you earlier and the stretcher-bearers told me you were all right. Thank the Lord for that."

Jodie smiled at Jackson as Hunter said to her, "I guess you know who that is."

"Yes. I saw you in Frederick, General, when the boy was hit with a rock."

"I saw you too, Miss Jodie, but it was not the opportune moment to ask Hunter for an introduction."

"General," Jodie asked, "why isn't it likely there'll be more fighting tomorrow?"

"The Yankees fought as hard as we did today. They need rest as badly as we do. And if George McClellan stays true to form, it'll take him a day to get his troops ready to fight again."

"I hope you're right, Tom," Hunter said. "We're going to be a long time getting to all the wounded men as it is. Another day like today, and we'll bury more than we carry away."

"But what if they go back to fighting on Friday?" Jodie asked. "It'll be the same thing then."

Jackson nodded. "General Lee knows that. I've got a hunch he'll pull us out of here before Friday."

"Be foolish not to," Hunter said, keeping his attention on what his hands were doing.

"I agree," Jackson said. "Hunter, I was told that Rance Dayton was brought to you with a hunk of shrapnel in his leg. He doing all right?"

"Yes. He's out there on the south side of the tent. There's a lantern in the corner not being used. Light it and go see if he's awake."

"I'm glad you didn't have to take the leg," Jackson said.

"So am I. He'll be fine in a few weeks...won't even walk with a limp once it's completely healed."

Minutes later, Jackson made his way among the wounded men. Most were asleep. He spotted Dayton and knelt beside him. The major blinked at the lantern light, then focused on the face of his old professor.

"Hello, General. I sure am glad to see you."

"Same here, Rance. I saw what you did out there today. You're a brave man."

"How'd you see that?"

"Binoculars. I also saw what those five men in your regiment did."

"Yes, sir. I was going to talk to you about them, sir. I sure would like to see them get some kind of commendation from General Lee."

Jackson grinned. "I've already got that in mind," he said, pulling a slip of paper out of his shirt pocket. "Got it down right here, with all their names. I talked to some of the men in the regiment."

"Thank you, sir. They deserve to be honored for it."

"I've got a meeting with General Lee and General Longstreet in a few minutes, Rance. But one more thing before I go…"

"I took care of it, sir."

Jackson eyebrows came up. "You did? When?"

"When I came to, lying right here. I've been such a fool to put it off, General. When my mind came clear, it hit me that if I'd been killed out there today, I'd be in hell right now. What a fool I've been. The Lord was so good to me. Men dying all around me. Even—even Billy Dean. I'm saved now, General. Thanks to you. If you hadn't pressed the gospel to me over and over, well…I know you've prayed for me all this time, too."

"You're right about that," Jackson said, brushing tears from his eyes. "I'm so glad you opened your heart to Jesus."

"Best thing I ever did, sir. There's nothing like the peace I have in my heart right now. But then you know that, don't you?"

"I sure do, Rance. Glad you know it now, too. I have to get going. I'll check on you again tomorrow."

Jackson returned the lantern to the tent and doused its flame. "Well, Doc, when are you and Miss Jodie going to get some sleep? You can't work all night, you know."

Hunter, without looking up, said, "We've got two more men who need attention real bad, Tom. After we take care of them, we'll get some sleep. When will you know if General Lee is going to pull out?"

"Maybe tonight. I'm due at his tent in about ten minutes."

"Let us know, will you?"

Hunter and Jodie bid him goodnight and were finishing up with their present patient when two stretcher-bearers appeared.

"Dr. McGuire," one of them said, "we have a man here who needs attention right now. We took him to the tent next door, but when Dr. Jensen examined him, he said you were the man to handle this one."

"All right. Just hold on for a minute. We're about done here."

It took Hunter thirty seconds to finish up, and then he nodded toward the man on the stretcher. "Put him on the table. I'll be right back." He carried the last patient outside as Jodie began preparations for the new one.

As the stretcher-bearers lifted the man onto the table, what Jodie saw took her breath. The man's midsection was a bloody mass.

One of the stretcher-bearers saw her flinch. "Grapeshot, ma'am. He's lost a lot of blood."

The wounded soldier was conscious. He looked at Jodie through droop-lidded eyes. She judged him not more than twenty years old.

Hunter returned and the stretcher-bearers disappeared back onto the field of dead and wounded.

Jodie watched Hunter's face when he took his first look at the young private. He winced and shook his head. The grapeshot had done too much damage.

Hunter kept his voice to a whisper as he said, "All we can do is try to alleviate his pain."

Jodie nodded. "He's awake enough to take laudanum. I'll get some."

A sound came from the soldier's quivering lips. "Doc—Dr. McGuire..."

"Yes, soldier?"

"I'm not gonna make it…am I?"

"Well, I—"

"I heard what you said. There's no…chance, is there?"

Hunter bit his lower lip. "No, soldier, there isn't. You've been lying out there on the battlefield for hours. You've lost a lot of blood. It's a wonder you're still alive."

"I've been told you're a…a Christian."

"That's right."

"Doctor, I was raised in a God-fearing home, but I'm not a Christian. I don't want to go to hell. Please…help me."

"You come from a Christian home?"

"Yes. I went through a prayer once…when I was nine. But it was just to please Mama. By the time I was twelve, Mama… Mama knew I hadn't meant it. I lived and acted like the devil. Broke her heart."

"What's your name, soldier?"

"Eddie. Eddie Watkins. There's a letter from Mama…in my hip pocket. Has her address in Memphis."

"Listen to me, Eddie."

"Yes?"

"Do you understand who Jesus Christ is?"

"God's Son."

"Virgin-born and sinless…"

"Yes."

"Died on the cross for your sins, as well as the sins of the rest of humanity…"

"Yes."

"You know you're a guilty sinner before God?"

"The worst."

Jodie prayed silently as Hunter quoted Scripture, making sure Eddie Watkins understood the way of salvation.

When Eddie had finished asking the Lord to save him, he gritted his teeth in pain, and said, "Dr. McGuire…would you see that my mama knows I got saved…before…before I died? Her name and address—"

"Is in the letter in your hip pocket," Hunter said, pulling the letter from the pocket. "Yes, I'll write to her."

Eddie's eyes were turning glassy. "Tell Mama I'll...I'll meet her in heaven."

"I'll tell her, Eddie."

Hunter and Jodie continued to work, trying to save more lives. It was 3:20 A.M. when they heard footsteps outside.

"Doc...Miss Jodie..." It was General Jackson. "I thought you were going to get some sleep."

Both of them were so exhausted they could hardly stand. Hunter turned bleary eyes on Jackson. "After this one, Tom."

"You wanted me to let you know what General Lee decided about pulling his army out of here."

"Yes?"

"He's a very discouraged man right now. Blaming himself for the whipping we've taken...the men who died. But his thinking is clear. He sees no reason to keep us here. We'll pull out sometime late tomorrow. Probably be after dark."

"He doesn't think McClellan will attack today?"

"No. We've taken a pretty good toll on them. Of course, he could wipe us out if he had a mind to. We're out of ammunition, but McClellan doesn't know that. If he came at us, it wouldn't take him long to find out. We'll be gone by sunup on Friday."

"There's no way you can take the wounded men with you, is there?"

"No."

"Then Jodie and I, and all the Confederate doctors will stay until we've done all we can."

*****

After less than three hours of sleep, Hunter and Jodie, who had slept on the floor amid the wounded, were fed a meager breakfast by the army cooks and went back to work.

Piteous moans and cries for water were still coming from the battlefields.

Stonewall Jackson was returning from the Sunken Road and heading toward the patch of woods that sheltered the Confederate medical facility. He was sickened as he let his gaze roam the valley. Like pages of a book, the battlefields told their story. Churned earth where cannon shells had exploded and blackened patches where they had burned the grass told of death, terrible and swift. The grass wore a garish red stain and quivered in the morning breeze. All around were the bloating bodies of dead horses and the broken, shattered artifacts of war.

The opposing armies—still under their truce—gathered their wounded who had survived the long night.

The general thought of home and his sweet wife, Mary Anna. He longed to hold her in his arms and feel her sweet warmth.

When he reached the hospital, he found Hunter and Jodie cleaning the operating table. They greeted Jackson and told him they felt refreshed after a brief sleep.

"Hunter, could I have a few minutes of your time?"

"Certainly, Tom. What can I do for you?"

"I need you to go for a little walk with me. I hate to take you away from your work, but this is important."

"Hunter," Jodie said, "I can go to the next tent and ask Dr. Jensen if he'll work in your place till you get back. He's got another doctor working with him at the moment."

"Go see if he can come right away. I'll put the next man on the table."

The general led Hunter to a long split-rail fence that bordered what the soldiers had dubbed "Bloody Lane" at sundown yesterday. His attention was drawn to a Confederate soldier at the fence on his knees with his rifle aimed across the road.

Hunter gave Jackson a quizzical look, then walked toward the man in tattered gray. The soldier wasn't moving a muscle as he stared along the barrel of his rifle with both eyes open. As Hunter bent low, he realized the man was not breathing. Then he saw the single bullet hole centered in the man's forehead beneath the brim of his ragged gray hat.

"What do you think of that?" Jackson asked.

"Death attitude."

"Death *what?*"

"Death attitude. Maybe more often called attitude of death."

"You know about this, Hunter?"

"It's rare, but not unheard of. Medical science hasn't been able to explain it, they just know that it happens. A doctor I graduated with at Harvard has done an intense study and written a journal article about it. Name's John Brinton. I read in the *American Medical Association Journal* that he's one of Lincoln's Corps Medical Directors."

"You say medical science hasn't been able to explain it?"

"Well, we know the preservation of these attitudes of death is not caused by rigor mortis. Dr. Brinton has determined that an unconscious muscle contraction at the instant of death can freeze a person's body position and facial expression. Look at this man's face. See how intense it is?"

"Yes..."

"Usually death relaxes the body muscles, and they go limp. But when this phenomenon happens, it freezes everything. See if you can take the musket from his hands."

Jackson took hold of the weapon, but the dead man's hands

were unmovable. "Hunter, it's like his hands are made of steel. Come with me. We've got some more death attitudes yonder. General Colquitt told me about them. He's waiting there now."

As they drew near the place where Sunken Road took its famous dip, Hunter saw bodies strung out for more than a half-mile. Most of them were Confederates, but there were a few blue uniforms. Many of the bodies were heaped three and four deep.

Brigadier General Colquitt and his aides were standing nearby, talking with three Union soldiers. When Hunter drew closer, he saw that two of the Union men were officers, and the other was a doctor.

"Tom! It's my old college friend, John Brinton!"

Brinton had been told that General Jackson was bringing Hunter to the scene. When he saw the man who had led him to Christ, he hurried to meet him. The two men embraced as Union Generals Fitz-John Porter and George Meade looked on with General Colquitt and his aides.

Hunter kept a hand on John's shoulder as they turned their attention to the other men.

"Maybe we can talk later," John whispered.

"Yes," Hunter said. "I've read what you've written about death attitudes, John. Interesting."

"Well, I was sent here by General Halleck when we knew the battle would take place." As he spoke, Brinton pointed up the road. "Some stretcher-bearers told me there are some more death attitudes up there. We'll have to walk on the high edge of the bank to get around the bodies here. I'll lead the way."

Within ten feet of each other they found three bodies in the attitude of death. One was on his knees, as if he had died while trying to get up. The other two were in almost the same position. They lay on their backs, heads slightly lifted, arms raised rigidly in the air, as if reaching toward heaven.

"What you see here, gentlemen," Brinton said, "is reaction when the bullets struck their hearts. Both men apparently lived a few seconds and reached for heaven. There was a final muscular action at the last instant of life, in which the muscles set and remained rigid and inflexible."

Brinton then told Jackson and Hunter about the Confederate captain who had been shot while mounting his horse at South Mountain. He died sitting straight up in the saddle.

Jackson had heard about Captain Errol Taylor's strange behavior and apparent capture by General Jeb Stuart. It looked like they could finally clear up that puzzle.

As the men were about to depart Bloody Lane, Brinton said that earlier that morning, Battery B of the 4th U.S. Artillery had found a Union horse in death attitude. The animal had taken a bullet in the brain while apparently in the act of rising from the ground. Its head was held proudly aloft, and its forelegs set firmly forward in a lifelike pose.

This amazed them all.

Later that afternoon, Hunter and Jodie crossed the creek on the middle bridge and visited the Union medical facility at Dr. John Brinton's invitation. Jodie was glad to meet Hunter's old college friend and was elated to meet Clara Barton. The two camps agreed that in the next few days the Union and Confederate doctors and nurses would work together to take care of the wounded.

CHAPTER TWENTY-ONE

Hunter was carrying a man outside who had just died on the operating table when General Jackson appeared in the lantern light.

"Lost another one?" Jackson asked.

"Yes," Hunter said, placing the body tenderly on the ground.

There was more room in and around the facilities since the wounded men who were able to travel had been picked up and placed in wagons for the trip home.

The general followed Hunter inside and nodded at Jodie, then said, "Well, we're ready to pull out. How long do you think you'll stay, Doc?"

"Probably three or four more days—till we've saved the last life we can."

"Well, you're a volunteer, Doctor. You don't have to report back until you want to. I doubt there'll be any big battles in Virginia for a while. You need a good rest. Take it. When you're ready to come back, they can tell you at C.S.A. headquarters in Richmond where I am."

"All right. I think I'll take a room at the same boarding house where Jodie lives in Frederick and spend at least a week there."

"Good idea. After I get my Corps settled back on Southern ground, I'm going home for a while, myself. If you contact Richmond and I'm not there, they'll tell you where to report in."

"Good enough, Tom," Hunter said, giving his friend a hug.

Jackson then turned to Jodie. "You take care of this good man while he's with you, honey."

"I will, General." Jodie raised up on tiptoe to plant a quick kiss on his cheek. "I'll see you sometime down the line."

"Well, if I'm not tied up in a battle when you two get married, I'll be there to kiss the bride."

Jodie laughed and thought how good it felt. There had been so much sorrow all around her for two days.

Robert E. Lee took his army back into Virginia without opposition from McClellan. Little Mac wired General Halleck in Washington, saying, "Our victory is complete. The enemy is driven back into Virginia. Maryland and Pennsylvania are now safe."

Tactically, the battle at Antietam had been a draw. The Federals had gained ground, but they had failed to dislodge the Confederate army from Sharpsburg. The Confederate withdrawal transformed a tactical stalemate into strategic victory for the North.

President Lincoln seized the opportunity to issue a document that would lend a new and deeper meaning to the bloodiest day in American history—the Emancipation Proclamation, which decreed freedom for the Confederacy's three-and-a-half million slaves. Within a short time this action would incite the Confederates to fight even harder against the Northerners.

In spite of the Union's victory at Antietam, Lincoln was angry with McClellan. In his eyes, Little Mac had once again failed to vanquish the enemy when he'd had the opportunity.

*****

Seven days after the battle, Hunter and Jodie returned to Frederick, having done all they could for the survivors of Antietam.

One of the first things Hunter did was write a letter to Mrs. Emily Watkins in Memphis, Tennessee. At least he could tell her that Eddie had opened his heart to Jesus before he died.

After a day of resting at the boarding house, Hunter and Jodie took a long walk on Friday afternoon, September 26. As they entered the woods, the lowering sun cast long shadows across the forest floor. A breeze began to stir the leaves and its invisible fingers fluffed Jodie's long silken tresses.

Hunter pointed to a fallen tree. "Let's sit down for a moment, sweetheart. I've been thinking."

"About what?"

"Our wedding. How about a December date? A little earlier than we had discussed before."

"Sounds good to me. Any special day?"

"Haven't gotten that far. I thought if you agreed on December we'd come up with the exact day together."

"Fine," she said, and smiled. "December it is."

Hunter pulled her close and kissed her tenderly. They sat together in silence, enjoying the sounds of the forest and each other's presence.

After several minutes, Jodie squeezed Hunter's hand. "You know what, Dr. Hunter McGuire?"

"What, Nurse Jodie Lockwood?"

"Do you realize how little we know about each other? At Lexington we had only a few days together. And the time was so short at Frederick...then at Sharpsburg there was hardly time to talk."

"I know all I need to know about you to be absolutely positive I want to spend the rest of my life with you. The rest I'll learn as time goes by."

"I don't have any doubts about marrying you either...but some things I want to know *now.*"

"Like what?"

"How about your middle name for starters."

Hunter laughed. "That's an easy one. It's Newman. I've told you about being adopted by Jason and Ellie McGuire when I was five."

"Yes."

"When they took me before the county magistrate to adopt me, they suggested that I carry the family n— Oh! I never even told you what my last name was before I was adopted."

"See what I mean? We need to learn some of the important things like that about each other."

"Well, I was Hunter Newman Jr. My mother's name was Florence, and I already told you my baby sister's name was Lizzie. When the McGuires took me before the county magistrate, they suggested I carry the family name as a middle name in honor of my real parents. So I became Hunter Newman McGuire. Now, Miss Jodie Lockwood...I don't know *your* middle name either."

"It's Elizabeth. My parents used to call me Jodie Beth when I was little. My Aunt Bertha—Mom's sister—still does."

"My baby sister's middle name was Elizabeth. That's why my parents called her Lizzie. So your name is Jodie Elizabeth?"

Jodie shook her head and brushed a lock of hair from her forehead. "No. Jodie is just a nickname. My name is actually Joan Elizabeth."

Hunter's smile faded. "Really? That's quite a coincidence. Lizzie's real name is Joan Elizabeth."

"You're kidding!" Jodie noticed a strange look in his eyes. "Hunter, what's the matter?"

He chuckled hollowly and ran shaky fingers through his hair. "Well, that you and my sister have the exact same first and middle name is really something. But..."

"But *what?*"

"I hadn't thought about it till now, but Lizzie's hair was black like yours, and her eyes chocolate-brown just like yours. And... and the two of you have to be very close to the same age. She was three years younger than me, the same as you."

"When is Lizzie's birthday? Do you remember?"

"I was only five when Mom died, and Lizzie and I were separated. It's in February, I think. Yes...February. But I don't remember what day."

Jodie raised a trembling hand to her mouth. "Mine's February 19. I was born in 1838. I assume Lizzie was too."

"I was born in '35, so Lizzie would've been born in '38. February '38." Hunter's chest felt tight. "But you were born in Tennessee. She was born in Virginia."

"Hunter, are...are we really thinking that I could be your long lost sister? I mean, this can't be, can it?"

"Jodie." Hunter tried to keep his voice steady. "These coincidences are really astounding, but that's where it ends. Like I said, you were born in Tennessee; Lizzie was born in Virginia." Hunter forced a laugh. "Besides, little Lizzie had a burn scar on her upper left arm. Mom accidentally spilled boiling water on her when she was about a year-and-a-half old."

The blood drained from Jodie's face and she began to unbutton her left sleeve at the cuff, methodically rolling it up. Her lips quivered as she said, "Was Lizzie's scar shaped like this?"

Hunter's eyes glazed with tears as he nodded.

"Hunter," Jodie whispered, squeezing his hand, "tell me I'm going to wake up and all of this will be gone."

"I don't understand..." was all Hunter could say. Then, "But you said you were born and raised in Tennessee."

"That's what I've always thought," Jodie said, looking at the scar on her arm. "But how do we explain this?"

"No, Jodie. This just has to be the strangest set of coincidences that has ever happened in all human history. The Lord would never let a thing like this happen to us. Weren't we just saying a little while ago how He so wonderfully kept us for each other for over seven years, then used the War to bring us together?"

"Hunter, didn't you tell me you've always wanted to find Lizzie, and have prayed that you would?"

"Yes."

"Well, I can't say I understand all that the Lord has done in our lives, but if I *am* Lizzie, at least God has brought us to each other."

Hunter stubbornly shook his head. "No. I'm *in love* with you, Jodie. How could I ever just love you as a brother loves his sister? And how about you? Could you just love me as your big brother?"

Jodie's tears began to spill over, and she couldn't speak.

Hunter folded her into his arms. "Sweetheart, we must believe that the circumstances are not what they appear to be. Somehow we've got to find a way to clear all of this up."

Jodie pushed back enough to look into his eyes. "Hunter, there *is* a way to clear it up. My Aunt Bertha can do it for us. We'll go to Athens, Tennessee. That's where she lives. I remember her telling me many, many times about being right there at our house when I was born. She can settle it for us, once and for all!"

Fifty-four-year-old Bertha Pittman, a widow for several years, hurried through the parlor to see who was knocking at her door. She peered through the heavy curtain and saw a tall, sandy-haired man with a small woman at his side. She opened the door a crack.

"Yes?"

A face appeared, exactly Bertha's height. "Hello, Aunt Bertha."

"Jodie Beth! Come in this house!"

They embraced for a long moment, then Bertha looked the handsome man up and down. "Jodie, you didn't go and get yourself married without writing to your Auntie, did you?"

"Not yet, but I want you to meet my fiancé, Dr. Hunter McGuire."

"I always knew that when my Jodie Beth found herself a man, he'd be as good-looking as she is beautiful!"

Bertha tugged at Jodie's hand. "Well, come in and sit down. I want to hear all about your nursing...and how you met this handsome doctor."

"Our time is a little limited, Auntie, so we'll have to tell it in brief. Actually we're here because we need your help."

Bertha guided them to a love seat in the parlor and took a chair facing them. "I can't imagine how you would need my help, honey, but I'm listening."

Together, Jodie and Hunter told their story.

"So..." Jodie said, "this is why we're here. I remember you telling me many times when I was growing up how you were right there in the house when I was born."

Bertha remained silent. Then her lips quivered and tears began to spill down her cheeks.

Jodie leaned forward. "Auntie, you were there when I was born, weren't you?"

Bertha left her chair and picked up a hanky from a small table. "Honey, I once swore to my sister and brother-in-law that I would never tell this, but now I have no choice."

The portly woman wept as she explained that back in the late spring of 1840, her sister, Bettieann, and brother-in-law, Jubal Lockwood, were on a trip to North Carolina in their wagon. They had gone to visit some of their old high school friends who had moved to Reidsville, some fifteen miles north of Greensboro. When they returned, Jubal and Bettieann had a two-year-old girl with them.

During their trip they came upon a wagon in the woods a few miles outside Reidsville. Apparently robbers had murdered the young couple they found, since there was no money on either person. In the back of the wagon, Jubal and Bettieann found the little girl. They also found papers showing that the couple had just adopted her in Virginia.

When Hunter and Jodie heard this, a hopeless feeling washed over them. Bertha saw it, but continued.

"Bettieann and Jubal had been married for nine years and hadn't been able to have children, so they took the little girl and the papers and headed back home to Tennessee. When they arrived home, Jodie Beth, they told me and your Uncle Harold what had happened. They figured they hadn't done anything wrong. After all, you needed a home."

Jodie leaned over and put her head in her hands.

"Jubal and my sister made Harold and me swear never to tell anyone about it, honey. They simply told folks hereabouts they had gone to North Carolina and adopted little Jodie Beth, which is what they called you right from the start. They liked the name Joan Elizabeth, which of course was on the papers, so they decided to let you keep it. No one ever questioned it, since they had often talked about adoption."

Hunter's voice had a dull tone as he asked, "Mrs. Pittman, did you ever actually see the adoption papers?"

"Yes, I did."

"Can you remember the name of the adoptive parents? The ones who were robbed and killed?"

Bertha put a hand to her temple, looking at the floor. "No, Doctor, it was just too long ago. I should be able to remember the name, but it just won't come to me."

"If you heard the name, would you know it?"

"Yes, I think I would."

"Was it William and Bessie Caterson?"

Bertha's eyes lit up. She snapped her fingers and said, "Yes, that's it! Caterson!"

"And Jodie Beth's original name, ma'am. Would you know it if you heard it?"

"I'm sure I would. I recall it had the word 'new' in it. Like

Newcomb, or Newberry, or something like that."

"Newman?"

"Yes! Little Jodie Beth's name had been Joan Elizabeth Newman!"

Hunter drove the rented buggy through Athens toward the railroad station, keeping an arm around Jodie as she stared vacantly ahead.

Numb of soul, Hunter felt his world slipping through his fingers like grains of sand. All the dreams he had for a future with Jodie were gone. He knew the precious young woman by his side was suffering the same feeling of loss.

"Jodie..."

"Yes?"

"At least I'm glad to know that my little Lizzie's all right. I do have to say it's good to have found her."

Jodie squeezed his hand. "And I didn't even know I had a big brother."

"But, Jodie, what do I do with my love for you? It isn't proper that I should feel this way toward my sister."

"Nor for me to feel this way toward my brother. I don't understand, dar—Hunter. I don't understand why the Lord would let it happen in a way that has so torn our lives apart."

"I don't either. But we'll just have to trust Him. Our God does no wrong. We'll have to cling to that. I'll take you back to Frederick so you can resume your nursing career. We'll keep in touch. The Lord has somebody for you, I'm sure. One day he'll walk into your life."

Jodie knew she could never love a man like she had loved Hunter. She would just bury herself in her career.

At the depot Hunter bought tickets for Richmond, then on to Frederick. Now that the battle at Antietam was over, the

Maryland trains were running pretty much on schedule again.

"Once we're over the initial shock of all this, little sister, we'll get together now and then. One day I want you to meet my adoptive parents. They've heard a lot about Lizzie."

"Oh, Hunter!" Jodie buried her face in her hands and sobbed.

Hunter folded her in his arms and wept with her.

The railroad car rocked and the steel wheels clicked rhythmically as Hunter and Jodie sat side by side watching the Tennessee countryside. Neither had spoken a word since the train pulled out of Athens. Now Hunter turned toward Jodie.

"I just thought of something," he said. "Tom Jackson was going to spend some time at home. He's probably still there. We could change trains at Knoxville and go to Lexington. Would you mind?"

"Of course not. General Jackson is your closest friend, and he will need to know, sooner or later, what's happened. Anyhow, I know it would be a comfort for you to see him."

Jodie loved Mary Anna Jackson immediately upon meeting her.

As they sat in the Jackson parlor, the general said, "I'm glad you caught me home. I'm heading back for duty day after tomorrow. Now, just what brought you two to Lexington? This is a long way from Frederick."

"Well, Tom," Hunter said, sighing, "Jodie and I have something to tell you and Mrs. Jackson."

Mary Anna waggled a finger at Hunter as she said, "Now, now, Doctor. I'm not 'Mrs. Jackson' to you. I want both you and Jodie to call me Mary Anna."

Hunter smiled and proceeded to explain the recent development in Jodie and his life. When he'd finished, Tom began rubbing the back of his neck and shaking his head. Finally he looked straight at his old friend and said softly, "Hunter, you need to go to Smithburg."

"Excuse me?"

"You need to go to Smithburg."

"Why, pray tell?"

"See if old Dr. Chet Riley is still alive. Tell him your story and ask him if it all makes sense."

"Why wouldn't it make sense?"

"I...I remember that when your mother gave birth to Lizzie—I was about thirteen years old—I overheard my Uncle Cummins and Aunt Ophelia talking about the Newmans' baby girl. There was a name brought into the conversation, and the only reason I can remember it is because it was the name of a teenage girl who used to live on a farm near McCann's Run, and then suddenly she wasn't living with her parents anymore. She had gone up north to live with some relatives. Her name was Elaine Worley. If Dr. Riley is still alive, ask him about Elaine Worley."

"But what can this Elaine Worley have to do with us?"

"I don't know. There's just something scratching at the back of my mind about her. Maybe it's the Lord talking to me, I'm not sure. All I can say is go ask Dr. Riley."

CHAPTER TWENTY-TWO

Hunter rented a buggy for the ride from Parkersburg to Smithburg. When he and Jodie arrived at the small town, Hunter was surprised that it actually looked familiar to him. But where was Dr. Riley's office?

The next corner looked very familiar. Instinct told him to turn and follow that street. When he rounded another corner, there it was, a half-block away. Dr. Chet Riley's office.

"You drive like you know where you're going," Jodie said.

"I didn't at first, but it kind of came back to me. The office is right up here."

The small building was still a doctor's office, but the sign read:

Gerald Bishop, M.D.
Physician and Surgeon

"Well, let's see if maybe they know where Dr. Riley might be," Hunter said.

Moments later, Hunter and Jodie entered the doctor's office to find the nurse-receptionist at the front desk.

"Good morning, folks. Which one is to see the doctor?"

"Neither of us, ma'am. I'm Dr. Hunter McGuire, and this young lady is Miss Lockwood."

"I'm Harriet Mulford. Is this a professional visit to Dr. Bishop?"

"No, ma'am. Actually, I came here to see Dr. Chet Riley."

"Oh, I'm sorry. Dr. and Mrs. Riley have both passed on. Both of them died in 1859, just two months apart. Dr. Bishop took over the clinic about five months before Dr. Riley died. Is there something I can do for you?"

"Well, ma'am," Hunter said, pulling at an ear, "I had hoped Dr. Riley could help me with a problem Miss Lockwood and I are facing. I don't think there's anything you could do."

"The problem," Jodie said, "involves some information Dr. Riley very possibly could have provided that affects both of our lives."

"Would there be anyone else in the community who might be able to help you? I know just about everybody. I was raised on a farm near here."

"I don't know who it would be, ma'am, but thank you just the same," Hunter said.

Harriet's heart went out to the couple. She could see they were quite distressed. "This information you were hoping to obtain from Dr. Riley...does it involve patients of his, or something like that?"

Hunter and Jodie exchanged glances again.

"I think so, ma'am," Hunter said. "Since you were raised around here, does the name Elaine Worley mean anything to you?"

Harriet blinked and thought for a moment, then said, "No, sir. Doesn't ring any bells. Was she a patient of Dr. Riley's?"

"I'm not really sure, but I assume so."

"Dr. McGuire, I don't mean to pry, but perhaps if I knew exactly what it was you were expecting to learn from Dr. Riley, I could help after all."

"Well, let me explain it, ma'am, and we'll soon see."

Harriet invited the couple to sit down, and they told her the whole story as briefly but thoroughly as they could.

When they had finished, Harriet said, "Well, bless your hearts. What a horrible thing to have happen. You know what? Dr. Riley's long-time nurse, Linna Bittner, may be able to furnish the same information. Linna's retired now, but lives here in town."

Hunter helped Jodie out of the buggy in front of Linna Bittner's small house and continued to hold her hand as they approached the porch.

"Oh, Hunter," Jodie said, "if this lady has no idea what General Jackson was referring to by naming Elaine Worley, we're at a dead end."

"I know, honey. But the Lord is with us. It's all in His hands. We've trusted Him with our souls for eternity. We've got to trust him with our lives for our time here on earth."

Hunter knocked on the door. There were instant footsteps, and the door opened to a bright-eyed woman with snow-white hair and a pleasant smile.

"Yes?" she said. "Is there something I can do for you?"

"Mrs. Bittner, I'm Dr. Hunter McGuire, and—"

"Little Hunter Newman? The boy adopted by Dr. and Mrs. Jason McGuire years ago?"

"Yes, ma'am."

"Please, come in. And this young lady is your wife?"

"Well...ah...no, ma'am." Hunter allowed Jodie to enter ahead of him. "Since you remember me, do you remember my little sister?"

Linna's eyes widened as she closed the door behind them. "Lizzie?"

Hunter smiled. "You have a terrific memory, ma'am. Yes. This is my little sister, Lizzie. Only she goes by Jodie now."

Linna looked stunned. "Well, isn't this wonderful? When did you find her?"

"You knew about the Catersons disappearing?"

Linna nodded. "Please," she said, gesturing toward an overstuffed couch, "sit down."

Linna sat in a chair across from them. "I know about the disappearance of the Catersons and little Lizzie because your adoptive father came here looking for them—what was it?—maybe a year or so after they had taken you to Boston."

"Oh, yes. I hadn't thought about that."

"My, both of you children grew up to be very good-looking. Of course, you were awfully cute when you were little. So when did you find her, Hunter?"

"On September 14, ma'am."

"*This* September 14?"

"Yes. I'm a volunteer surgeon for the Confederate army, and I was with General Stonewall Jackson at the Antietam battle. I'm his Corps Medical Director."

"Really! Well, how is Tommy?"

"He's just fine, ma'am. Well, anyway, Jodie—Lizzie to you—was in Frederick, Maryland. She's Dr. Harvey Roberts's nurse at the clinic there."

Linna's eyes brightened. "A nurse! That's wonderful, dear."

Jodie smiled.

"General Lee passed his army through Frederick on Sunday, before the battle at Sharpsburg. There was Jodie—Lizzie—on the street. We hadn't seen each other for—well, I started to say twenty-two years. But we had met in Lexington seven years ago for a brief time, and then I lost track of her."

"Which brings us to why we're here, Mrs. Bittner," Jodie said. "We're facing a serious crisis in our lives. Because Hunter and General Jackson are very close friends, we talked to him about it. Not knowing that Dr. Riley had died, General Jackson sent us here to ask him a question. The nurse at Dr. Bishop's office thought you might be able to help us."

"I'll certainly try. Exactly what is this crisis?"

Jodie remained silent as Hunter told Linna Bittner the story. When he brought up the name of Elaine Worley, Linna looked as if she would cry.

"I see you know her name," Jodie said. "What can you tell us about her? General Jackson seemed to think that Elaine would be the key to our dilemma."

Linna pulled out a hanky and dabbed at her tears. "I was sworn to secrecy on this, children. But after hearing your story, I can't keep it from you. Bless your hearts. What a horrible experience for you."

Linna wiped tears again. "The Worley family lived on a farm near McCann's Run. One day Ralph and Edna Worley brought sixteen-year-old Elaine to Dr. Riley. I'll never forget the look on their faces. Elaine was so pale and just stared at the floor. She was pregnant out of wedlock. Ralph and Edna were terribly devastated and ashamed. They couldn't bear to face the community with such a scandal hanging over them. The boy who fathered the baby had left Virginia. His name was Bobby Henderson. No one knew where he had gone.

"The Worleys told Dr. Riley in my presence that they would keep Elaine inside the house until she gave birth to the baby. In the meantime, they wanted Dr. Riley to help them find someone in a distant town or city who would adopt the baby.

"Dr. Riley agreed to help them. Ralph and Edna told him they would tell the community that Elaine was staying with relatives up north for a few months. Now, children, I want you to understand that I heard all of this with my own ears."

Hunter and Jodie nodded, listening with rapt attention.

"At that time, Hunter, your mother was carrying her second child. You were three years old."

"Yes'm."

"Florence—your mother—was having complications with the pregnancy. Dr. Riley was making house calls almost every day. Of course, you were too young to understand what was going on, Hunter."

"Yes'm."

"When Florence's time to deliver drew near, Dr. Riley brought her to the clinic so he could keep an eye on her. During the nights, either he, Mrs. Riley, or I stayed with her. Some nights, your father was there, too. Thora Kemp was keeping you at her house. You probably remember Thora."

"Yes."

"Well, your father was there at the clinic when your mother delivered."

Jodie and Hunter hung on Linna's next words.

"The baby was stillborn."

Hunter's mouth went dry.

Jodie's heart thumped against her ribs as tears filled her eyes, and she scooted forward on the couch. "Mrs. Bittner, I'm Elaine Worley's daughter, aren't I? I'm Elaine Worley's daughter!"

"Yes."

Jodie flung herself into Hunter's arms, sobbing, "O Hunter, I'm not your sister! I'm not your sister! You're not my brother! You're my precious husband-to-be!"

Linna cried with them as she watched Hunter and Jodie weeping for joy and praising the Lord. Finally, the overjoyed couple settled down enough to listen to the rest of the story.

"Elaine gave birth to her baby girl at the Worley home that same night. Dr. Riley left Florence and Hunter Sr. with me at the clinic.

"When Dr. Riley returned, he told the Newmans that since their baby—a girl—had been born dead, he had a newborn baby girl they could adopt if they wanted her.

"Dr. Riley made them promise to keep secret what he was about to tell them, even if they decided they didn't want to adopt the baby. When they were told about Elaine, and that she had given birth to a healthy girl just an hour before, the Newmans were elated, saying they would take her.

"Dr. Riley told them everyone must believe the little girl was the baby Florence had brought into the world. They could never tell a single soul, not even you, Hunter. They made the promise and took the little black-haired, brown-eyed baby girl home the next night.

"Of course, I was sworn to secrecy too. Say! It just struck me why Tommy Jackson would bring up Elaine to you, though he didn't really know why."

"We'd be interested to know that," Hunter said.

"Well, one day a few months later, Tommy's Aunt Ophelia Jackson came to the clinic for some medicine. We were alone while I was filling the bottle. Ophelia said she and Cummins suspected that Elaine Worley's real reason for dropping out of sight was that she was pregnant by the Henderson boy she'd been running around with. She asked if it was so.

"I tried to lie about it, but Ophelia saw through me. In order to keep it from going any further, I told her the whole thing. I knew she would have to tell Cummins, but I asked her never to let it go beyond that. She promised she wouldn't, and as far as I know, it never did. From what you told me, Tommy must have overheard part of the conversation when Ophelia told Cummins."

"God let him overhear it," Jodie said. "He knows the end from the beginning. And way back there He was working all of this out."

"No reasonable person could deny that," Hunter said. "Well, we'd better be going." Hunter rose to his feet and helped Jodie up.

On the porch, Linna put her hand on Jodie's arm. "Is it going to bother you, honey? Knowing that you're Elaine Worley's daughter?"

Jodie looked into Hunter's eyes as she replied, "Not in the least. I'm just so happy to know that I'm going to become Mrs. Hunter McGuire!"

*****

Jodie clung to Hunter's arm as they drove out of Smithburg and headed north for Parkersburg. When they reached a wooded area, he tugged at the reins and pulled off the road onto a grassy spot.

"What are you doing, darling?" she asked.

Hunter turned on the seat and took Jodie into his arms. "I know at times my faith grew a little weak, sweetheart, but down deep I just knew the Lord wouldn't do a thing like that to us."

"I did too, but my faith wavered sometimes, just the same."

"You know what?"

"What?"

"On that windy day in Frederick, the Lord really brought *two* people to me on the wings of the wind—the woman I love and my sweet little Lizzie!"

EPILOGUE

The Federal Sanitary Commission in Washington, D. C., reacted to the horrible carnage of the Antietam battle by bringing in supplies and materials, as well as food, to treat the wounded men on both sides. Before the last hospital barn, house, or tent was closed, and the last wounded man sent from the Sharpsburg area, the Commission had distributed over twenty-eight thousand pieces of dry goods, shirts, towels, bed ticking, pillows, and other necessities; thirty barrels of bandage for dressing of wounds; some thirty-two hundred pounds of farina; twenty-six hundred pounds of condensed milk; five thousand pounds of beef stock and canned meats; four thousand sets of hospital clothing; several tons of fruit, plus crackers, tea, sugar, coffee, and tin cups. They provided medical supplies such as opium, chloroform, and surgical instruments.

All of these supplies were donated by volunteers in the Northern communities or bought with money donated by people of the North.

*****

On October 26, 1862, nearly six weeks after the Battle of Antietam, General McClellan finally set his army in motion. President Lincoln had visited him in the field on October 4, expressing his displeasure that McClellan had not vanquished the Confederate Army of Northern Virginia when he had the opportunity. McClellan gave his reasons for not doing so, but Lincoln was not convinced they were valid. However, he decided to give McClellan one more chance.

His army reinforced to 110,000 men, McClellan sent his vanguard across the Potomac five miles south of Harper's Ferry. He would pursue Lee and annihilate his army.

General Lee was still suffering from chest pains but had recovered from his depression over the devastating loss of men at Antietam. He moved to thwart McClellan's advance by once again dividing his army. On October 28, he left Stonewall Jackson's Corps, including Dr. Hunter McGuire, in the Shenandoah Valley and took the other half of his army on a swift sixty-mile march southeast through the passes of the Blue Ridge Mountains.

By the time the Federal vanguard had reached Warrenton, Virginia, Lee had established himself at Culpepper Courthouse, twenty miles to the southwest. From this position, he could oppose a Federal march on Richmond.

To Abraham Lincoln, this meant that McClellan's slows had allowed the enemy to get away again. McClellan had failed the final test.

On November 5, Lincoln had papers drawn up relieving McClellan of his command and replacing him with Major General Ambrose E. Burnside. McClellan was instructed by Lincoln to return immediately to his home in Trenton, New Jersey, where he was to await "further orders"—orders which would never come. George B. McClellan had fought his last battle.

On November 11, 1862, McClellan boarded a train at

Warrenton Junction. Thousands of weeping Union soldiers were there to see him off. The general stepped onto the rear platform of his coach and calmed the distraught soldiers by saying, "Stand by General Burnside as you have stood by me, and all will be well. Good-bye, lads."

The train steamed out of the station, carrying the beloved McClellan away from the War. Later, Colonel Edward Cross of the 5th New Hampshire wrote, "A shade of sadness crossed his face. He carried the hearts of the army with him."

OTHER COMPELLING STORIES BY
AL LACY

Books in the Battles of Destiny series:

☛ *A Promise Unbroken*

Two couples battle jealousy and racial hatred amidst a war that would cripple America. From a prosperous Virginia plantation to a grim jail cell outside Lynchburg, follow the dramatic story of a love that could not be destroyed.

☛ *A Heart Divided*

Ryan McGraw—leader of the Confederate Sharpshooters—is nursed back to health by beautiful army nurse Dixie Quade. Their romance would survive the perils of war, but can it withstand the reappearance of a past love?

☛ *Beloved Enemy*

Young Jenny Jordan covers for her father's Confederate spy missions. But as she grows closer to Union soldier Buck Brownell, Jenny finds herself torn between devotion to the South and her feeling for the man she is forbidden to love.

☛ *Shadowed Memories*

Critically wounded on the field of battle and haunted by amnesia, one man struggles to regain his strength and the memories that have slipped away from him.

☛ *Joy from Ashes*

Major Layne Dalton made it through the horrors of the battle of Fredericksburg, but can he rise above his hatred toward the Heglund brothers who brutalized his wife and killed his unborn son?

☛ *Season of Valor*

Captain Shane Donovan was heroic in battle. Can he summon the courage to face the dark tragedy unfolding back home in Maine?

Books in the Journeys of the Stranger series:

☞ *Legacy*

Can John Stranger bring Clay Austin back to the right side of the law...and restore the code of honor shared by the woman he loves?

☞ *Silent Abduction*

The mysterious man in black fights to defend a small town targeted by cattle rustlers and to rescue a young woman and child held captive by a local Indian tribe.

☞ *Blizzard*

When three murderers slated for hanging escape from the Colorado Territorial Prison, young U.S. Marshal Ridge Holloway and the mysterious John Stranger join together to track down the infamous convicts.

☞ *Tears of the Sun*

When John Stranger arrives in Apache Junction, Arizona, he finds himself caught up in a bitter war between sworn enemies: the Tonto Apaches and the Arizona Zunis.

☞ *Circle of Fire*

John Stranger must clear his name of the crimes committed by another mysterious—and murderous—"stranger" who has adopted his identity.

☞ *Quiet Thunder*

A Sioux warrior and a white army captain have been blood brothers since childhood. But when the two meet on the battlefield, which will win out—love or duty?

Books in the Angel of Mercy series:

☞ *A Promise for Breanna*

The man who broke Breanna's heart is back. But this time, he's after her life.

☞ *Faithful Heart*

Breanna and her sister Dottie find themselves in a desperate struggle to save a man they love, but can no longer trust.

☞ *Captive Set Free*

No one leaves Morgan's labor camp alive. Not even Breanna Baylor.

☞ *A Dream Fulfilled*

A tender story about one woman's healing from heartbreak and the fulfillment of her dreams.

Books in the Hannah of Fort Bridger series:

☞ *Under the Distant Sky* (coming February 1997)

Solomon and Hannah Cooper knew the journey West involved risk. They just didn't realize they were gambling with their lives.

Available at your local Christian bookstore